STRIVERS
ROW

During the 1920s and 1930s, around the time of the Harlem Renaissance, more than a quarter of a million African-Americans settled in Harlem, creating what was described at the time as "a cosmopolitan Negro capital which exert[ed] an influence over Negroes everywhere."

Nowhere was this more evident than on West 138th and 139th streets between Adam Clayton Powell and Frederick Douglass boulevards, two blocks that came to be known as Strivers Row. These blocks attracted many of Harlem's African-American doctors, lawyers, and entertainers, among them Eubie Blake, Noble Sissle, and W. C. Handy, who were themselves striving to achieve America's middle-class dream.

With its mission of publishing quality African-American literature, Strivers Row emulates those "strivers," capturing that same spirit of hope, creativity, and promise.

Shades of Jade

VILLARD / STRIVERS ROW / NEW YORK

Shades
of Jade

A NOVEL

GLORIA
MALLETTE

To Arnold, ever discerning;
Khadijah Bandele and Muslimah Toliver,
ever encouraging;
Debbie Buie, forever believing;
Curtis Richard, forever a friend.

The heart doesn't lie, it feels what it feels,
it loves who it loves.

—GLORIA MALLETTE

ACKNOWLEDGMENTS

IN THIS WORLD we do nothing alone. There is always someone—family, friend, stranger—extending a helping hand.

To my friend Carl Weber, himself an author and the owner of the African American Bookstore, thank you for heralding *Shades of Jade* to your customers; and to other bookstore owners, thank you for being so giving.

To my sister in spirit, Karen Quinones Miller, thank you for sharing your storehouse of knowledge so selflessly, for lending an understanding ear, and, above all, for being my friend.

A gracious and heartfelt nod to my editor, Melody Guy, for her vision and for presenting me with this wonderful opportunity.

Much appreciation to my agent, Claudia Menza, for taking me on when others had no confidence in my ability or belief in my potential.

A humble thank you to the African-American distributors and bookstores that took a chance on putting self-published copies of *Shades of Jade* on their shelves and pushing it to their customers.

A very special thank you to the marvelous ladies of the numerous book clubs that have chosen *Shades of Jade* as a club selection. To those of you whom I have not met, I am honored. To those of you

whose meetings I have attended, thank you for making me feel so special. It's been my pleasure.

Last but certainly not least, a standing ovation to the street vendors of Brooklyn, Queens, Manhattan, and the Bronx for selling my books to all who approached them. Because of you, the word-of-mouth network extended well beyond the streets of New York City. You guys are truly my heroes.

Shades of Jade

Chapter 1

SPENT, SHE LAY on her side, her knees drawn up to her stomach, her arms crisscrossed gently cradling her tender breasts, humbly licking her wounds, quietly comforting herself. Holding her eyes closed, she tried to will away the ache between her thighs, though she knew it would eventually subside. Always the pain of being with Louis lingered longer than the pleasure of his passion; and always he stayed longer than he needed to—or rather, longer than she wanted him to. Telling him that she had a busy day tomorrow and needed her rest didn't move him along any faster, but telling him that it was 9:15 did—he had an hour's drive ahead of him out to Long Island. Yet it wasn't the lateness of the hour that motivated him, it was not wanting to be made to lie about where he was coming from. He cheated on his wife with a clear conscience, he just didn't like lying about it—he prided himself on not being a liar. As far as she knew, cheating and lying were one and the same, but that wasn't any concern of hers; she just wanted him to go.

At the door, "Just one more kiss" turned into three more long, deep kisses. "I always hate leaving you," he said.

"You know what they say about all good things."

"And you're certainly a good thing."

Riiiing!

"I'd better get that," she said, trying to pull herself out of his smothering embrace.

He held her tighter. "They'll call back."

Riiiing!

Her neck and face were suddenly hot. "Let me get that."

"Let it ring," he said, nibbling on her left earlobe.

Riiiing!

"Louis," she said, pulling her head away so that her earlobe slipped out of his mouth. She was repulsed by his refusal to let go of her.

He pecked her on the lips. "I wish there were two of me."

Riiiing!

Feigning a syrupy smile, she planted her hands firmly but gently on his chest and pushed him out the door into the hallway. "Sorry, you're just one man," she said, pushing the door up.

"See how you treat me?"

The telephone rang no more.

"Go home. You made me miss my call."

"If it's important . . ."

"They may not call back. Louis, please go home before . . ."

Riiiing!

"I'm answering that. I'll talk to you tomorrow." She closed the door and locked it. She could hear him laughing on the other side of the door. "Go home!"

Riiiing!

"See you, baby love," he said through the door.

She dashed for the telephone in the living room. "Hello?"

"Slut."

Click.

Chapter 2

IF IT WAS GOING to rain, Marissa wished the sky would just go ahead and open up, let it pour, get it over with. But the fine, dreary drizzle that had persisted all afternoon, coupled with the high humidity blanketing the city like a steambath, was making her skin clammy and her nerves fragile. It did nothing to brighten her mood after that nasty telephone call last night, nor did it give her a shot of much needed energy, and it certainly didn't make her feel pretty. About all it did do was first wimp out her hair and then frizz it up once it dried. What she wanted most to do after work was go straight home and fall into bed. However, Charmaine had asked her over for dinner earlier in the week and she had accepted, but now she was wary. Since it was supposed to be "just us girls," why didn't "just us girls" just go out to a restaurant like they usually did? And why had Charmaine gone through the trouble of making a pan of lasagna large enough to feed ten people? The more she thought about it, the more it felt like a setup.

"Anyone else coming over?"

Charmaine didn't look up from the lettuce leaves she was washing. "Not that I know of."

"What about Gregory?"

"He had to work. Would you get out a tray of ice?"

"No one else is coming?"

"Girl, don't be so paranoid," she said, diligently patting the lettuce leaves dry with a paper towel.

Marissa eyed her suspiciously. "You make me paranoid," she said, taking a single blue ice tray from the freezer. She sat it on the counter. If there had been a setup planned, she would have been pissed, and it would be partly her own fault—she never turned down a free meal and tonight she didn't have a dinner date. Eating out was expensive in New York City, especially if she had to pay for it herself. She hated going into a supermarket, which also played a part in why she accepted the invitation. As far as she was concerned, food shopping was for housewives and she was as far away from being a housewife as Elvis was from being alive. Whenever a cashier asked for more than fifty dollars of her money, it was for a pair of shoes or a blouse or something else she could wear. Her cabinets and refrigerator didn't know what it was to hold much more than Ritz crackers, peanut butter, a can or two of tuna, instant coffee, cream, cheddar cheese, mayonnaise, and ice cubes.

Marissa filled two glasses with ice cubes and again eyed Charmaine. The last time she tried to play matchmaker, she had set her up with some obnoxious, computer-programming specialist who thought every woman within the sound of his voice should feel honored by the privilege of his company. He boasted that he had had so many women that he could tell within minutes what it would take to get a woman in bed. She didn't know how that was possible, since within minutes he disgusted her. Charmaine dismissed her as being too picky—thank God for small favors.

When Charmaine kept glancing over at the wall clock and holding up dinner with a lame excuse about waiting for the dinner rolls to brown, Marissa knew it was Gregory she had been waiting for all along when he "happened by." Besides, when the doorbell rang, Charmaine left the plastic wrapper from the already brown store-bought dinner rolls on the counter in the kitchen in her haste to open the door for him. She could have at least got French bread: tacky, just like this setup. That Gregory didn't use his keys confirmed her

suspicion. It was a good bet that one of his friends would "happen by," too. Now, that was something to worry about. Gregory was no model for *GQ* and his nine-year career as a correction officer was drab and unimpressive. Most of his friends were correction officers, too, so what was there to look forward to?

"Look who's here," Charmaine announced.

She didn't bother looking at Gregory, but at Charmaine Marissa glared. "We have to talk."

"What's happening, Marissa?" he asked flatly.

"Not much," she answered, her tone the same.

"Marissa, you don't mind if Gregory eats with us, do you?"

She felt put upon. "Why would I mind?"

"Good," Charmaine said, throwing her arms around Gregory's neck.

Marissa wanted to snatch Charmaine bald. Disgusted, she turned her back to them. This was not going to be a fun evening. She and Gregory never had much to say to each other after "What's happening?" In fact, he had no conversation beyond prisoners and basketball—two topics well outside her sphere of interest. But obviously not Charmaine's, as she had stomached him for five years and was going to be marrying him in four weeks. Everything was "simply wonderful," she had said more than a dozen times. Great. Marissa was happy for her. That's why she had agreed to be her maid of honor.

"I'll be back," Marissa said, excusing herself. She left the two of them hugged up in the kitchen and went into the bathroom at the back of the apartment to check her hair. It looked like she felt, frazzled. Using Charmaine's comb, she tried to comb some style and body back into her hair. No matter who was coming, she would look her best, but then, she looked her best even when she took her garbage to the incinerator. That's just the way she was.

The sweet, seasoned smell of tomato sauce was just as inviting in the bathroom as it had been in the kitchen. At least she would have a tasty meal. Still, it irritated her that Charmaine was again trying to set her up with someone she thought was a good catch—any single man. The last time she told her to mind her business—this time

she'd tell her to kiss her ass. On second thought, the more she thought about it, she was not that hungry and she was no longer the child made to sit through a boring visit with her grandmother's "oldest, dearest" childhood friend. Therefore, why should she subject herself to the company of a man she already knew she was not going to like?

Putting Charmaine's comb back on the organizer over the toilet, she gave her hair a final fluff just as the ringing of the doorbell signaled that the mystery man had arrived.

"Damn!"

For an instant her stomach fluttered, but she calmly wet her fingertip on the tip of her tongue and ran it over her eyebrows.

There was a tap at the door. "Marissa, dinner's ready."

She opened the door. "I'm not staying."

Charmaine immediately put her hands up on either side of the doorjamb, holding Marissa just inside the bathroom. "You can't leave."

"Oh, no? Watch me," she said, starting to push against Charmaine's right arm.

"Marissa, damn, it's just dinner."

"Then why did you have to lie?"

"I didn't. Greg was supposed to be working, but his schedule was changed this morning. When he called this afternoon and said he was coming over with a friend, I didn't think it would be a problem."

"It might not have been, if you had told me about it."

"Yeah, well, I know how you are."

"That's exactly why . . ."

"Charmaine!" Gregory called from the living room.

"Coming!" she called back, dropping her hands off the doorjamb. "Look, Marissa. It won't kill you to meet Levi, he's . . ."

"Levi?"

"Yes, he's a nice guy."

"Oh, damn," Marissa said, rolling her eyes up to the ceiling. "With a name like Levi, he probably picks a banjo with his toes."

"He does not; he's not country."

"Charmaine! We eatin' tonight or not?" Gregory yelled.

"I said, I'm comin'!" Charmaine replied.

"I don't feel good about this."

"Please, Marissa," Charmaine said, starting to back down the hallway, "it's just dinner. C'mon."

"You owe me," Marissa said, following hesitantly behind her. There was no way she wasn't going to tell her about herself—later. By the time she got to the living room, a weak smile she used with coworkers she didn't particularly like was on her lips.

The mystery man was already sitting at the table in the far corner of the living room with Gregory, and both had just popped cans of beer, but only Levi was pouring his into a glass. The first thing she noticed about him was how much hair he had on his head—damn near an afro—he was a dinosaur. Strike one. She wanted to about-face and get out of there, because strike two was boldly drawing her eyes—he wore a red, black, and green plaid flannel shirt, which reminded her of the shirts her father used to wear as a street paver for the city.

"Greg," Charmaine began, "would you do the honors? I have to get the rolls. Marissa, I'll be right back." Leaving the room, she didn't look at Marissa.

Marissa felt like she was just pushed on stage. She wanted to strangle Charmaine. But . . . she looked down at the table. The lasagna was already on the table, which was set with four place settings. Two cans of beer sat at Gregory's left elbow.

"Marissa," Gregory said, "this is my man, Levi."

She barely looked at him. "Hi."

"Levi and Greg go way back," Charmaine said, carrying in the dinner rolls on the aluminum pan they were packaged in. She sat the pan down on the corner of the table.

"Yeah, back to high school, when we were young and fly and could get all the girls," Gregory said, taking a swig of his beer.

Placing her hands on her curvy hips, Charmaine glared at him. "I beg your pardon. All *what* girls?"

"Did I say all the girls? I meant to say where I first dreamed of meeting you," he said smoothly, pulling her down onto his lap.

"See how quick the boy lies?" she asked, softly pushing her

elbow into his stomach. "You better start remembering your lies. You told me that all you did in high school was pant after your basketball."

"I remember you panting after Sarice Wilson and her double-basketball chest," Levi volunteered.

"That's cold, man. You supposed to watch my back."

"I am. I'm trying to keep you honest."

Charmaine elbowed Gregory hard in the stomach.

"Oooh," he said, rubbing his stomach. "Baby, you the one who won my heart." He kissed her. Charmaine pouted.

Lowering her eyes, Marissa felt like retching. She wished she could twitch her nose and disappear.

Levi could see Marissa's discomfort. He stood and extended his hand to her. "Nice to meet you, Marissa," he said, leaning across the table. "Excuse my clothes, I came straight from work."

That was obvious. She extended her own hand, but then she suddenly coughed and pulled it back to cover her mouth. A quick glimpse of his rough, dry-looking hand, and the grime under his fingernails, made her cringe. Strike three.

"Are you all right?" he asked, withdrawing his hand.

"You want some water?" Charmaine asked.

She shook her head no. "I'm fine. It was just a little tickle," she said, swallowing to wet her throat. She could see that Levi wasn't bad-looking, but a man with dirty fingernails and rough-looking hands that looked like they could shred a pair of nylons definitely was not touching her.

Sitting down again, Levi reached for his glass. That was as phoney a cough as he had ever heard. Eyeing her covertly, he began sipping quietly on his beer.

Charmaine nudged Gregory in the side to get him to look at the way Levi was looking at Marissa. He looked but he frowned.

Taking her seat across from Levi, Marissa kept her eyes lowered as she took her napkin off the table and lay it across her lap. The sneaky way he was looking at her made her feel uneasy, but at least it wasn't the hungry look men on the prowl in bars give every po-

tential one-night stand, which is why her one and only visit to a bar without a man at her side was her last. Like this was going to be the last time she let Charmaine play her for a fool. She was here now, so she'd finesse it. Crossing her legs, she looked up. "So, Levi, what do you do? Are you a plumber?"

"You could say that."

"You could also say carpenter, electrician, roofer, mason, etcetera," Gregory volunteered. "Levi's a contractor. He remodeled my mother's bathroom. You should see it."

She wasn't impressed. "A jack of all trades, huh? Is there anything you can't do?"

"I can't tap dance, but I can handle just about anything else," he said, placing his left arm over the back of his chair, his eyes lingering still on her face.

Inexplicably, there was a nervous flutter in her stomach. "Not very modest, are you?" she asked, pulling her eyes away from him and looking at Charmaine.

"Marissa is kind of impressive herself," Charmaine said, getting up off of Gregory's lap and going over to sit in her own chair across from him. "She's the business manager where we work."

Staring at her, Marissa tried to tell Charmaine with her eyes that she was telling too much of her business.

"A lady with some authority, huh? I like that."

Gregory grinned. "I bet you do."

Looking at Gregory, she began fingering her fork. If he thought he was being cute, he wasn't. For the life of her she didn't know what Charmaine saw in him, he was so obnoxious. Looking back at Levi, she glimpsed a flirtatious twinkle in his brown eyes. He really wasn't a bad-looking man. He had beautiful, long, black eyelashes and the deepest, most sensual dimples she had ever seen on a man. Too bad he wasn't her type. Yet the sudden attraction she was feeling, although puzzling, made her flush. What was wrong with her? She never gave men that got dirty for a living the time of day, and certainly none had ever made her feel this way. He looked at her and smiled. Taken aback, she glanced angrily at Charmaine.

The look on her face confused him. She looked angry. Still, he'd try to make the best of the evening. "So, Marissa, what do you do to have fun?"

"Watch television," she answered dryly.

Wait a minute. Attitude? He wasn't here for that. "Great."

Why should she tell him that she liked going to the theater and spending Sunday afternoons in art galleries. She doubted whether he had ever been inside an art gallery; a photo mart seemed more his speed.

"Tell the man what you like," Charmaine coached, prodding Marissa with her foot under the table, until Marissa kicked her, making her jump.

"Baby," Gregory said, "can we eat now?"

Charmaine glared at Marissa. "Yeah, baby, give me your plate."

He passed it across the center of the table, bypassing Marissa and Levi.

Charmaine took Gregory's plate. "Levi, I'll tell you what Marissa likes. She likes plays and eating out."

Any minute Marissa was going to scream bloody murder. Charmaine was really being a bitch. "Charmaine, stop."

"Yeah, babe, leave it alone," Gregory said.

"What?"

"Don't play with me, Charmaine," Marissa warned. Under the table, she began twisting her gold bracelet repeatedly around her wrist. She wished that it was Charmaine's neck.

Levi could almost see the static bolts shooting from Marissa's eyes. He didn't know what was going on, but he wasn't here to play their game.

"Marissa, relax. Look, I have an idea," Charmaine said, scooping out a large square of lasagna oozing with tomato sauce and ricotta and strings of mozzarella. She laid it on the plate and handed it to Marissa to pass back to Gregory. "Levi, why don't you invite Marissa to the dance next month that Gregory's club is giving, she's a great dancer."

She gaped at her. Did Charmaine not hear her?

Gregory took a gulp of his beer.

Charmaine looked straight-faced at Marissa.

"Charmaine, let it go," Levi said, feeling awkward. Whatever was going on between the two of them, he wasn't about to be put in the middle.

Charmaine looked at Marissa wide-eyed. "What's wrong with you people? We're all friends here," she said, scooping out another square of lasagna. "Levi, pass me your . . ."

Suddenly pushing her chair back, making a loud scraping sound on the parquet floor, Marissa stood up. Her napkin slipped to the floor at her feet. They all looked up at her. "Charmaine, may I speak with you . . . privately?" she demanded, though she did not wait for an answer. She stepped around her chair and stormed out of the room without looking back.

"I told you this was a bad idea," Gregory said as Charmaine got up to follow behind Marissa. "She's gonna kick your butt."

"Oh, shut up!"

Gregory laughed.

"What the hell was that all about?" Levi asked.

"Stupidness," Gregory said, waving his hand at Charmaine's back. "Let's eat. Serve yourself. That damn Marissa is a pain in the ass."

"It look to me like it was Charmaine baiting that hook. Now tell me why."

Chapter 3

IN CHARMAINE'S BEDROOM, Marissa paced like a caged tiger. This time the woman had gone too far; embarrassing her like that, putting her on the spot in front of a handyman, all the time grinning, trying to be cute. Who the hell does she think she is? Her mother?

"What's wrong?" Charmaine asked from the doorway.

"What the hell do you think you're doing?"

She quickly closed the door. "What did I do?"

"Don't play that Miss Innocent crap with me!"

"*Shh!*" Charmaine whispered, stepping around Marissa to sit down on the bed. "Levi might feel bad if he hears you."

"I don't give a damn! You didn't seem to care much about *my* feelings while you were playing matchmaker."

"Was what I did so wrong?"

"Damn right. Do I look like I want a handyman?"

"Don't knock it until you try it; besides, he's single."

"So is the pope. Are you going to set me up with him?"

"With all of his money, I'm surprised you haven't gone after him by now."

"Go to hell," Marissa spat, pivoting on her heels and reaching for the door.

"Wait!" Charmaine said, standing quickly and reaching out for Marissa's arm before she could open the door.

She pulled back out of her reach. "I'm leaving."

"That was uncalled for. I'm sorry, all right? But the truth is, Marissa, I've listened to you for the past six years whine about having to do so many things by yourself because the married men you see have to spend their weekends with their families."

She folded her arms across her chest. "Obviously, I won't be whining to you anymore."

"Oh, come on, Marissa, you know it never bothered me; but you'll whine the rest of your life if you don't stop overlooking good single men like Levi."

"Charmaine, I don't know where the hell you get off thinking that you know what's best for me."

"I didn't say I . . ."

"Yes, the hell you did. You're always butting in my business; and for your information, I don't wear a sign on my forehead saying MARRIED MEN ONLY NEED APPLY. They come after me, I don't go after them. And if I don't like men, single or otherwise, like Levi, that's my damn business, not yours."

"Oh, I forgot, you only like Mr. Married Executive with the BMW or Mercedes and the six-figure income, right?"

"My choice—my business."

"Fine, if it works for you."

"It does."

"Really?" Charmaine asked, sitting down again and crossing her legs. "Then why do you spend every holiday whining about having to find something to do or somewhere to go? And why have you gone through a bushel of married men and not one has left his wife for you?"

Glaring at her, Marissa wanted to slap her face, but thought better of it. Women who fought like harlots were the lowest form of life in her book; but she sure as hell didn't have a problem with never

speaking to her again. She didn't see why it was Charmaine's business who she slept with as long as it wasn't with her man. God forbid. The haughty look on Charmaine's face said she thought she had put her in her place or something, but she had better think again.

"I have asked no man to leave his wife for me, but believe me, if I wanted any one of the men I see, I could have him simply by snapping my fingers," she said coolly, snapping her fingers. "From here on, stay the hell out of my business."

Shrugging her shoulders, Charmaine said, "No problem. Then I'll just say this and I'm out of it. I suggest you stop living your life through these men and what they have."

"What the hell is that supposed to mean?"

"You should listen to yourself sometimes. This guy has a Mercedes; this guy has a five-thousand-dollar Rolex; this one makes one hundred and fifty thousand a year; that one has a twelve-room house. Marissa, what you fail to comprehend is that *they* have; their *wives* have. You don't have."

Marissa felt her face tighten. It was true, she did speak a lot about what the men in her life had, but that was because she was proud of them, she wasn't trying to be ostentatious in any way.

"Believe me, honey," she said, determined to not let Charmaine get the last word. "I get more than my share."

"You know something, Marissa, I often wonder if you like a man for himself or for what he has to give you."

"That's not for you to wonder about, is it? Besides, as I see it, there is no shame in wanting a successful man who can give me what I want. If he happens to be married, so be it."

"So be it, huh? Well, one of these days you're gonna mess with the wrong woman's husband."

"Am I supposed to be quaking in my boots or something?" she asked, raising her voice.

"*Shh!*" Charmaine said, pointing at the door.

She flipped her finger at the door. She didn't care what Gregory or Levi thought of her, so she didn't care what they heard. Neither one of them could do a damn thing for her. "If a woman has a problem

with me, she had better look at her husband. I didn't twist his arm to be with me."

"You don't say no to an invitation to dinner from a gold band wearer, either."

"That's my prerogative. If a man was satisfied at home, he wouldn't be inviting me out in the first place."

"I can't speak on that, but how do you explain that you've been seeing Terrence for more than ten years and he still goes home to his wife? His children are grown. What's wrong? Can't you pull him?"

Glowering, she sucked her teeth. Terrence was the one man she truly loved and Charmaine knew that. She also knew that he loved her, too, but he loved his children more, which she understood. His children adored their mother and he feared losing their love and respect if he were to leave. His own father had left his mother when he was twelve, and the divorce had devastated him and his two brothers. He said he never felt the same about his father again. That's why she knew he'd never leave his children's mother, no matter what their ages were.

"Charmaine, I don't know why the hell I'm standing here taking this crap from you, you're no saint yourself."

"I never said I was."

"Does Gregory know you cheated on him with Ross Hilton on the job?"

Charmaine stood up. She looked anxiously at the door. "You are such a bitch."

"So are you. How does it feel to be put on the spot?"

"You tell me, you're the one that has to sneak around."

"Hey, at least the men I sneak around with have money and class. Can you say the same?"

"Until you said that, I didn't know how stupid you were."

"Stupid? I have my MBA," she said smugly, knowing that Charmaine regretted not finishing school.

"Good for you. Then you should know that money and class are not synonymous. Even the poorest man can outclass the man with millions. It's not about what's in one's bank account or on one's

back or in one's driveway, it's about attitude; it's about the way one carries oneself; it's about what's inside," she said, pressing her hands to her chest. "Why don't you give a thought to Terrence's wife the next time you screw him."

She smirked. "You're jealous."

"If that's what you want to believe, believe it."

"I do. I have the life you wish you had. Your man works every day as a prison guard, yet you go wanting. And worse yet, it took you a lifetime to get him to commit. I wonder why."

"You're . . ."

"Maybe after the wedding, he'll be more generous, but not with you."

"Let me tell you something," Charmaine began, pointing her finger in Marissa's face.

She shoved Charmaine's finger out of her face. For a dangerous second they glared at each other.

Charmaine put her hands on her hips. "There isn't a thing I want that I can't get for myself," she said, no longer speaking softly. "But you're not going to get me off on that jealousy tangent because that's bull. You might be trying to hurt my feelings, but I'm not trying to hurt yours. I care enough about you to want you to be happy, and seeing other women's men won't *ever* make you happy."

"Hey, happiness is relative. I'm satisfied with my life. Can you say the same?"

"I'm getting married. Are you?"

She smirked. "You have nothing to boast about."

Charmaine narrowed her gaze. "Go on, Marissa, keep on being flip. The men you see don't give a damn about you. They get what they want and go on back to their wives, leaving you to look at your four walls or the next married man. You've taken fornication and adultery to a new art form, haven't you? Tell me, how many men are you seeing anyway? Three? Four? One is usually enough for most women. By the way, I hope they all use condoms."

Marissa's neck and cheeks flushed hot as embers. From the time she was a teenager and had to deal with jealousy from pimpled-face ugly girls, she had always felt that men made better friends for her

than women—they weren't so envious, so conniving, so catty. Why in the world did she let herself stray from that and become friends with this vicious woman scowling at her? But that's all right, Marissa thought; like marriages, friendships can be dissolved, too. She scowled back. "I got a man for all occasions, honey. One to love me; one to wine and dine me; and one to buy me whatever my heart desires. You should be so lucky." Then rolling her eyes, she turned and yanked open the door. She stormed out of the room.

"I got all that in one man, honey!" Charmaine shouted.

She said nothing more as she headed for the living room.

Charmaine lifted her arms out to her sides, then let them drop heavily. "Damn! How in the world did this happen? My God, it was only supposed to be dinner. Marissa!"

In the living room, Marissa rushed past Levi and Gregory and snatched up her shoulderbag and jacket off the chair near the door.

Levi's lasagna was only half-eaten. He picked at the remainder while Gregory chomped down on a dinner roll. Neither one looked up from his plate.

Charmaine ran past them to catch up with Marissa as she rushed out of the apartment. "Marissa, don't leave like this." Standing out in the hallway, Charmaine watched her run down the stairs. "I'm sorry!" she called to her. When Charmaine couldn't see her anymore, she listened to the *clickety clack* of Marissa's heels as she ran down the three flights of stairs to the first floor. When she heard the door slam shut, she went back into the apartment. Gregory looked at her as if to say "I told you so," while Levi stood at the window looking out.

He saw Marissa run out of the building to her car. He watched her recklessly pull her Lexus out in front of an oncoming car in her haste to flee. The other car screeched to a halt. The driver honked his horn angrily at her several times as she sped off. "I wouldn't want to be on her bad side," Levi said.

"She don't scare the almighty Charmaine," Gregory said, turning the beer can up to his mouth.

"What's that supposed to mean?" Charmaine asked.

"Like she said, you shoulda minded your own business."

She shrugged her shoulders. "I don't see what was so wrong with what I did."

"You never do," Gregory said, taking a big swallow of his beer, emptying the can.

"Don't start with me; and how come you don't ever use a glass?"

Locking eyes with Charmaine, Gregory crumpled the can up in his hand and then, sneering, smashed it into the table.

Chapter 4

LEVI LOOKED AT Charmaine and then at Gregory. Both looked agitated. "I think I'll head on home."

"Naw, man, sit down and finish your dinner," Gregory said. "Since when you let some woman ruin your appetite?"

"Hey, my appetite's fine. I thought you two might want to be alone."

"No, Levi, stay," Charmaine said, looking at Gregory, although he avoided looking back at her. "Greg, you act like you're mad at me. I didn't know she'd get that upset. Levi . . ."

"Leave him out of it," Gregory ordered, reaching for a beer. He pulled it away from its plastic holder and offered the can to Levi.

He remained standing. "I'm all right," he said, touching his glass. It had about two warm swallows left.

Gregory pulled back the ring on the beer top and popped open the can. Charmaine and Levi both watched as he slowly filled his glass. The foam rose to the top and spilled over onto the table. Lifting the glass, he slurped at the foam.

"You think I was wrong, don't you?"

"Not now, Charmaine," he said, shoveling a heaping forkful of cold lasagna into his mouth.

Ignoring his dismissal, she turned to Levi. "Levi, I didn't think she'd . . ."

"C'mon, baby. Levi'll think we don't know how to treat company."

She began wringing her hands. "I'm sorry I ruined your dinner, Levi."

"Don't worry about it," he said, sitting down.

"I just didn't think she'd get so upset."

"Charmaine, let . . . it . . . go."

She shot Gregory an angry glance as she turned on her heels and rushed out of the room.

Levi looked at Gregory when the force of the door slamming at the back of the apartment shook the walls—a loud reminder that there was a reason he was still single and worked hard, long hours. In fact, he'd rather stick his hand in a clogged sewer drain before he'd trade places with Gregory tonight.

"Damn!" Gregory said, slamming down his folk. "Now I gotta hear mouth all night because her little 'itch of a friend didn't go along with the script."

"What script?"

If he heard Levi, Gregory did not answer. He shoved his plate to the center of the table. "I told her a million times, don't put me in the middle of this garbage with her and her stuck-up friend."

"Look man, I ain't got time for this," Levi said, pushing his own plate away and starting to get up from the table.

"Naw, man, wait a minute. I shouldn't've invited you. Just because you're the best man don't mean you have to hang with the maid of honor, especially that maid of honor. And you know what pisses me off? I knew how stuck-up the girl was. She got her own agenda and men like you and me ain't got no place on it. And Charmaine knows this, man. She nagged me to death to invite you."

"What for?"

"I guess she thought you had enough money hidden under your mattress to pique Marissa's interest."

"How do she know what's under my mattress?"

"Man, women know. Charmaine figured that since you work six days a week, wear only work clothes, drive a fifteen-year-old car, and live in your mother's basement apartment, that you're hoarding the dollars."

"Yeah, well, I have a dollar or two, and it's not under my mattress; but since I don't wear or drive my money, how was Marissa supposed to become interested in me?"

"Man, don't ask me. That's why I didn't want no part of this mess. In fact, I don't understand why Charmaine even bothers with the girl in the first place. She claims she's her best friend, but if you ask me, I don't think she likes Marissa all that much."

"If she don't like her, then why is she the maid of honor?"

"Hell if I know. I just know that she talk about her all the time like she don't. Man, I get tired of 'Marissa did this,' 'Marissa got this,' 'Marissa and some married man that.' I gotta tell you, I get tired of hearing her damn name."

"When they were arguing, seem to me I heard her say something about jealousy."

"Jealous of what? Charmaine ain't got nothing to be jealous of her for."

"Well, she is a real good-looking woman, and I guess she got the right to choose her playmates."

"Man, for one thing, she ain't all that good-looking."

"One man's opinion."

"Yeah, well, whatever. But, man, it's more than a matter of choice, the girl's shallow. Listen to this," Gregory said, pushing his chair back from the table. "Charmaine told me that they were out at a club one night and this suited-down dude couldn't take his eyes off Marissa. Dude showed class; he sent over a bottle of white wine. Charmaine said he was looking at the girl like he could eat her up, toenails and all. Seems she was eyeing him back, too. That is until the dude comes over and starts talking."

"What did he say?"

"Man, it wasn't what he said, it was his mouth."

"What? He had green teeth?"

"No, he had one big, broken tooth up front; snaggletooth dude. The girl got her prissy ass up, told Charmaine to come on, and left the dude with egg on his face."

He couldn't help but snicker. "Cold."

"Damn right. She didn't know who that dude was or what he had. She said, 'If a man can't afford a good dental plan, he can't afford me.' The dude don't know how lucky he was."

"She's a tough one, all right. It'll take a sledgehammer to knock down that attitude."

"Man, I know you ain't thinking about doing no swinging."

"It might be an interesting challenge."

Gregory's jaw hit the table. "You got to be kiddin'. That girl ain't nothing but trouble. I wouldn't touch her with a ten-foot pole."

Charmaine threw herself facedown across her bed and began flailing her legs hard against the mattress. She could not believe what she had done. Gregory didn't have to tell her that she had crammed both feet down her own throat, she already knew that.

Grunting loudly, she flipped suddenly onto her back, spread her arms and legs wide out to her sides, and stared up at the ceiling.

The bedroom door opened. "Levi's gone."

"Marissa will never forgive me."

Gregory strolled into the room and plopped down hard onto the side of the bed. "Life goes on."

"Damn," she said, annoyed that he had shaken her when he sat down hard on the bed. "One of these days you're gonna break my bed."

"Hey, don't take it out on me, it's your girlfriend you're pissed with."

"You're the one that just tried to break my bed."

"I'm going home," he said, starting to get up.

Sitting up, she quickly grabbed onto his arm. "No! Don't leave. I'm sorry."

"Don't be sorry, just don't be taking it out on me."

"I didn't mean to, but I feel awful," she said, falling back on the bed. "I just can't believe I did that."

"I wouldn't let it bother me."

"You wouldn't, but I'm worried."

"She'll get over it."

"I don't know. Greg, I knew full well that Marissa would be furious with me if she thought I was trying to get her with Levi, so I didn't tell her about him. I tried to make it seem like you all were just stopping by."

"That's where you messed up."

"I know, but the truth is, I wasn't really trying to pair her with him in a romantic sense. Since you asked Levi to be your best man, I figured it was only right they meet before the wedding rehearsal. I should have told her that's what the dinner was for, but I know how she is. She's so paranoid about meeting single men. And then when I saw her draw back in disgust when Levi went to shake her hand, I almost lost it."

"Yeah, I saw that, that was deep. The girl is full of herself."

"Gregory, that's just Marissa. She didn't mean to be insulting, I know that. She's particular, that's all."

"So if you know that, why did it bother you?"

"Because sometimes I hate that she's the way she is. I just lost it. Before I knew what I was doing, I went at her, baiting her to get her even madder."

"From what I heard, and I heard a lot, you enjoyed every minute of it."

"At first I did, but I swear to God, I didn't mean for it to go that far. Not that Marissa would believe me. I'm not jealous of her, nor am I worried that she'll go after you after we get married."

"She couldn't get next to me on my deathbed."

"I know, baby, but her screwed-up attitude about seeing married men galls me. No matter how many times she explains or justifies her preference only for married men with money and position, she'll never convince me that she's right. Between you and me, I don't think there's a person on earth who can convince her that she's wrong."

"Probably not."

"Yeah, but as long as it wasn't you she was having an affair

with, I should have kept my mouth shut. I really do care a lot about her."

"Charmaine, get a clue. Your girlfriend don't give a damn about you. The girl is out for self, period."

"No," she said, sitting up again, "that's not completely true. Marissa's been there for me when none of my other friends were."

"So?"

"Greg, that's a big thing. Having a good friend to lean on is important to me."

"That's what I'm here for."

"Sure, you're here, most of the time, but Marissa's been here even when I've had problems with you."

"What problems? You telling her our business?"

"Calm down," she said, kicking off her shoes. "If it wasn't for Marissa, I wouldn't be marrying you. She's the one that told me to do what I had to do to make myself happy."

"You had doubts about us?"

"Greg, I had questions like every bride-to-be," she explained. "You may not like her, but Marissa's been a good friend to me. She was with me at the hospital when my father almost died in that car accident."

"I was at work. I didn't know your father was in any accident."

"I know, but Marissa sat with me at the hospital for hours holding my hand and running errands for my family. And remember the time when I was diagnosed with a lump in my breast? It was Marissa who stayed out in the waiting room while the surgeon removed that cyst. Thank God, it was benign."

"If you had told me, I would have been there, too. I can't expect to be there for you if you don't tell me what's going on."

"Greg, it's not like I was trying to keep you out; that was just something a woman shares with another woman. Would you have understood my fears, my doubts, my concerns?"

"Neither of us will ever know the answer to that, will we?" he asked, standing and going over to the door. "I'm going home, I'm tired."

"Then stay here."

"Not tonight, babe. With the mood you're in, I won't get any sleep."

She let him go; he didn't much like talking about Marissa anyhow. He didn't think any of her good virtues outweighed her one bad virtue of having affairs with married men. She didn't quite agree with that, which is why she had to stop letting it bother her. Marissa had been a better friend to her than some of her own sisters. Even when Greg made her life miserable, which was more than a handful of times, Marissa had listened without judging, without advising, and until today, had said nothing bad about him. Although she had hoped that her best friend and her man would get along, she was willing to settle for the cordial amenities they exchanged when they were in each other's company. After all, she didn't much like some of his friends, and she was definitely tired of hearing their inmate stories, yet she was cordial to them. That's the least of how she should have been with Marissa tonight. She had judged her. She was wrong.

Chapter 5

AS SOON AS Brandon opened his door, Marissa pushed past him into the apartment, ignoring his cheery "Hey, girl" greeting.

He looked her up and down as she whirled around in his entrance foyer, started to say something, then changed her mind, whirled around again and strutted off into the living room. He watched her flop down into his favorite wing chair and drop her shoulderbag onto the floor at her feet. Flipping his hand at her, he closed the door before going into the living room himself. Stepping right up to her, he stared down at her.

"You're in a lovely mood, my dear," he said, bending and picking up her shoulderbag. He flung the long strap over his shoulder on top of his colorful, lavishly embroidered caftan. "Hard day at the office?"

She rolled her eyes up at him as he sashayed back and forth in front of her, modeling her shoulderbag.

"It works," he said. "It's unisex."

"Give me back my bag."

"Oh, now you want it back after you see how good it looks on me. Just like a woman," he said, dropping the bag by the strap onto her lap. "I'm going to get some apple juice. Want some?"

"No."

"Well, you need something cold to cool your hot ass down," he said, leaving the room.

Ignoring the remark, she opened up the flap of her bag and dug down into the side pocket until she found her emery board. Angrily, she attacked her already well-manicured blood-red nails. Driving was usually a calming experience for her because she enjoyed sitting behind the wheel of her Lexus, but even after the twenty-minute drive from Charmaine's apartment to Brandon's, she was still wound up as tight as a top. The ugly things Charmaine said were still bouncing around loudly in her head. All this time she thought Charmaine was the one female friend she could trust. She told her everything about her life; about her men; about what she wanted out of life—all of which went against her usual close-mouthed nature with women. Unlike men, women could be vicious when they were jealous, which is why she invested very little time in them. If she had gotten even a hint that Charmaine was jealous-minded, she would have never told so much, much less associated with her.

"Every time I go in that kitchen, I cringe," Brandon said, coming back into the room. "Those old wooden cabinets have so much paint on them that the doors are as thick as a slab of cement."

"You say that every time I come here. Why don't you have them stripped and stained?"

"I would if that was all that was needed. I need new countertops; new appliances; a new floor."

"Then move."

"No, I like it here. I think I'll remodel the whole room."

"Whatever," she said, flipping her hand backward. She couldn't be so bothered.

"So tell me, miss, what's got your gluteus maximus up on your shoulders?" he asked, sitting his long-stem champagne glass of apple juice down on the coffee table before lounging on the sofa. He didn't drink anything harder than ginger ale, but he loved the classy look of champagne glasses and used them all the time.

She dropped the emery board back inside her shoulderbag, and

then sat it on the floor alongside her chair. "I'm so mad, I could scream."

"That I can see. The question is, why?"

"The why is Charmaine Spencer and her meddling," she said, slipping her arms out of her jacket.

"Do tell."

"The woman invited me to dinner so that she could set me up with some friend of Gregory's that she had to know I would not be the least bit interested in. I was mortified."

Brandon rolled his eyes comically. "Not another one of those blue-collar workers who wouldn't know an aria from a frog croak."

Not the least bit amused, she squinted her eyes at him.

"Oh, lighten up, it could have been worse. She could have introduced you to a gold-tooth, medallion-wearing homeboy."

Still she stared at him.

"Moving on," he said, flipping his hand at her. "I know he was single, but was he a good-looking hard body?"

"You can joke if you want, Brandon, but no one, and I mean no one, can tell me who I should or should not be seeing."

"I don't know what you're so angry about, you knew she was a prude about you seeing married men."

"My life is none of her business."

"Hey, that's what I say, but maybe she thought you might want her man once they were married. After all, you never limit yourself to just one."

Flabbergasted, she leaped to her feet. "I would have to be dead and walking this earth as a zombie to want the likes of Gregory the prison guard. There isn't a thing he can do for me except maybe introduce me to the commissioner of corrections. And for your information, I choose to see more than one man because I'm not sitting around waiting to see one man once a week for anybody."

"Girl, sit down before you blast off and put a hole in my ceiling."

"I don't know why I came over here," she said, snatching up her jacket. "You think everything's funny."

"Now, look," he said, sitting up and planting his hands on his thighs, "don't go getting testy with me, Miss Marissa; I didn't do a

thing to you. If you want me to act like I feel sorry for you, or act like my feelings are hurt, too, because of what Charmaine did to you, then maybe you best go on home, because I'm not so bothered."

She huffed. She folded her arms. She cut her eyes away.

"Marissa, stop playing the victim."

"I'm not playing the victim. That woman . . ."

"Okay . . . okay, but this is not the first time 'that woman' put you on the spot. Either get used to it, or tell her to stop, or disown the friendship. I am not going to let you bring me down because you're down. Heaven knows, I get more than my share of days like this."

Duly chastened, she sat down again and crossed her legs. She would have left, except Brandon was the only person she knew that didn't act like she drowned a sack of baby kittens because she went out with married men. She dropped her jacket over the left arm of the chair.

"You let yourself get too upset, Marissa. You need to find a way to channel your negative energy—a hobby, exercise, music, something positive."

"That's why I came here; you're good at calming me. And you know what? I feel just fine."

"Hey, I'm your friend, sweetie. You and Charmaine have had this drama before, so what's new in Dodge?"

"What's new is that I'm really sick of it."

"Then put a stop to it. You two have got this thing going on between you that I haven't quite figured out yet. Give me time, I will. Meanwhile, stop telling her your business. You don't tell any of your men about each other, do you?"

"I'm not stupid."

"Then stop telling Charmaine about your men; that's the only thing you all seem to argue about and you're the one that gives her the ammunition to fight you with. Keep it to yourself. You don't even have to tell me, unless you want to. But, you know how much I love hearing about all those fabulous men."

She smiled in spite of herself. "I'm not even going to tell you anything anymore."

"I don't care," he said, pretending to pout. "I'm not going to tell you about my man, either. So there."

"So there to you, too," she said, smiling and flipping her hand sideways at him.

"Seriously, Marissa. Who you see is your business. However, I do feel that you deserve a man that's yours alone. That might be how Charmaine feels."

"Who cares?"

"Obviously not you. See, I've never been good about sharing what I have—not even when I was a kid; and now that AIDS is 'making us pay' for our promiscuity, I definitely have no intention of sharing if I have any say about it, and for the most part, I do. That's why I kicked Gary, the cheater, out. Remember him?"

"Barely."

He stretched his eyes in surprise. "How could you forget such a gorgeous man as Gary? He was Adonis himself. Girl, you just don't know a hunk when you see one."

"Remember, sweetie, your idea of a hunk and my idea of a hunk are two different animals."

"Believe me when I tell you, a hunk is a hunk, no matter what his chosen profession."

"I'll just have to take your word on that."

"You're still young yet, you'll learn. Anyway, do what makes you happy."

"Well, thank you very much," she said sarcastically.

"No need to thank me. Just learn to live with how some people feel about you dating married men."

Recrossing her legs, she said, "That's their problem, not mine."

"It's yours if you don't know how to handle it. I learned early in life to keep my business out of the public eye. What I do behind closed doors does not hurt anyone but me," he said. Then as an after-thought, "That is, unless I let it."

"I'm not hurting myself or anyone else."

"If you feel that way, then why let yourself get so worked up?"

"Because," she began, then, thinking better of what she was about

to say, she clammed up. She didn't want to admit that although she dated married men, she did, on a rare occasion, sometimes feel guilty about getting the money that maybe their children needed for braces or shoes. Which was why she never wanted to know anything about their home life, their wives, or their children. In fact, she forbade even Terrence to discuss his two children. He accepted her explanation that talk of his family suppressed her sexual desire, and that was the last thing he wanted to do. She simply didn't want to make their existence her reality. Yet she never felt guilty about the wives because if they were doing what they were supposed to—be it in bed, in the kitchen, or in the living room—then their men would not be seeking out her company.

Getting up off the sofa, Brandon picked up his empty champagne glass at the same time. "Marissa, I believe you get yourself all worked up because you are a sweet, sensitive, misunderstood soul."

Nodding in agreement, she said, "I think so."

"Poor misunderstood baby. You walked out on Charmaine, didn't you?"

"Damn right. I was not about to hang around for more of her verbal terrorism, or sit there and pretend to be amused by a man that didn't interest me."

"In that case, you did the right thing—be true to self, I say. I'm going for a refill. Can I bring you something?"

"Maybe a little white wine."

"No problemo," he said, walking off into the kitchen with a flourish of his caftan.

She smiled. Behind his apartment door, away from the eyes of the world, Brandon was probably more feminine than she was, if that was possible. He never exaggerated his mannerisms, he just came across as refined. Looking around, everything about his co-op apartment was refined, too. There was nothing masculine, dark, or bold about his eclectic selection of contemporary and traditional furniture. In the low light, his ice blue walls trimmed in white wrapped the room in a cloak of mellowness. There was always a scent of strawberries in the air from the incense sticks placed in strategic

spots around the apartment. The ambiance was soft, soothing, and sophisticated. Very few people were privy to glimpse the real Brandon Wallace. He knew whereof he spoke when he said that she should either get used to how people felt about her seeing married men or keep it to herself. He lived a double life himself. He was a psychiatrist. At work and in public, no one would guess that he was gay. He dressed conservatively and acted butch, all of which effectively camouflaged his refined mannerisms.

Interestingly, he said he never wanted to be a woman, but he felt that he had to let his feminine side breathe once in a while. He felt strongly that if men in general got in touch with their feminine side every now and then, they would not rape or abuse women. It was the macho attitude, he said, that caused men to harm women in the first place, which was probably true. Nonetheless, wouldn't his patients love to get him on the couch?

His choices never did bother her, other than when they met seven years ago and she was attracted to him herself. It was kind of hard on her ego to be rejected by a single man, the first she was interested in in years. But then they became fast friends, calling each other constantly to gossip. It was a month before he told her that he was gay. She was shocked at first, then felt a kind of selfish relief that he was gay and did not spend his time with another woman, which helped to restore her bruised ego. She became his cover; his "date" whenever he had an affair to attend. He took her to the best formal affairs, the best restaurants—they always had a ball. His colleagues thought she was his woman. He got a big kick out of that.

"Oh, Marissa, did I tell you that Phillip and I are getting pretty serious? You have got to meet him. I think he's the one."

"That's what you said about Gary three years ago," she said, taking the glass of white wine he handed her.

Going over to the wall unit, he turned on the stereo. A CD was already in the deck. The soulful voice of Patti LaBelle filled the room.

"Gary would still be the one if he didn't roam like a wildebeest," he said, speaking loudly. "I don't play that, AIDS is vicious. I like myself and life too much to play with a propane torch."

"Geez," she said, sticking a finger in her right ear. "Turn it down a little."

"Oh, you're so boring," he said, popping his fingers, closing his eyes, and swaying to the music. "You have to play Miss Patti loud to feel the thrill. Don't you just love her?"

"I could love her even more if you turned her down a couple of decibels."

He turned down the volume. "Party pooper. Oh, let me show you what Phillip bought me for our second-month anniversary. I can't wait for him to get back in town."

"Where is he?"

"Paris."

"I envy him."

Chapter 6

GETTING THROUGH two weeks without speaking to Charmaine had been anything but easy for Marissa. Since they didn't work in the same department or even on the same floor, it wasn't difficult to avoid bumping into her, but the telephone was a constant reminder that she was only two floors away. The first week Charmaine didn't bother Marissa, but in the last two days she had left three messages. Marissa tossed every one without reading them. While it wasn't fair to put her assistant, Vivian, in the middle, she told her to stop writing down the messages from Charmaine. She wasn't ready to talk to her on any level—business or not. Besides, it was never business Charmine wanted to discuss—it was her wedding. Well, too bad, it was going to have to go on without her.

Actually, Marissa had been excited about being the maid of honor. It was going to be her first time in a bridal party. Her sister Denise had gotten married at city hall, and she wasn't close enough to anyone else to be asked to participate in their wedding. Be that as it may, she had been willing to be in Charmaine's wedding party despite the fact that she didn't think that Charmaine needed to be marrying Gregory. He was such a nobody, and he was too satisfied with

his little job. No big dreams, and no little ones, either, according to Charmaine; but it wasn't her place to tell anyone what to do with their lives, certainly not when she welcomed no one's opinion about her own.

Still, Marissa could have slapped her own face for breaking her own rule. She had, for years, been against friendships or love affairs developing in the workplace. Soured relationships made for bickering coworkers. In her book, they were both taboo. That is, until she needed a shoulder to cry on. Terrence had left her because his wife was suspicious of his staying out late three and four days a week. From the start, they couldn't get enough of each other, so when he stayed away for three weeks and didn't call, it hurt her to her heart. She found herself crying at the oddest times and in the wrong places. It was Charmaine who had held her hand in the bathroom at work and listened to her blubbering. Then one day Terrence was waiting for her outside her apartment when she got home from work. In the end, the one day a week they managed to see each other was better than nothing.

Meanwhile, she and Charmaine had become close on and off the job. Now she regretted that she had shared so much of her private life; it left her vulnerable. Of course, she realized that she wasn't being very professional by not taking Charmaine's calls, but she seethed with anger every time she thought about Charmaine's sneaky attempt at matchmaking.

On Fridays after work, along with several other people from the office, Marissa and Charmaine would usually meet to have a drink at the watering hole down the street. For the last two weeks, Marissa had avoided that scene altogether. All afternoon her inner voice had been pushing her to sneak out of the office at four-thirty, and she was glad she listened. As the elevator door closed, she saw Charmaine exiting the elevator across the hall. More than likely she was trying to catch her off guard in her office. If Charmaine was anything, she was persistent.

"She's gone for the day," Vivian said.

Charmaine's shoulders slumped. "Did she get my message?"

Vivian's eyes shifted over to the telephone sitting on the corner of her desk. "She's been so busy. I'll tell her that you stopped by."

She shook her head before turning away from Vivian, who wasn't looking at her anyway. Vivian was standing at an open file drawer, busily fingering through the files looking for the right file to insert the paper she held in her hand.

It was no secret that Marissa wasn't speaking to her, everyone seemed to know. She had been asked about it several times but always she managed to get by with "We disagree like everyone else." Knowing Marissa, as closemouthed as she was, if she was asked, she wouldn't give up even that much. Marissa trusted a very select few, and Charmaine had been one of that few, that is until she messed up. She owed her an apology.

Marissa resolved to let her so-called friendship with Charmaine remain distant. It was the best way to avoid another argument and the prolonged anguish. She was still feeling miserable and she was counting on her date with Wayne to cheer her up. He was always good company. She hadn't seen him in two weeks but they usually got together on a Friday night for dinner, conversation, and sometimes a movie. They went out freely as there was no chance of bumping into his wife, who rarely came into Manhattan or Brooklyn from their home up in Mount Vernon. It was just as well, as there wasn't much for them to do behind closed doors. Though he had tried several times to make love to her in the first month they knew each other, he had failed. He said he had been impotent since his late thirties, but he thought that his strong desire for her would transcend nearly fifteen years of deflation with his wife and help him rise to the occasion. It didn't, and it was a shame. He seemed such a passionate, attentive man in his foreplay that she knew surely that she was missing out on something wonderful. She felt as badly for herself as she did for him, though she'd never fully appreciate what it was for him to be impotent. She did, however, understand the pain she saw in his eyes when he said, "You should have known me when I was a young man. I was insatiable." There was no need to remind

him that when he was twenty-five, she was a mere five years old. It
would not have happened then, either.

He wanted so badly to make love to her, that once he had tried
putting a rubber band snugly around the base of his penis. Something he had heard from some old man who was probably drunk.
Supposedly, he was supposed to get an erection when he got the desire and the pressure of the rubber band tightened, damming up the
flow of blood until it burst through and made him swell. It never
worked. She played along, laying in wait until he grew tired of
fondling her, or sometimes until he built her up to the brink of a
somewhat sweet sensation that vanished quicker than it took to get
to that point. That, she was used to. That elusive sweetness had always been out of her reach. At times it was more frustrating than not
having sex at all.

But poor Wayne, he tried hard not to cry. "I don't feel like a man,"
he had said.

She had taken his head gently against her naked breast and caressed him. "That's the problem with men," she said, "you all think
your manhood is in your pants. Give me a caring, sensitive man I
can talk to, who can talk to me in turn, then I'm satisfied."

He lifted his head and looked into her eyes. "Will that be enough
for you? Will you still want to see me?"

"As far as I'm concerned, good conversation can be as satisfying
as good sex. And keep in mind, all sex isn't necessarily good."

"Speak for yourself."

"I stand corrected," she said, stroking his well-defined biceps,
"but there is plenty to do besides going to bed."

He had kissed her tenderly on the breast, and for a long while,
they had lain as innocently as two babes in each other's arms with
their naked bodies touching. It was the last time. She had never regretted her decision to continue seeing him. He treated her well, and
once in a while, a gift of a gold bracelet or earrings or a necklace
was evidence of their friendship. She was more than satisfied, because after all, she wasn't in it for the sex. She had enough of that
with Terrence and Louis.

She had yet to find out what Eric could do for her. They had only met two months ago, and had gotten together only five times. In fact, they hadn't even had sex yet. She told him she was taking time out after breaking up with a long-time love. It never paid to be too easy, and really, two sexual partners was her limit. If she started with him, then either Louis or Terrence would have to go, and she wasn't ready for that yet. At forty, Eric was younger than her other men and was just getting his new dental practice off the ground. He was but an interesting diversion once in a while.

Of course, Wayne knew that she was seeing someone besides him, he wasn't stupid. She was single, she had needs. Therefore, sitting on her hands like a schoolgirl while waiting for his Friday night visits wasn't happening. The particulars were kept out of their conversations, but he knew. That's why she was comfortable enough with him to tell him about what Charmaine had done, minus, of course, the part about her seeing married men. He laughed.

"I wish I had been there to see you pitch a bitch."

"I can assure you, it wasn't pretty," she said, kicking off her shoes.

"I bet it wasn't, but, actually, I feel sorry for the guy."

"I don't. Anyone who consents to being set up on a blind date should expect rejection, especially if the other party, me, didn't have a clue."

"You're right."

"I know I am," she said, pulling her arms out of her blazer while he held onto the lapels. "Sight unseen, you don't know what you're in for."

"True," he agreed, handing her the blazer to hang in the hall closet. Then taking off his own suit jacket, he handed it to her also. She hung it alongside her own blazer before closing the door.

"Go on into the living room, I'm going to put water on for coffee."

"I'll come with you," he said, pulling at his tie knot to loosen it. "Of course, I'm glad he's not your type. He might have a problem with us seeing each other."

"Wayne, our friendship is one any man I see will have to accept."

He sat down at the oak and glass table. "I hope so, though I have to admit, I might be a little jealous."

"Don't even go there," she warned. "You can't even begin to talk jealousy when you have a wife."

"It's a man thing, Marissa. We're jealous by nature. We don't like anyone touching what's ours."

His statement irked her. Going over to the sink, she turned on the faucet and began filling the teakettle with cold water. She looked back at him. "Women belong to men, huh?"

"Marissa, don't go getting feminist on me. It's just a figure of speech."

"No, it isn't. This has been going on since the first caveman grunted: 'You ma woman.' "

"Are you saying that I think like a caveman?"

"If the rusty sole fits," she said, looking at him pointedly.

"Well, a man will be a man."

"Which is why, from the dawn of time, men have freely touched as many women as they damn well please and get a pat on the back for it. Women, on the other hand, when we do something similar, we're called whores."

"Different standards, Marissa. I didn't make up the rules."

"No, you only live by them," she said disgustedly. She took the kettle over to the stove. Turning on the gas, she bent down slightly to peer under the kettle as she adjusted the flame. Straightening up, she continued, "Wayne, do you know that most women are in a relationship with somebody, and so are most men for that matter?"

"What's your point?"

"My point is this: men, like yourself, have affairs and so do women like me, and women like your wife."

He started shaking his head.

"Therefore, some other man is always touching somebody else's woman, maybe even *your* woman."

"Nobody better not touch my wife."

"They better not?"

"That's right."

Sitting two coffee cups and saucers onto the counter, she chuckled to herself as she scooped a heaping teaspoon of instant coffee grains into each cup. "I give up."

"Admit it, you women wouldn't have us any other way."

"Keep thinking like that, okay? You'll find out," she said.

"Sue us. Instinctively, men are territorial."

"You're cavemen. Think about it this way, Wayne. Your wife, I'm willing to wager that unless she's frigid, she's been putting her Friday nights to good use while you're out with me, and I don't blame her—and you shouldn't, either. She's probably doing what you would if you could."

His eyes clouded over. She had been dying to say that to him for a long time, and looking at the blotchy, ruddy shade he turned and the sudden tight lines around his mouth, he didn't like it one bit.

Riiiing!

"My wife isn't like that, she's very religious and highly moral."

Riiiing!

"Okay. Then I'm wrong. But you're . . ."

Riiiing!

"Darn. I forgot to put on the answering machine," she said, getting up from the table and rushing into the living room. She waited for the phone to ring again. She always let it ring at least four times before answering. She didn't want anyone to think that she was sitting idly by the phone, ever.

Riiiing!

"Hello?"

"Stay away from my man."

"What?"

"Stay away from my man or I'll kill you," the voice said low and threatening.

She inhaled sharply. Her heart leapt in her chest. "Who is this?"

A loud *crack* came through the receiver as the person on the other end slammed down the phone. She jerked the receiver away from her ear and stared at it.

"What happened?" Wayne asked from the kitchen door.

Hanging up the telephone, she stared down at it.

"Marissa? You look sick. What did they say?"

"I don't believe this," she said, going back into the kitchen.

For a moment she sat with her eyes closed with her hands cupped around her nose and mouth. The threat came from so far out of left field that it shook her to the core.

"Would you please tell me what happened?"

She lowered her hands. "Some maniac just called and said, 'Stay away from my man.' "

His eyes bugged. "Who?"

"I don't know."

"Was it a man or woman?"

Gawking at him, she said, "A man? No man would call here and say, 'Stay away from my man.' It was a woman."

"I mean, what did she sound like?"

"I don't know. She sounded like a woman, like me, like anybody. I don't know."

"You spoke to my wife once. It wasn't her, right?"

Marissa locked eyes with him while trying to remember what his wife's voice sounded like. She had called his house several times over the years but had heard his wife's voice only once when she answered the telephone. She had hung up immediately so she had only heard a brief "hello." Who could tell from that? The truth is, she had never given a thought to anyone's wife ever calling her. Especially Wayne's wife. She didn't consider what they were doing wrong—they weren't sleeping together. In fact, she could easily meet his wife and be a friend to her, too.

"My wife's voice is high-pitched. You know, kinda squeaky. Her voice is unmistakable—she sounds almost like a little girl. She's about the size of a little girl, too, but her voice gets kind of raspy when she has a cold, but she was fine when I spoke to her this afternoon."

Shrugging her shoulders, she was struck by his nervousness and his determination to make sure she understood what his wife's voice

sounded like. "I don't know voices, Wayne. Besides, your religious, highly moral wife wouldn't be calling me and saying that she was going to kill me, would she?"

"That definitely does not sound like my wife. My wife is scared of her own shadow."

She stared at the reflection of the overhead light in the table. "Then why do you sound so frantic? Are you worried that it might truly be your wife?"

"No! I just wanted to know who you thought it might be."

"I can't say if it was your wife or the wife of Attila the Hun. In fact, I can't tell you who it sounded like because I don't know the voice."

Wooo!

They both started. The whistling of the teakettle shattered the momentary silence. Leaping up from the table, Wayne raced to the stove and turned off the fire as she stared down at her long, red tapered nails. He lifted the teakettle with a pot holder and began pouring water into each of their cups while she picked under each nail of her left hand with the thumb nail of her right hand. Repeatedly, she clicked each nail before moving on to the next. Staring blankly at nothing, she wondered if the threat was real.

He sat a cup of black coffee in front of her. The silver spoon handle rose up out of its opaque depth. Coming back to the table with his own cup, Wayne splashed his coffee over onto the saucer as he sat down again. "Are you seeing another married man?"

He was looking at her like he already knew the answer. He was probably hoping that the finger could be pointed at someone else. She looked down into her cup. Slowly, she began stirring the blackness into a swirl; the word *yes* had caught in her throat. When she looked at him again, he was scooping two heaping teaspoons of sugar into his cup from the sugar bowl.

He stirred. "You don't have to answer."

She continued to stir.

With his spoon still in the cup, he cautiously sipped at the edge of his cup, his lips barely touching the white china.

"Maybe I should call the police," she said pensively.

Wayne sat his cup down with a clank. He pulled his chair closer to the table. "They'll want to know who you're seeing."

"I'm guessing; that could be a problem for you, huh?"

He rubbed his chin. "They might want to question my wife."

She glanced up at the wall clock. It was 11:15, time for Wayne to go home to his wife. He was more concerned about her anyway, even though he had already said that it definitely was not her voice.

"Marissa, I can't involve my family. You understand that, don't you?"

"Sure do," she replied dryly. The fear that his wife might be contacted by the police was crystal clear in his words. His wife's continued ignorance of their relationship was more important to him than her safety. As innocent as their relationship was supposed to be, it wasn't innocent enough for his wife to know about it. Still, it would make more sense to her if it were Terrence's or Louis's wife. For each of them, sex was a big part of their relationship and being that they weren't exactly young roosters, she wondered if they had the energy to do for their wives what they did for her. Three weeks had passed since Terrence's last visit—his mother-in-law was visiting and he didn't want to make her suspicious of his late nights; he always said she was more observant than his wife. Still, neither his wife nor Louis's wife had ever called her before. Maybe one of them had finally found her telephone number in her husband's wallet. Wives were notorious for snooping whether they suspected their husbands of cheating or not.

"Marissa, have you ever been threatened before?"

The call two weeks ago came to mind. She had forgotten all about it. Telling Wayne about it now would only make him more nervous. Taking a quick sip of her coffee, she flinched. "Why?" she asked, standing up. The bitterness had shocked her out of her stupor. Going over to the refrigerator, she took out a small container of cream.

"Maybe it's someone from your past."

"I don't think so. Forget the call. It was probably a prank, a random call."

"But you're unlisted."

"So," she said, sitting down and pouring the thick white cream

slowly into her cup. The blackness instantly vanished into a rich mocha. "Kids randomly dial telephone numbers all the time. Wayne, I am not going to let a stupid prank call scare the wits out of me. In fact, I hope whomever made the call goes straight to hell."

He took another sip of his coffee. "Just the same, maybe you ought to consider changing your phone number."

"I am not going to get paranoid about this." Then waving her hand as if to shoo away a fly, she said, "Enough of this. Do you want to catch the last half of the news?"

Wayne pulled his shirt cuff above his watch. "I think I should get going."

"Already?"

"Yeah," he said, pushing away from the table and standing up. "I got a lot to do around the house tomorrow morning to get ready for my daughter's party. She graduated from Columbia."

"Congratulations. I'd send a card, but you know . . ."

"I know," he said, reaching for his cup.

"Leave it," she said, getting up from the table also. Together, they walked to the hall closet. She helped him slip into his jacket.

"Listen," he said, "call me if you get another call."

"It's the weekend."

"Say you're calling about a promotional survey or something. I get calls like that all the time."

Unlocking the door, she pulled it open. "Maybe."

Lowering his head, he kissed her on first the right cheek and then the left. "I'll call you next week," he said, starting off down the hall.

She didn't wait until he rang for the elevator—she closed the door, double bolted it, and rushed into the living room to switch on the answering machine. She turned the volume level to high so she could hear whomever was calling from anywhere in her three-room apartment.

Only after she got out of the shower did she feel like she could sleep. Lying in bed on her left side, as was her norm, she left her window blinds up so that she could see the night sky. The twinkle of the stars never failed to lull her into the bosom of sleep.

Chapter 7

"HI, THIS IS Marissa. If you leave a message, I'll call you back. 'Bye."

Beeep!

Silence.

Click.

Her eyes popped open. Just as quickly, she snapped them shut against the bright sunlight streaming through her bedroom window. Twice during the night she had been awakened by her own recorded voice followed by dead silence and finally the click of someone hanging up. She hated weak-kneed people. Whomever it was had plucked her last nerve. If this woman had something to say to her, then she should say it and stop the childish games.

The notion of turning off the answering machine and disconnecting the telephone was quickly discarded when she realized that she might miss a call from Terrence or Louis. It didn't happen too often on a Saturday, but either one could get the afternoon or evening free. If not, she stood a good chance of spending another Saturday night polishing her nails and watching a rented video. First one to call, first one served was her motto. Hopefully, it would be Terrence. Louis was as generous as he was passionate, but he was not sensitive

to her emotions, though she had no problem with that; she wasn't seeing him for that reason. She preferred Terrence. He was sensitive and affectionate and was probably the closest to love she had been in for more than ten years, and right now, she needed him. For the most part, she grabbed hungrily at any time he could spare, and savored it for all it was worth. That's why she had canceled out Louis for him more than once.

Clutching the spare pillow to her chest, she turned onto her side away from the window and sighed. Just the thought of Terrence made her ache for him.

Riiiing!

She glanced over at the brass alarm clock on the nightstand next to the telephone. It was 8:35, too early on a Saturday morning for a telephone call—unless it was Terrence.

Riiiing!

"Hi, this is Marissa. If you leave a message, I'll call you back. 'Bye."

Beeep!

She waited.

"Marissa, pick up the phone. I know you're there. You realize, don't you, that people who screen their calls are subconsciously trying to be the proverbial fly on the wall? Who is it that you're trying to avoid?"

She reached over to pick up the telephone.

"I must tell you—"

"Tell me what?" she asked, her head sinking back into the pillow with the telephone receiver pressed to her ear.

"Screening calls, are we?"

"Brandon, it's too early. What do you want?"

"My, we're testy already."

"With good reason. This damn phone has irritated me all night. Someone keeps calling and—"

Beeeep! The answering machine disconnected itself.

"—hanging up."

"Have you reported it to the telephone company?"

"Not yet."

"You should, and ask them about a Caller ID box while you're at it."

"That's a good idea."

"Meanwhile, I got a call last night from your girlfriend Charmaine."

"So." Marissa sat up. She crossed her legs Indian style and rested her left elbow on her left thigh.

"She wants to talk to you. She thought I might pass the word on and perhaps encourage you to speak with her."

"I do not want to hear anything she has to say."

"Maybe not, but she did say that she was sorry, and to me, she sounded sincere."

Pursing her lips, she fixed her gaze on a colorful print of a jazz ensemble on the far wall.

"Marissa, at least she's mature enough to admit that she was wrong, and although I didn't tell you before, she called me the same evening you two fought. She admitted it then, too."

"Brandon, I could care less. I just want her to leave me alone."

"Did you forget that you're her maid of honor?"

"Not anymore."

"Marissa, that's not right and you know it. The wedding is a week away and she's counting on you."

"That's not my problem."

"Girl, don't hurt yourself trying to be nice. Look, I'm going to be at the wedding and I hope to see you there."

"Don't count on it."

"I see this isn't getting us anywhere. Look, I said I'd give you the message and I did. She said she would like to meet you for dinner tonight—her treat. Call her."

"Thanks, but no thanks."

"Sweetie, holding grudges clogs the arteries."

"Brandon, do I tell you what to do?"

"Oh, well, message delivered. I have several runs to make today. I'm redoing my kitchen. If your mood swings north, call me later."

There was an audible click in her ear when he hung up. She hung up, too, knowing that he was annoyed with her, but she didn't care.

She fell back against the pillow and nestled in its softness. A hell of a thing to have to be reminded of Charmaine the first thing on a Saturday morning. Neither she nor those annoying hang-ups were going to ruin her day. Wait a minute. Maybe it was Charmaine calling and hanging up. Except it didn't sound like her. To be fair, the last time—a week ago—Charmaine called, she had left a message. Hang-ups didn't seem to be her style. Though it might be a cheated-on wife's style. But which one?

She wasn't about to drive herself crazy trying to figure out who was harassing her. That's why she had to get out of the house. If she stayed in, there was nothing to do but clean and there was only so much cleaning she had to do. A flick of the feather duster across the furniture; a quick push of the vacuum throughout the apartment would take less time than it would take for her to take a shower, dress, and hit the road, but she wasn't in the mood for being domestic when she could go shopping. She could always use some new clothes. Something pretty—something sexy.

Admittedly, this is when she missed Charmaine; she usually went along for the ride. While Charmaine often ended up buying an outfit or a pair of shoes herself, she'd complain all the way to the cashier that she couldn't afford it. It wasn't that she couldn't afford to spend money on herself, it was that she and Gregory were trying to save thirty thousand dollars for the down payment on a house. If she thought Charmaine would listen to her, she would tell her to wait until she and Gregory were married a while—a year or two—before she made a financial commitment like that. Suppose they had problems from day one? But then, that wasn't her concern, either, was it? She no longer wanted anything to do with the wedding or the friendship. The pity of it was, she had already spent money to have her dress made—a waste. That's what she gets for trying to be a friend. She should have made Charmaine pay for her dress, like she did for her two bridesmaids, then she wouldn't be out two hundred and seventy-five dollars. But no, she had to be understanding about her plans to buy that damn house.

Throwing both her legs over the side of the bed at the same time, Marissa pulled her nightgown over her head and, flinging it onto the

bed, rushed into the bathroom to take her shower. The quicker she got out, the better she'd feel. She didn't want to spend her day either musing about Charmaine or waiting for Terrence to call. Besides, if the telephone did ring, answering it might be an invitation to let whoever it was that was harassing her into her life to upset her further.

Chapter 8

WHIPPING OUT HER credit cards and prowling through the designer outlets in Paramus vanquished Marissa's blues. After five hours of shopping, she treated herself to a lunch of shrimp creole and wild rice. She sprightfully left New Jersey behind and by the time she crossed the East River back into Brooklyn, she was singing along with the oldies but goodies on the car radio. Shopping always had that effect on her. She had no idea how much she spent, but she had two hot new designer suits to wear to the office and a really sassy, slinky, black dress to wear out to dinner with some lucky man. Once home, as was her habit, she tried on all three outfits again before hanging them in her closet. It was the full-length mirror hanging on the back of the closet door that she trusted—not the one in the stores designed to flatter and give an illusion of a perfect fit. If she looked good in her own mirror, then she kept the outfit. If not, it went back to the store. Luckily, all three still looked good on her.

That little ritual out of the way, she dared to check the answering machine. She had purposely avoided going into the living room right away. The message indicator signaled that there were three messages. She pushed the Play button. While the tape rewound, she

waited with her eyes shut in anticipation of hearing either silent messages or a vile threat.

"Hey, baby love. I'm uptown on Eighty-ninth Street. I'll be finished up here 'round seven. Beep me before seven, if you're free."

Beeep!

Damn, Louis would be the one that would have a free evening. Twice a month he got together with four other men to jam, as he called it. He had been playing a saxophone since high school. Sometimes they played in local clubs, but mostly they entertained themselves.

"Rissa, please do me a favor. Can you baby-sit Sean and Corey for me tonight? Willie got theater tickets from one of his customers and I really wanna go. Call me as soon as you get in. 'Bye."

Beeep!

"Not tonight, sister dear," she said to the answering machine. She loved her nephews and didn't mind keeping them—they usually had fun together—but horsing around or watching a kiddie video was out of the question tonight.

"Marissa, I know you don't wanna talk to me, but I realize I was wrong. Would you please call me?"

Beeep!

"Please leave me alone, Charmaine," she said, pushing the rewind button. Picking up the telephone she dialed Louis's beeper number. That done, she dialed Denise's number. "Hi, Niecy."

"Hey, sweetie," she answered, sounding out of breath. "I didn't know if you were going to get back to me. I got the girl downstairs to baby-sit."

"Is she trustworthy?"

"Oh, sure. I've used her before."

"What are the tickets for?"

"*CATS,* finally," she answered excitedly.

"That's nice. I saw—"

"Rissa, I'm trying to get dressed. Can I talk to you tomorrow?"

"Sure, go ahead. Have fun."

Her feelings might have been hurt if it wasn't for the fact that

Denise got to go out so rarely that this was an occasion. Along with her full-time job as a registered nurse, she was the consummate wife and mother. Where she found time in the course of a day to do anything for herself besides getting dressed was a mystery. The thought of being saddled with that much domestic responsibility sent chills up Marissa's spine.

The telephone rang less than a minute after she hung up.

"Hello?" she asked cautiously.

"Hey, baby love," the melodious baritone voice said.

"That was quick."

"I was waiting to hear from you. Wanna get together?"

"Of course."

"I'm dressed rather casually, chinos and a shirt. What do you wanna do?"

"Nothing special," she lied. She had hoped that they could have gone somewhere nice so that she could have worn her new black dress, but chinos?

"Then let's stay in. I'll pick up some Chinese food."

She silently sucked her teeth. Chinese food meant that she was in for a long night.

"I have something for you."

She perked up. "What?"

Beeep!—the call-waiting signal sounded in her ear.

"Don't you like surprises?"

"You know I do, but hold on a minute, I have another call."

"I'm getting off," Louis said quickly. "I'll see you in an hour."

Beeep!

"Okay," she said, pushing the flash button to pick up on the other call. "Hello."

"Hi, Marissa," Charmaine said.

"Damn!" she mouthed, sitting down hard on the arm of the love seat.

"Please, don't hang up."

She said nothing. She sighed loudly.

"I want to apologize," Charmaine said, speaking quickly. "I was

wrong. I will never say or do anything again to hurt or embarrass you. Will you please forgive me?"

Crossing her legs, Marissa began to shake her foot rapidly. Oh, how she wanted to hang up.

"Please, Marissa. I really am sorry. I was thinking about postponing my wedding until we can resolve this."

She sighed dejectedly. "Don't do that," she said, remembering how excited Charmaine had been when Gregory finally relented and let her set the date. No one was going to blame her if this wedding did not happen.

"I consider you my best friend, Marissa. My wedding will not be the same without you. I can hold off until you feel comfortable enough to be around me again."

"I'm sure Gregory would love to hear that."

"Well, that's how I feel. Gregory knows that."

"Look Charmaine, I'm still upset, but . . ."

"I understand, you have a right to be."

"Then you understand I need a little more time. . . ."

"I know, that's why I'm going to postpone—"

"No."

Charmaine was silent.

"Don't put off your wedding."

Charmaine remained quiet.

She realized that the ball was bouncing in her court, waiting to be returned. "Damn," she mouthed to herself again.

"Can I come by tonight to talk for a minute?"

"I have plans tonight. Maybe tomorrow—afternoon?"

"What time?"

"Two-thirty?"

"I'll be there."

"I have to go now," she said, hating herself for giving in.

"I'll see you tomorrow," Charmaine said, sounding a lot cheerier than she sounded when she first called.

She hung up without saying good-bye. "I'm such a wimp," she said, glancing at the VCR clock. She had about forty-five minutes to

shower and get ready for Louis. Leaving the answering machine on, she stripped and jumped under the hot shower. She thought she heard the telephone ring, but there was no need to wonder about whether or not it was Terrence, he would have called by now.

It wasn't until she had lotioned, perfumed, and draped herself in luscious, silky black lounging pajamas that she remembered that the telephone had rang. The solitary "Whore," said low and nasty followed by a click, unnerved her. She erased the message without a second's hesitation. Dumbfounded, she sat on the edge of the love seat hugging herself tightly.

This didn't make any sense. Why would someone suddenly start harassing her? Had Terrence or Louis or Wayne or even Eric slipped up and left her telephone number laying around? They should have all known it by heart by now.

Buzzzzzz!

She jumped up and reached over and turned down the volume on the answering machine. If the telephone rang again, she did not want Louis to hear ugly words, or silence. Shaking her hands to release the tension, she rushed to the intercom box on the wall near the door and pressed the talk button.

"Yes?"

"Miss Jenkins, the tall gentlemen, Mr. LaSalle," Maury announced.

"Thank you," she said curtly, releasing the button.

She hated that. There were days when she wanted to put her fist through the line and punch Maury in the mouth. "The tall gentleman" was his way of saying, "Let me describe him to you in case you don't remember." "The distinguished gentleman" was the way he described Terrence. While Wayne was "the muscular gentleman," he simply announced Eric as "Dr. Grayson." Of course, none of the guys thought anything was wrong with the way he announced them; that's because it was flattering to their egos. They thought she was upset for nothing, but she knew that Maury was being flip about the number of men that called on her. Even he dismissed her when she spoke to him about it, by explaining that he described all visitors in one way or another, he said it made his job less boring. It didn't help

when none of the other tenants complained. She was waiting for someone really fat to visit her to hear how he'd announce them. Smart-ass.

The first thing Louis did when she opened the door was take her into his arms, push his tongue into her mouth, and kiss her long, deep, and passionately. He greeted her the same way every time they got together. Fortunately for her, he kissed well—and dry. She hated a sloppy, wet kisser who left her mouth full of spit and her face wet. When he finally released her, he handed her the shopping bag he carried—heavy with Chinese food.

"There's enough here to feed an army," she said, taking the bag into the kitchen.

"I know you like chicken and broccoli, but you like shrimp, too," he said, sitting down at the table. "I wanted steak, so I got a little of everything."

She began lifting out one hot container after another and sitting them on the table. There must have been three containers of starchy white rice alone. The strong smell of soy sauce filled the room.

She placed the containers of rice side by side. "Do you want to eat now?"

He chuckled. "I'm hungry," he said, "but not for food."

"Oh really?" she asked coyly. "What are you hungry for?"

Slowly licking his lips, he answered, "You."

She sat the empty shopping bag in the chair. Then like a sleek cat on the prowl, she slinked around the table to stand in front of him. He took her hand and pulled her down onto his lap. They kissed. She could feel on the underside of her thigh how much he wanted her, but before he got started, she needed to ask him something first.

His hand slowly moved down her back. "I said I had something for you."

Oh, well. Perhaps it was not his wife harassing her. "What is it?" she asked sweetly, playing along because Louis liked to make a big deal of trying to surprise her, even though it was usually money he gave her.

"It's in my left inside jacket pocket."

Slipping her hand inside his jacket, she pulled out a small sealed,

blank envelope. Acting coquettishly naive, she asked again, "What is it?"

"Open it and find out."

Slowly tearing back the flap with her fingernail, she was pleased to see that there were several one-hundred-dollar bills inside. She didn't want to show her eagerness by counting them right then and there. She placed the envelope on the table.

"What's this for?"

"Last week you said you wanted to buy a few clothes. I can't go with you, but I can pay for them."

Hugging him tightly, she smiled to herself knowing that he always took her hints to heart and saw no reason to tell him that she had already gone shopping. "You're so sweet."

"I try to be," he said, grinning from ear to ear while one hand caressed her waist, and the other eased up the inside of her thighs.

She kissed him gently on the lips.

He groaned softly.

"Thank you," she said, starting to get up.

"Where are you going?"

"To my bedroom. You wanna come?"

"Sure do," he answered seductively. His voice had dropped an octave.

She glanced back at him and smiled. He followed her like a hungry dog.

Chapter 9

IT WAS ELEVEN o'clock Sunday morning before Marissa was able to crawl out of bed. She was exhausted. Louis didn't leave until two o'clock in the morning, and he had been practically insatiable. He left with his belly full of lovemaking and Chinese food. It was amazing to her that his desire increased as he got older. No matter how many times they got together during the course of a month, his desire was just as strong. Again, she had to wonder if his wife was satisfying him at all, or if maybe he was insatiable. While she had always gone the distance with him, she couldn't imagine herself having to satisfy him every night—he'd put her in an early grave. Amazingly, with all of their lovemaking, he had never been able to take her to the summit and over the top, and as far as she was concerned, if he couldn't do it, no one could.

Before Charmaine rang the bell, Marissa had eaten a plateful of leftover chicken and broccoli and fried rice. She knew that she was not going to be able to face her on an empty stomach.

At the door, Charmaine pulled her into her arms, which wasn't so much unusual as it was awkward, under the circumstances. It was an uneasy embrace, yet it released a bit of her tension. Charmaine

wanted to sit in the kitchen like old times as they had had many a gabfest there, but she suggested the living room instead. The last thing she wanted to do was sit in a straight chair.

"Thank you for letting me come over."

She didn't know what to say to that, except "You're welcome," which sounded silly even to her own ears.

"Your dress is ready," Charmaine said. "I'm picking it up Monday after work. It looks really great."

"What about your gown?"

"They need another few days to finish it. It looks good so far. I've scheduled rehearsals for Friday night. Can you make it?"

"I'm sure I can."

"Good. Then I need to call the minister tomorrow and confirm. I can call Gail and Lisa when I get home."

"Call them now."

"You don't mind?"

"Girl, please."

Charmaine got up and went over to the telephone sitting on the table. As she dialed, she looked at the blinking light on the answering machine. "You have a few messages."

"I'll check them later," she said casually. The last thing she needed was for Charmaine to hear someone calling her a whore on the answering machine. It would only validate her argument about her and married men, in addition to confirming what she'd said only two weeks ago: "One of these days you're gonna mess with the wrong woman's husband."

With her calls to her cousin Gail and her sister Lisa made, Charmaine sat down again. For the next hour they talked about the wedding and her planned three-day honeymoon trip to St. Thomas. It was the best she and Gregory could do, considering their desire to find a house.

"Marissa, I need to say something to you."

Marissa could about guess what that was. "We don't really need to rehash what happened. Just let it go."

"I will, but please, give me a minute."

There was that annoying persistence again. Charmaine was going

to make her listen while she purged. Marissa hated that. She folded her arms brusquely across her chest.

"What is it you have to say?"

Charmaine began rubbing her hands. "Marissa, I am so sorry."

"You've said that already. Let's just forget it."

"Okay, but I wanted to make sure that what happened doesn't change our friendship in any way."

She looked away and then back again. "Charmaine, life is about change; people are about change. In fact, my father used to say all the time, 'Friends come and go; enemies accumulate.' "

"And which am I?" Charmaine asked, no longer rubbing her hands.

"We'll always be friends, Charmaine, I'm not saying that we won't. I'm just saying that change is inevitable. It's good for both of us."

She stared at Marissa. "You know something? I don't think you've ever been really comfortable with our friendship."

"Here we go," she said, angrily recrossing her legs. This was the very reason she did not want to talk, garbage that had nothing to do with their argument was coming out.

"You're uncomfortable now, aren't you?"

"Charmaine, is there anything else I need to know about the wedding, about the rehearsal?"

"No, but I need to say this, Marissa. When we first became friends, I could tell that you didn't trust me."

"That was your own perception, Charmaine, and had nothing to do with anything I did or said to you."

"Not that you're aware of. In fact, until that day you first talked to me in the bathroom about Terrence, probably because you had no choice, you—"

"I always have a choice."

"Okay, but until that day you never said more than ten words to me."

"So what. Am I a bad person because of that?"

"Marissa, do you know that everyone was saying that you were stuck up?"

That didn't surprise her. "A bunch of women, I'm sure."

"Yes, but that's because you only talked to the men—especially the administrators and executives."

"That's my business."

"Sure it is, but women don't like being ignored by a sister, it makes them think that you're either stuck up, or a tramp."

She glowered. "They can kiss my ever-loving ass. I don't give a damn what they think."

"I'm just telling you what was being said about you."

"I don't care, Charmaine. Whoever was saying or thinking that about me needs to get a life and leave mine alone; but personally, I don't give a damn what any of those jealous bitches said about me. I'm not there to kiss their asses, I'm there to do a job."

"I just want you to know that I never thought that about you. I—"

"I don't care if you did or not," Marissa said, suddenly pushing herself up off the sofa. She began to pace, her arms folded across her breasts. "I let no woman's opinion, or man's, either, for that matter, infringe upon who I am."

Charmaine's eyes followed her. "Marissa . . ."

"Women have never liked me. Even when I was in high school, girls did not like me. They were jealous of me, they talked behind my back."

"Why do you think they did that?"

She stopped pacing and whirled around to face Charmaine. "Because I was better-looking, better-dressed, and certainly had more class than any of them."

"Nobody could touch you, huh?"

"That's right, and it's the same way now."

This time Charmaine arched her brows. She sat back. "If you say so."

"Jealousy is an ugly thing, Charmaine. What else could it be, but jealousy?"

Charmaine slowly rolled her lips inward.

"That's why I like men, I don't have to worry about them being catty. I've never done a damn thing to any one of the women on the

job, and I've never stooped low enough to gossip about any one of them. I have a life."

"So have I, but, Marissa, can you honestly say that our friendship hasn't meant something to you? That it didn't feel good to have a girlfriend to lunch with; to shop with; to care about you; to share private thoughts with? Can you say that a woman doesn't make a better friend than a man?"

She stuck her right leg out to the side and glared at Charmaine. "From my perspective, no. Women betray each other every day, they tell each other's secrets. Even the things I've told you about myself made me vulnerable to your betrayal."

"Betrayal?" Charmaine asked, uncrossing her legs and sitting up straight. "Marissa, I haven't betrayed you. I agree that secrets friends share can make them vulnerable; however, I've never betrayed you."

"Charmaine, that's exactly what you did a few weeks ago. You used what I'd told you about my love life to try to set me up with the very kind of man I don't like, and then you shot your mouth off with him in earshot about everything you knew about me. If that's not betrayal, what is?"

"Wait a minute," Charmaine said, gripping the arms of the chair. "Before you say another word, let me come clean on that so-called setup. That wasn't supposed to be a setup. Levi is Gregory's best man. I just wanted the four of us to get together before the rehearsal. It came out looking like a setup because of the way you were acting."

Marissa tapped herself on the forehead. "Oh, it's my fault it came out looking like a setup. And how did I unwittingly do that?"

"You were acting snooty."

Dropping her arms to her side, Marissa narrowed her eyes to slits. "You're no different from the women I know who are jealous of me."

"Don't be paranoid, Marissa."

"Paranoid my ass. Don't you be a bitch."

Stretching her eyes wide, Charmaine chuckled dryly. "You know

something, Marissa? This would be funny if it wasn't so damn sad. I am sorry that I upset you, okay?"

"Don't patronize me, Charmaine."

"Okay, look, Marissa. I am not gonna let this conversation put us back where we were two weeks ago, but you're wrong. I, for one, am not jealous of you."

Too bad she didn't take the bait, it would have been the perfect excuse to kick her ass out of her apartment for good. "Then if you're not jealous, what's the problem?"

"It is certainly not jealousy, though, at times, I may have been a little envious, but that's all."

"Envy, jealousy, same difference."

"Not really."

She stomped over to the window, looked out, and then whirled around. "Charmaine, I'm not about to play word games with you. I don't need you in my life pretending to be my friend."

"I'm not pretending," Charmaine said, getting to her feet. "I am your friend."

"*Humph!*"

"Marissa, understand what I'm trying to say. I am not jealous of you, your accomplishments, or anything you might have. I'm happy for you. However, I do happen to envy your drive to go after what you want. I am envious of your meticulous nature, your professionalism, and your fearlessness in standing steadfast in your convictions. Ten years ago I would not have been able to sort out my feelings like this, but thanks to you, I can now. I've learned a lot from you."

"And how was I, in my snooty, paranoid way, able to teach you anything?"

"By being honest about your feelings; being true to yourself; being forthright with me; and by being very self-assured."

Marissa was taken aback. Had Charmaine really understood all those things about her? She crooked her head and looked at her sideways.

"When we first talked at length, I realized then that you weren't stuck-up or conceited."

"Oh? A few minutes ago you said I was acting like that at your house with Gregory's best man."

"You were, but that's because you were mad at me."

"You bet your ass I was," she said, walking away from the window and sitting down again on the sofa. "You have no idea how close I was to shoving that lasagna down your throat."

"Oh, I think I have an idea," Charmaine said, sitting down again herself. "Can we forget that day?"

"I wish you'd stop saying that you're sorry. It's wearing me out."

"Fine. Then we're okay, right?"

Marissa wanted to be immature and say no, but she realized that this was the first time any one of her so-called friends, besides Brandon, ever had the guts to think that she was worth hanging on to as a friend. She never cared much for staying friends with anyone who pissed her off anywhere near that bad, and she had kissed off many burdensome acquaintances. But Charmaine, apparently, was nothing like those pretenders. She seemed to care—for real. What would it hurt to give in? Did she have anything to lose? No, not really. Letting out a long sigh, she felt the tenseness in her neck and shoulders subside.

"We're just fine," Marissa finally said.

Charmaine smiled and she, too, breathed a sigh of relief.

Chapter 10

HAVING PROCRASTINATED long enough, Marissa turned up the volume on the answering machine and pushed the Play button.

The first message: A long, drawn-out silence.

The second message: A long, drawn-out silence.

The third message: "Rissa, call me tomorrow. The play was great."

The fourth message: "Hey, sweet lady," Eric said. "I wanted to just say hi. Can't wait to see you. I'll try and call you later."

The fifth message. "I'm warning you, bitch. Stay away from my man."

The machine clicked off.

A chill seized her heart. This woman had no intention of leaving her alone. "Dear God," she said, closing her eyes and quickly re-opening them. This time she didn't rewind the tape. She sat on the arm of the love seat and stared at the answering machine. She didn't have the foggiest notion as to who could be threatening her. If Wayne or Louis had indicated that their wives were suspicious, then she would have a clue. She didn't mention anything to Louis about the telephone calls because she didn't want him to back off; she would lose a lot of money if he did—he was the main reason she had

been able to get her car. If he thought his wife knew, he might stop seeing her altogether. After seeing the way Wayne had acted, she could only imagine how Louis or Eric might act. Terrence, however, would never desert her, but this woman was trying to mess up her good thing.

Riiiing!

She sprang up off the love seat and snatched up the telephone. "Who is this?"

"It's me," Denise said. "Geez, who were you expecting?"

Relieved, she exhaled sharply. When she inhaled, she started to cry.

"My God, Rissa! What's wrong?"

Struggling to get control of herself, she began to sniffle repeatedly.

"Rissa, talk to me."

"Someone keeps calling and threatening me."

"Who?"

"It's a woman, but I don't know who it is."

"A woman? Why is some woman threatening you? Did you call the police?"

"I can't, not yet," she answered, wiping her face dry with her free hand. "I don't know who it is."

"So. They can trace the—"

"Niecy, she doesn't stay on the phone but a second."

"Well, what is she saying in that second?"

"One time she said she was going to kill me."

"What?"

"At first I thought it was a crank call, but she's called four times. Twice she left a message on the answering machine. Plus, I keep getting hang-ups."

"Marissa, this doesn't make any sense. Why would anyone wanna kill you? I mean, you're not involved in anything illegal, are you?"

"Of course not!"

"Well, there must be a reason for this, Marissa. What is it?"

She did not want to tell her that it was someone's wife. Denise had been on her back, lecturing her for years about going out with

married men. Her argument with Charmaine was mild compared to the arguments she and Denise had. A few times, they had gone for months without speaking afterward. Now, it was something they didn't even talk about.

"It's somebody's wife, isn't it?"

Closing her eyes, Marissa slapped the palm of her hand against her forehead.

"Marissa, answer me. You know damn well it's somebody's wife. Did you think that no one would ever say anything to you?"

Frowning, she threw her head back and groaned.

"Even if no wife ever did say anything to you, Marissa, what are you trying to do? End up like Aunt Loretta? Do you wanna be a shriveled-up old maid who waited forty-two years for some married man to be free? Her children have never carried the name of their father."

"That's Aunt Loretta's problem. I am not having children and I am not waiting for anyone."

"Seems to me you are. I bet you're still seeing Terrence, aren't you?"

"Denise, I do not want to talk about this."

"I know you don't think he'll marry you after all this time."

"Denise."

"Aunt Loretta didn't get her man, you know. When his wife died, he went and found himself a new girlfriend. What do you think is gonna happen to you?"

Grimacing, she stomped her foot. She wanted to scream. Instead, fresh tears poured from her eyes.

"Marissa, I do not have time to be worrying about you, I got my own damn problems to worry about. Do you ever think about anyone besides your own selfish behind?"

"Shut up!"

"Goddamnit, Marissa, you brought this on yourself. I have told you and told you, stop messing with other women's men. Some women don't play that shit."

"Stop it! I can't—"

"Girl, don't you know there are women who will kill you over a man? Do you think for a minute—"

"Denise, pl—"

"—that you won't get hurt? You need to get your own damn man and—"

Bang! Marissa slammed the receiver down with such force, she thought she might have broken it. She felt like she couldn't catch her breath—like her throat had closed up. Balling her fists up, she lifted them up to her head, pressing hard, trying to still the sudden pounding. She was not going to let herself be scolded or lectured to like she was a witless child; and she had no intention of being harassed all evening by the faceless, nameless voice on the answering machine. She switched it off.

Riiing!

She grabbed the phone on the first ring. "Denise, I have enough to deal with right now. I don't need you—"

"Don't you *ever* hang up—!"

"Denise, please! I cannot deal with whomever is threatening my life and you haranguing me at the same time."

"Yeah, well, you reap what you sow."

She gritted her teeth. "Good-bye, Denise."

This time she didn't slam down the receiver, she calmly sat it in its cradle, then she reached in the back and pulled out the telephone line. She would argue with Denise another day, as she was sure there were at least another hundred arguments waiting to be unearthed in their future. For now, she didn't have the stomach or the stamina. Her nose began to sting, warning her of the tears that were threatening, but she steeled herself against them as she went from the living room to the bedroom to disconnect the telephone in there. Tonight no one would call her, no one would leave a message. Tonight she would cut herself off from those who judged her. Tonight Marissa would sleep without interruption.

Chapter 11

SLEEP ELUDED MARISSA most of the night, mostly she napped in between shifting from one position to another. Every time she looked at the clock, it appeared to have only moved fifteen to twenty minutes ahead. She tossed and turned until 5:00 in the morning, then she blacked out from exhaustion.

The sudden, harsh buzz of the alarm clock at 6:30 startled her awake. Her hand shot out toward the clock, knocking it over backward as she fumbled to switch it off. She was more tired than she was before she went to bed. Monday mornings were rough to begin with, but this one was worse by far. The clothes she chose to wear on Mondays were usually dressier because they made her feel alert and glamorous. This morning, she pulled on a pair of black slacks and a tailored white blouse. There was nothing glamorous about the way she was feeling.

It wasn't until after she had dragged herself out of the apartment and was on her way down in the elevator to the garage that it dawned on her that she hadn't reconnected her telephones. Shrugging her shoulders, she continued on to the underground garage with one other woman and headed for her car. Right away, she saw that there was a note under the windshield wiper. It was probably a note from

Julio, asking her if she wanted her car washed. Besides doing maintenance work in the building, he freelanced as a car washer. He did
pretty well, too. Ten dollars a car—hand washed and waxed. She
gave the car a quick once-over. It could use a wash. White was hard
to keep clean, but Julio kept her car spotless.

She pulled the note from under the wiper, unlocked the car door,
threw her pocketbook across to the passenger seat, and slid
smoothly behind the wheel. With the note still in her hand, she
turned the key in the ignition. The engine came alive instantly,
purring softly. As was her habit, she would give the car a minute to
warm up. Unfolding the note, she expected to see Julio's scrawl
telling her when he was available.

"Bitch, I don't need a telephone to reach you. I can put my hands
on you any time I want. Spread your legs with my man again, I'll
kill you."

Her mouth dropped open. Her eyes widened. For a minute her
breath caught in her throat. Her stomach flipped. She sat frozen,
staring at the note in her hand.

Suddenly, *tap . . . tap . . . tap* on the window next to her.

Startled, Marissa jumped.

"Hey, Miss Jenkins," Julio said, his face just inches from her on
the other side of the window.

She crumpled the note up in her hand and tossed it onto the floor
on the passenger side. She then covered her face with both hands
until her heart stopped racing.

Julio tapped again. "You all right?"

She wasn't all right, but she pressed the button and lowered the
window.

"You all right?"

"You just startled me, that's all," she said. "I've been watching too
many horror movies lately."

"Maybe you oughta stop, you look like you was about to flip out."

"Believe me, I was."

"I can wash your car this evening, if you want."

"Sure. I'll be home around six."

"Catch you later," he said, running his hand along the hood of the

car before he turned and went back to wherever he was before he scared her out of her mind.

Rolling the window back up, she sat staring at the crumpled note on the floor. Whomever it was not only knew where she lived, but knew her car, too. Not just anyone could get into the garage—a key was needed, although she had seen people enter when the garage door was open and a car entered or exited. Until now, she had never been concerned about security. At the monthly co-op meetings, the few times the need for a security guard in the garage was broached, the majority of the membership had voted against it because of the additional fee that would be tacked onto their monthly maintenance cost. Her no vote had not been because of cost—she just didn't see why it was necessary. At the next meeting, she would champion the need for a security guard with a vengeance.

Until then, there was always the police. However, she feared that they would lose no time questioning her about the men in her life. Then they would surely want to question their wives. She could not carelessly expose them to this. Since Wayne was certain that it was not his wife's voice, then it was Terrence, Louis, and Eric that she would have to speak to without scaring them away. She'd let them handle their own wives. In which case, the note was important; perhaps one of them might recognize the handwriting. Reaching over, she retrieved the note and stuffed it inside her pocketbook. Then, putting her car in gear, she drove slowly through the garage to the exit. Rolling down her window again, she reached over to the control box and pressed the green button. The garage door began to lift. It was possible for anyone to get in while the door was up. She had come in herself while other cars were leaving or entering. Yes, she was going to have to demand security down there, Marissa thought as she drove slowly out of the garage and up to the street.

Chapter 12

MARISSA CALLED TERRENCE the minute she got into the office. He was an early bird like her and was about to go into a meeting.

"Can't talk right now," he said, "but I was planning to see you tonight anyway. Why don't we meet at Armondo's around six."

Marissa agreed, and as soon as she got off the line with him, she dialed Eric. He was already with a patient, while Louis was away from the office for the day. Louis, she beeped.

Five minutes passed. "Hey, baby love. I was thinking about you this morning," he said. "I'd love to play hooky with you right now."

"Louis, I have to ask you something, but I don't want you to get upset."

"Why would I get upset?"

"Does your wife know about us?"

"What do you mean?"

"Has she ever asked you about me? Has she ever mentioned my name?"

An uneasy silence came through the telephone line. She pressed the receiver to her ear. "Louis?"

"Did my wife call you?" he finally asked in a hushed voice.

"I've been getting calls from a woman. She said that I had better leave her husband alone. Does your wife know?"

"I don't think so. She never said anything to me."

"Look, forget about it. I was just checking."

"I don't like this. It must be my wife. You're not seeing anyone else, are you?"

She rolled her eyes. Again, that question. Why did they have to keep asking that question? "No," she replied.

"Don't worry, I don't know how she might have gotten your number, but I'll take care of it."

"No, Louis, let it go for now. If she hasn't said anything to you, then maybe it'll go away. Just stay home for a few weeks. Let her think it's over and then just be more careful, that's all."

"I don't wanna stop seeing you."

"It'll be just for a few weeks. We've gone longer than that when you've gone away on vacation."

"All right, but I'll call you."

"That's fine."

"When we get together again," he said, his voice sounding husky, "I promise you, it will be special."

Rolling her eyes again, Marissa said, "I'll count the days."

"Talk to you tomorrow."

" 'Bye," she said, hanging up the telephone.

Buzzzzzz!

Pressing the intercom button, she said, "Yes, Vivian."

"You have a call on hold. I told her you would call her back, but she wanted to hold."

Looking at the second flashing light, she asked, "Who is it?"

"A Mrs. LaSalle."

Her heart skipped a beat. LaSalle was Louis's last name. "Did she say what she wanted?"

"She wouldn't say. Do you want me to get rid of her?"

"I'll take it," she said, pushing the button, ready to confront her antagonist. "This is Miss Jenkins."

"Well, Miss Jenkins, this is Mrs. Louis LaSalle. I have just five words for you: Stay away from my husband."

Marissa's hands began to shake. "How did you get this number?"

"Never you mind. Just listen."

Who the hell did she think she was? For a second, Marissa took the telephone from her ear. She looked at it before bringing it back.

"Miss Jenkins, I am not about to get down and dirty, but I suggest strongly that you prostitute yourself with another man."

"Prostitute! I—"

"Louis and I have been married thirty-two years. I have invested a lot of time in my marriage, and I am not about to lay down and die so that you can have my husband, nor am I willing to continue sharing him with you now that I know you exist. If Louis opts to leave me for you, mark my words, dear, the only thing he'll have to offer you is a token and a Tic Tac."

"Mrs. LaSalle, I suggest you speak to your husband. Meanwhile, stop calling my house and never leave me another threatening note again, or I will go to the police. You have a good day."

Marissa hung up quietly, although every nerve in her body screamed. She pushed back from her desk and stood up. She took a deep breath and blew it out through her mouth. This was a nightmare. Slamming both hands down on the desk, she shook her head in disbelief. This was getting uglier, but at least now she knew who the caller was. She had to warn Louis.

He answered his beeper right away.

"Louis, your wife just called me."

"Damn."

"I think you'd better call her."

"What did she say?"

"To stay away from you."

"Damnit. How the hell did she find out?"

"Damned if I know."

"I'll get back to you."

He hung up while she still held the telephone to her ear. She could not help but feel that it was most likely over between herself and Louis. Mrs. LaSalle didn't sound like a woman willing to let her man go, and Louis didn't make any overtures like "I love you, not my wife."

It didn't matter, really. She didn't want any more out of Louis than she was already getting. Actually, she didn't think she wanted any man permanently. "Come see me" and "Come live with me" were two different animals. There was no one she wanted to spend every waking hour with for the rest of her life, including Terrence. As good as she felt when her men visited, that's how good she felt when they went on their merry way. She didn't have to cook for them; she didn't have to wash their dirty clothes; she didn't have to play nursemaid; nor did she have to argue over petty things. Kiss-kiss, bye-bye worked fine for her. It would hurt for a minute if she could not be with Louis anymore, but she would get over it. As it was, her plate was full anyway.

Knowing where the threat was coming from made her feel infinitely better. She sat down and turned her attention to the paperwork on her desk.

Vivian buzzed her again. "Marissa, your sister is on line one."

"Tell her I'm in a meeting and that I'll call her later."

Marissa didn't know when she was going to be able to speak to Denise again without getting upset. They could use a break from each other. When they fought as kids, Momma used to make them kiss and make up right away. She hated that. As soon as they were left alone, they'd fight again, this time without making any noise, until one or the other won. Of course, the winner was determined by who wasn't crying. She cried more often than Denise. That's because Denise was a hard-ass and didn't even cry when she was hit by Momma. They were adults now, and Momma was in Florida living a life of retired bliss. Kissing and making up with Denise wasn't about to happen any time soon as far as she was concerned.

Over lunch, she and Charmaine talked about the wedding rehearsal. When she pulled her appointment book out of her pocketbook, the crumpled note popped out and rolled onto the table. Charmaine pointed it out to her, but she said it was garbage. After lunch, she left it behind, ripped into pieces to be tossed by the waiter.

Over dinner, Terrence talked about the successful bid his computer software company had made to design an invoice program for

a small chain of hardware stores. Twice she yawned into her dinner napkin. Back in her apartment, she nestled in his arms, playing with the curly hair on his chest as they lay in bed, still glowing from the warmth of their lovemaking. There was always a sense of complete calm when she was with him. Their lovemaking was never hurried, never intense; just slow and steady, no fireworks, but satisfying.

He lifted a clump of hair away from the side of her face and slowly began twirling it around his finger. "You said you wanted to talk," he said.

She snuggled deeper into his arms. "It wasn't important. I just missed you, that's all."

"I've been really busy running."

"At work?"

"At home. My—"

Her lips stopped his words. She climbed on top of him and made him forget his thought of home. When he spoke again, he said, "I have to go to Chicago for a few days in three weeks. I was hoping you could go with me."

They had the best times when they took little trysts out of town and didn't have to watch the clock or look over their shoulders all the time for people Terrence knew. "Call me in the office. If my calendar isn't clear, I'll clear it," she said, now lightly massaging his soft stomach.

"Good. I'm going to be pretty busy between work and home until then, so if you don't see me, don't worry."

"You can't be that busy."

"Marissa, things are pretty rough at home right now."

"Oh, okay. At least call me."

"I will. I'll definitely call you at the start of that week to let you know that everything is set. We can go to the airport from here."

"Okay, but I'm going to miss you."

"I'll miss you, too," he said, extracting himself from her embrace. "As much as I hate to get up out of this bed, I'd better. I have a breakfast meeting scheduled for eight o'clock in the morning."

She rolled onto her back. "Busy, busy," she said.

Terrence got up slowly off the bed. "Maybe a bit too busy."

Marissa watched as he went naked into the bathroom to take his shower. Laying and reveling in the warmth of where he had lain, she remembered that she had not reconnected her telephones. Pulling on the short, pale pink kimono she had laying at the foot of the bed, she went about reconnecting the telephone lines. As an afterthought, she switched on the answering machine. She could only hope that Louis was able to make his wife understand that they were through. Until she was convinced, he would have to keep his distance. Having an irate wife on her back was not part of the deal. If he couldn't make peace with his missus, then they were going to have to part company permanently.

As soon as Terrence left, she took a hot bath and got back into bed. The last thing she saw was the dark, starless sky.

Riiiing!

She stirred.

Riiiing!

She lifted her head to look at the clock. From the soft hall light she could barely see that it was one o'clock.

Beeeep!

"Hi, this is Marissa. If you leave a message, I'll call you back. 'Bye."

"Hey, slut. Did Mrs. LaSalle give you a piece of her mind?"

Chapter 13

WHAT THEY SAY is true—a watched pot never boils, and a watched clock stands still. Daybreak seemed an eternity away as Marissa paced the minutes into hours. From the minute the call came, there wasn't a hint of heaviness in her eyelids. She had sat up in bed and had not been able to lay her head down since.

How could she have been so stupid to have let her guard down? Mrs. LaSalle's call had taken her by surprise and she had been so nervous that she hadn't realized that the voice was different. If it wasn't Mrs. LaSalle, then who? More importantly, who did she know that would know how to contact Mrs. LaSalle? After some thought—no one. Denise and Charmaine both knew about Louis, but she wasn't sure if they knew his last name. Giving out last names wasn't a habit of hers. Whether they knew or not, she couldn't see either one calling Louis's wife and snitching on her, no matter how wrong they thought she was. Neither would try to hurt her like that; at least she didn't think they would. The sad thing is, she couldn't call either one to talk to them about it. They'd only say, "I told you so." If only she could recognize the voice. She had replayed the message over and over again before rewinding the tape, racking her brain mercilessly, and still she didn't know.

Daylight greeted her as she dozed, wrapped in an old afghan on the sofa in the living room. There had been no other calls throughout the night, yet she had been too perturbed to go back to sleep. But now she felt stupid. She was in her own apartment, behind locked doors, no less, where no one could harm her, and she had sat up all night. The phone calls were real, but her own imagination scared her more. Suppose one day this person lay in wait for her outside her door? What she needed to do was put the calls and the note in perspective. She needed to speak to someone a whole lot saner than herself.

"Hi, Brandon. Forgive me for calling so early, but I wanted to catch you before you left for work," she said, feeling badly about the way she had behaved on Saturday when they last spoke.

"This is a surprise. I didn't think I'd hear from you this soon."

"Well, surprise," she said yawning loudly. " 'Scuse me. Look, I know you're getting ready for work, but I need to talk to you. Can we meet for lunch or, if it's more convenient for you, after work?"

"I'm not going into the office, I'm working from home today. Tomorrow I'm going to Washington for a conference. You can come over any time you like."

As tired as she was, she needed to take the day off herself. "I'm going to try and leave the office by one."

"I'll be here. Is everything all right?"

"Not really. I'll tell you everything when I see you."

"Fine. I'll see you later then."

"Brandon?"

"Yes?"

"Thank you," she said, quickly hanging up the telephone. She felt like she had to thank him. He was the only one that would hear her out without judging her.

Though it was still early yet, she was dressed and out the door by seven, instead of her usual eight o'clock. Guardedly, she stepped out of the elevator down into the garage. She saw no one, and for a brief moment, she strained to hear sounds of anyone lurking about. Hearing nothing, she walked quickly toward her car eleven spots from

the elevator. The two parking spots next to her car were empty, giving her a full view of her car and its two flat tires.

"Damn," Marissa said, approaching the car, thinking that she might have run over glass or nails in the street. When she got right up to the car, she saw that her tires were slashed. Her mouth dropped open. Staring at the tires, she saw that the gash on each tire was about four inches long. It had to have taken a sharp knife to do that. Her back suddenly stiffened. She looked anxiously around the garage. No one else seemed to be down there but her. She began to feel uneasy. It wasn't until she was going around the front of the car to check the tires on the passenger side that she noticed that her windshield was cracked into a spider's web of circular veins spreading outward from a jagged gaping hole in the center. Laying in the front seat was a dirty red brick. She gasped. She gawked at her car in disbelief. A weak cry escaped from her.

She felt extremely vulnerable standing there all alone in the underground garage of concrete walls. She began backing away from her car when, behind her, she heard the elevator door open. She jumped. She started to run in the opposite direction, but thought better of it. The other direction was deeper into the huge, underground garage. It was well lit, but isolated. Suppose someone was laying in wait for her there? Her odds were better that a neighbor or a maintenance man was getting off the elevator. She hid behind a pillar. Her heart was in her mouth until a man and woman she recognized came into view. They walked straight ahead toward their car, not even looking in her direction. She started to call out to them, but what could they do? The first thing she had to do was get out of the garage.

She ran back to the elevator and frantically jabbed at the button. The doors opened up right away. Her finger shook when she pushed the button for the lobby. There was no need to go all the way up to her apartment; she used her cellular phone to call the automobile club to request the tow service. Flipping the phone shut, she walked up to Maury where he stood, waiting to open and close the door for people coming and going. He didn't have to open the door for

anyone, but he did for most everyone in anticipation of a larger Christmas tip. He opened the door for her to leave.

"I'm not going out," she said.

"You're down early this morning, Miss Jenkins," he said, smiling at her. He let the door close slowly on its own.

And it's none of your business, she wanted to say. His nosiness irritated her on a good day; and as much as she hated to, she had to ask if he had heard anything about her car.

"You came on at six this morning, right?"

"Sure did," he answered, pushing aside the visitor's sign-in book and sitting down on top of the small desk next to the door reserved for the doormen. "Can't wait till I get back on my regular shift tomorrow. I prefer being on from four to midnight."

Of course he did. It was too quiet during the day when everyone was out at work—no in-and-out traffic to gossip about. "Did you speak to the night doorman before he left?"

"Sure did."

"Did he mention if he heard anything or if anyone reported anything suspicious in the garage during the night?"

Maury practically jumped off the desk. His eyes danced with excitement. "Did something happen in the garage?"

If he didn't know, she wasn't telling him. "No, I just wanted to know if anything did happen," she said, pulling open the door herself and stepping outside onto the walkway far enough away from the building so that Maury couldn't follow her out. While she waited for the tow truck, she pasted on a smile and nodded or said good morning to her neighbors. She prayed that no one would sense her anguish. The longer she waited, the angrier she got. Whomever was doing this was controlling her life and she wasn't having it. She had to regroup and take back that control. The only way to do that was to find out who was doing this to her.

The minute the tow truck pulled into the block, she called a car service. For the first two blocks the taxi followed behind her vandalized car. It was like watching her child being taken to the hospital. The tears that came were for her car and for herself. With the

tears came her decision to go straight to Brandon's; she was too tired and maybe a little too scared, after all.

Brandon was standing in the hallway when she got off the elevator. He was holding his door open with his foot. "I thought you were coming over around two."

"Things happen," she said meekly.

"Like what?"

"Ugly things."

For a second, he studied her face. "Honey, you look like scrambled eggs. Have you been crying?"

Covering her mouth with her hand, she tried to hold back the sudden urge to cry.

He put his arm around her shoulders and took her into the living room where, together, they sat down on the sofa. "What's wrong?"

For a minute, she gave in to the tears and sobbed on his shoulder.

He patted her gently on the back until she was all cried out. "Talk to me."

She wrung her hands repeatedly before she could speak. "Someone has been threatening me."

"What? Who?"

"I think it's the wife of either Terrence or Eric, I don't know which. She calls my house all hours of the night. Yesterday, she left a note on my car."

"Can I see it?"

She started to open her pocketbook, then remembered, "I left it on the table in the restaurant yesterday."

"We could have taken it to the police."

She let the reference about the police go over her head. "This morning, I went to get in my car and the windshield was shattered with a brick and all the tires were slashed."

"Are you kidding?"

"I wish I were," she said, wiping her face.

"Where's the car?"

"I had it towed to the dealer."

"Did anyone see anything?"

"I don't know. I asked that old nosy doorman but he didn't know anything. Brandon, I don't know what to do. To make matters worse, Louis's wife called me yesterday at work and—"

"No!" he said, gawking at her.

"She did."

"What did she say?"

"She wants me to stay away from Louis."

"Of course."

"Brandon, because of that call, I thought it was her threatening me. I told Louis and he said he would speak to her, but then I got this call last night and the woman asked me if Louis's wife gave me a piece of her mind."

"We're calling the police right now," he said, reaching for the telephone.

She grabbed his arm. "No. Don't."

"Why not? Do you need to have your skull busted with a brick before the police know what's going on?"

She shook her head sadly. "I don't want people to know that I'm seeing four married men. And what about Terrence and the others? This could mean a lot of trouble for them."

"You can't be worrying about that now."

"Please, Brandon. Right now I need you to help me deal with this. I figure if I call Terrence and Eric first, I can get them to question their wives."

"Suppose they won't?"

"Why wouldn't they?"

"Because they would be telling on themselves. It's like saying, 'I've been cheating on you for years, and by the way, are you threatening my mistress?' Do you really think any of these men are going to tell on themselves for your sake?"

She felt numb. "Apparently not Louis or Wayne, and I wouldn't bet on Eric, but Terrence, most definitely, will be concerned about my safety. He might not tell his wife directly, but he would try to find out if it were her, and somehow stop her."

"Sweetheart, don't delude yourself. You need to report these threats to the police."

"I can't. At least not yet," she said, balling up her fist. "But if I ever find out who's doing this to me, I'm going to beat the hell out of her, no matter whose wife she is."

"Oh, really? Marissa, get a grip. First off, I can't see you fighting, and secondly, suppose you get killed?"

"Then she's a better woman than I am."

Taking her hand into his, he gently patted it. "Honey, did you get any sleep last night?"

"Not after that call, not a wink."

"I didn't think so, because you're talking out of your head. Why don't you take a nap?"

"I have to call Terrence and—"

"It's too early to call Terrence or Eric and in the condition you're in, they might think you're crazy. You should rest first."

She thought about it. Her nerves were fried and she was tired.

"Give me the number to where your car was taken, I'll check on it. After you've rested, you might reconsider calling the police."

From the side of her pocketbook she pulled out the dealer's business card. She gave it to him. "I am sleepy," she admitted, checking her watch. It was 8:15. "I need to call my office in forty-five minutes."

Standing up, Brandon pulled Marissa to her feet. "I'll call Vivian. I'll tell her that you had a family emergency."

She felt weepy. "I am so glad you're my friend," she said, hugging him.

"I am sweet, aren't I? Now, if you don't mind sleeping on my sheets, use my bed. I'd change the bed, except I can't get to the linen closet," he said, nodding in the direction of the closet in the back hallway.

For the first time, she noticed that the apartment was in disarray. Groceries were on every available table in the living room and hallway. Dishes were in boxes on the floor along with silverware and pots and pans stacked everywhere else. A brand-new

refrigerator and stove stood side by side in front of the two windows.

"What's going on in the kitchen?"

"I'm having it remodeled, remember? The contractor should be here in a few minutes. I'll show you later. Right now," he said, nudging her toward the bedroom, "go to bed."

Chapter 14

THE SQUEAL OF a drill broke through Marissa's cocoon of sleep. Though in a fog, she knew right away that she was not sleeping in her own bed because of the satiny sheets she slept on. If satin didn't make her sweat, she'd have them on her bed, too, they felt so sensually divine.

The drill squealed again, indicating to her that the contractor Brandon mentioned was apparently at work in the kitchen. She sat up and checked her watch. It was three o'clock. That was more than a nap, but no denying it, she did feel better. Throwing back the covers, she sat on the side of the bed in her bra and panties until she could wake up fully. What had happened the night before and early this morning with her car seemed like days ago, but she knew it was only hours ago. What she had to do was uppermost in her mind. She had to call Terrence.

The sound of banging replaced the drill. That was her cue to get dressed. While she was tucking in her blouse, she caught sight of her face in the large wall mirror across from the bed. Her eyes were puffy and beet red from crying. In fact, her whole face was puffy from sleeping so hard. Not wanting anyone besides Brandon to see

her, Marissa stuck her head out into the hallway and called out to him.

He came running immediately. "How do you feel?"

"Better," she said, opening the door for him to come in. Together they sat down on the side of the bed.

"You still don't look too good."

"Well, you look good enough for both of us," she said, referring to his well-groomed casualness. He was wearing sharply creased jeans and a black T-shirt that showed off his flat stomach and nicely toned arms. He certainly looked butch.

"Don't drool," he teased.

"If I ever get out of this mess, I just might enter a nunnery."

"I seriously doubt it. Chastity is not your style."

She punched him in the arm.

"*Oww,*" he said, pretending that she hurt him. "Seriously, Marissa. Have you decided what to do? Are we calling the police?"

"I need to speak to Terrence first."

"Before you do that, do you want something to eat? I went out and picked up some fruit and sliced turkey."

"Not right now. I need to call Terrence before he leaves."

Standing, Brandon lay his hand on Marissa's shoulder. He massaged her briefly. She closed her eyes. It felt good.

"Make your call. I'll be in the living room."

"Okay."

She waited until he closed the door before she dialed Terrence at work.

"Hey, babe," he said. "How you doing?"

"Not too well."

"What's wrong?"

"Terrence, I didn't want to have to bother you with this," she began cautiously, "but I think I'm being harassed by your wife."

"My wife?"

"She's been threatening me. This morning, she broke my windshield."

"Marissa, what the hell are you talking about?" he snarled. "My wife could not've done anything like that."

His sudden anger startled her. She brought her right hand to her left breast. "Terrence, do you know that for a fact?"

"Damn right. Are you crazy?"

"You know I wouldn't make up anything like this. Your wife has been calling me."

"No, the hell she hasn't. If you're screwing somebody else's husband . . ."

Her mouth fell open.

". . . then you need to talk to *him*. My wife is no gutter slut. Even if she could, she wouldn't lower herself for the likes of you."

She cringed from the cruelty of his words. "How can you talk to me like this?"

"I'm a busy man, Marissa. I don't have time for your maniacal accusations. If you so much as accuse my wife of harassment again, I'll slap you with a libel suit so fast you'll wish you never knew my name."

Terrence slammed down the telephone, sending a loud crack through Marissa's ear. She dropped the telephone to the floor. She held both her hands to her wide-open mouth, trying hard to stifle a scream. So tense were the muscles in her shoulders and neck, a sharp pain shot up the left side of her neck into her head. The absolute absurdity of his words crushed her. Never would she have dreamed that Terrence thought so little of her. Never. Not Terrence. He was the one she cared most about. The one she loved. If she was still asleep, she wanted desperately to wake up. From her throat, cries strained to burst from her.

Snatching up the pillow, she smothered her face deep into the satin and wailed. She fell sideways onto the bed and drew herself up into a tight ball, crying pitifully.

"Marissa! My God," Brandon said, rushing into the room. "What happened?"

Words would not come; only moanful sobs tore from her throat.

Brandon sat down on the side of the bed next to her heaving body. He began rubbing her back like he was ministering to a crying child. "Let it out," he said softly.

For a while she sobbed. For a while she let herself mourn the loss

of the love she had for Terrence as she felt it seep from her soul. It was over, his words said so.

Though her tears still flowed, her wailing stopped as she struggled to tell Brandon what Terrence had said. Not even an eyebrow arched when she told him about the ugliness of his words.

"How do you feel about yourself after what he said?"

"I feel worthless," she said, sitting up, but hugging the pillow still. "I felt like he was saying that I was a tramp and his wife was a saint."

"Do you see yourself that way?"

"No, but he's put his wife's feelings above mine."

Brandon snapped his fingers in her face. "Wake up, Marissa! Terrence has always put his wife's feelings above yours. You knew about her, she didn't know about you. That adage, 'What you don't know won't hurt you' applies here. He was always protecting his wife, that's why he never flaunted his affair in her face. Terrence's wife, and you'll find that the others' wives, also, are vitally important to them or they would have been biting at the bit to leave them for you a long time ago."

"I never wanted any of them to leave their wives, but I never wanted to be used by any of them, either."

Brandon leaned toward Marissa and looked deep into her eyes like he was trying to see if she was all there.

She rolled her eyes and looked away. Her mother used to look into her eyes like that when she knew she was lying.

"Ask yourself, Marissa, who was using whom?"

"He . . ."

He held up his hand just inches from her face, silencing her. "Did you know that Terrence was married from day one?"

"No, not right away."

"When did you find out?"

"A few weeks later, but—"

"Wait a minute. Before you answer, consider all the aspects of your relationship with him. Did he make you any promises? Did he ever ask for anything other than what you were willing to give? Did he say he loved only you?" he asked, ticking off each question with

his fingers. "Did he beg you to fall in love with him? Did he ever offer to leave his wife for you? And, finally, did you want him to?"

She stared at him.

"If you can answer yes to any or all of those questions, then he used you. Marissa, after all this time, if you went along with the program that you both apparently agreed to, and you got everything you wanted—be it sex, money, that fancy car, or the illusion of love—then you used him."

Numb, she stared at him. For the first time she realized that she hadn't even had a sip of water all day. Her throat was so dry it hurt, though not as much as her feelings. She could not and would not have imagined that Terrence felt something for her other than love.

"Marissa, did he use you, or did you use him?"

Returning Brandon's intense gaze for a minute, she frowned before squeezing her eyes shut. Tears slipped out anyway. Slowly she began to rock with the pillow hugged tightly to her chest. She knew that she was responsible for her actions, and that she could not blame anyone but herself for believing that Terrence was anything other than what he represented himself to be—a cheating husband who wanted his wife and his plaything—her. Brandon was right. Terrence never did make her any promises. From the beginning he said that he would never leave his wife, and she had convinced herself that she didn't want him to, but all along, deep down inside, that is exactly what she had hoped for. She was guilty of using him.

Brandon lightly rubbed her arm, enticing her to open her eyes. "I think you should hold off calling Eric until tomorrow."

She nodded in agreement.

"Marissa, I know you say you get everything you want out of a man without the demands of a full-time relationship, but it's more than that. You have a good job, which means you can get what you want for yourself; and a single man can be just as good to you, if not better than a married man. You're going to have to look inward and find out why you're cheating yourself out of a real relationship with a man who will put you first."

A steady stream of tears spilled down her cheeks. From the tissue holder on the nightstand, Brandon plucked out two white tissues. As

gently as one would dry the eyes of a weeping child, he dried the tears on her cheeks.

"You're a special person, Marissa, you deserve someone just as special."

" 'Scuse me," a man's voice said suddenly.

She glanced over Brandon's shoulder at the man standing in the open doorway. Stunned, she quickly shielded her face with her hand and turned away.

Brandon looked back over his shoulder and saw Levi. He got up quickly and went to meet him at the door.

"I didn't mean to interrupt," Levi said apologetically, looking past Brandon at Marissa. "I need you to decide where you want the handles to be placed on the cabinets. I'm ready to drill the holes."

Pulling the door up behind him as he stepped out into the hallway—forcing Levi to back up—Brandon closed the door. "Put them where you think best."

"That's a personal decision. It might seem minor, but some people like their handles horizontal, some like them vertical. This one is your call."

"I hadn't thought about it. Wait a minute," he said, opening the door again just enough to stick his head inside the bedroom.

Marissa was holding her head with both hands. She kept shaking her head and saying, "I don't believe this . . . I don't believe this."

"Will you be all right for a few minutes? I need to go into the kitchen."

Without looking at him, she continued shaking her head.

"I'll be right back," he said, again closing the door. To Levi he said, "Okay," as he headed toward the kitchen.

Lagging behind, Levi looked at the closed door for an instant before he rushed to catch up with Brandon.

In the bedroom, Marissa lay down again with the pillow hugged tightly to her body. She didn't question why Levi was in Brandon's apartment, it was apropos—everything was going wrong in her life and he seemed destined to bear witness to her comeuppance.

.   .   .

Levi had been unable to concentrate on his work since hearing her cry. He didn't know who it was at first, but seeing that it was the one and the same belligerent Marissa, he was really curious. "How is she doing?"

"Not too good," Brandon answered while placing a white porcelain and brass handle horizontally on a cabinet door above his new white porcelain sink. He pulled back a little to look at the handle. Turned it vertically; looked at it critically; turned it horizontally again; then vertically again. "Vertical."

"That's what I would have chosen."

Brandon handed the handle to Levi. "I didn't realize you had to drill holes for the handles. I thought the holes came already drilled."

"When you buy quality cabinets, the manufacturers let you choose your handles and the way you want them put on."

"That's why I buy quality. I like this," Brandon said, admiring the gray marble countertop, "but it's longer than my old counter; are you sure the refrigerator will fit in this space?"

With a ruler and pencil, Levi began marking notches where he planned to drill the screw holes. "It'll fit," he said. "Say, isn't that Marissa in the bedroom?"

"That's right; you do know her, don't you?"

"Not really. I met her a few weeks ago at Charmaine's. She didn't hang around long enough for me to get to know her."

"Oh, yes, I do recall hearing something about that," Brandon said with a little smile dancing on his lips. Standing behind Levi, he let his eyes roll across and down his back to his firm-looking tush, and back up again to his exposed forearms and biceps, which left no question about their definition and tonality. Clearing his throat, Brandon continued to smile to himself. He watched as Levi moved from one cabinet door to the next with his ruler and pencil. Being slightly bowlegged enhanced Levi's appeal. Brandon looked away before he could be caught looking. Charmaine had highly recommended Levi and he was more than pleased with the way his kitchen was coming together. This was the first time he was home while Levi worked in the apartment as he had trusted that Charmaine

would not recommend a crook, which is why he had given him the keys to come and go as he pleased. In all that time, he had forgotten that he was the guy who Marissa had run out on. Levi might not be her type, but he certainly was his. However, that was something that Levi would never know. Instinctively, he knew that Levi was a full-blooded hetero male with eyes only for a woman. While he didn't concern himself as to what Levi might have thought about his less-than-masculine-looking apartment, he was careful not to reveal his feminine persona. That was not for his eyes.

"The last time I saw her," Levi was saying, "she was fighting mad. Seems like she's upset again. Is this her natural state of being?"

Folding his arms across his chest, Brandon leaned back against the counter behind him. He watched as Levi squatted in front of the lower doors. "She's having a rough time right now," he said. "The day you met her, she was upset that Charmaine was trying to make choices for her."

"I got the gist of that from their argument."

"Marissa's good people, especially when one gets to know her."

Still squatting, Levi sidled over in front of the next cabinet. "Doesn't seem like one will ever get to know her," he said, his back still to Brandon. "One's not her type."

"Oh, I wouldn't say that," Brandon said, looking at Levi's upper back muscles flex as he reached up to the top of the counter to get the door handle. "In fact, she thought you were quite charming."

Standing up, Levi turned and cut his eyes at Brandon before he crossed to the cabinet on the other wall. "I don't believe she said that. She didn't hang around long enough to find that out."

"She just needs time to warm up. Give her a chance, you might like her," Brandon said, starting out of the kitchen. "I'm going to make some turkey sandwiches. Why don't you join us?"

"Thanks, but I had lunch."

"At least sit down and have a soda with us."

"Maybe."

Chapter 15

MARISSA WOULD NOT hear of leaving the bedroom to go into the living room to eat. For one thing, she had no appetite for food, and no appetite to see Levi. If he even had an inkling about what was upsetting her, and put that together with what he must have overheard her and Charmaine arguing about, he'd laugh in her face.

"If you won't come to the food, then the food comes to you," Brandon said, pushing the door open with his foot. "Turkey on a nice, fresh roll with a slice of Swiss and a sweet slice of tomato. 'M'm! M'm! Good!' "

She didn't stir.

Brandon stood over her. "You're going to squeeze my poor pillow to death."

"I'll buy you another one."

"Marissa, I will not permit you to lie there and die in my bed. So get up, sit up, and eat up."

She raised her head off the pillow enough to look up at Brandon standing over her, holding a silver serving tray. "I can't."

"Yes, you can," Levi said, pulling a chair up to the bed and sitting down.

"Oh, God," she groaned, pulling the pillow she'd held against her body up to cover her face.

Levi unfolded a standing serving tray on which Brandon sat the tray he held.

"You must forgive her, Levi, Marissa's kinda shy today," Brandon explained, going to the far corner of the room. Hefting a sizable leather-and-wood chair, he carried it back to the bed. He sat it down on the other side of the serving tray before he flopped down in it. "There's your soda, Levi. I know you said you didn't want a sandwich, but I made you one anyway. Marissa, we both know that you're there, we can see your beautiful legs."

She tried to draw them closer to her body.

"Actually, I think Levi has the better view of them. You wouldn't want to switch places with me, would you, Levi?"

He did have a nice view. "I'm comfortable where I am."

Firmly holding her skirt to her thighs, Marissa sat up quickly, almost kicking the serving tray when she swung her legs over the side of the bed. With both hands, while glaring at Brandon, she tried to brush her hair back. She didn't have to see it to know that it was a mess.

"Your hair looks fine. Right, Levi?"

"To me it does," he replied, popping the ring off the top of the soda in his hand.

"See," Brandon said, biting into his sandwich. A piece of tomato slipped from between the roll and fell onto the tray. Picking it up, he tossed it into his mouth, then licked the mayonnaise off his fingers.

Marissa was so angry, she felt sick. "Brandon, what are you doing?"

Biting into his sandwich again, Brandon pointed to his full mouth, indicating that he couldn't speak.

Levi picked up half of a turkey sandwich, and he bit into it. Right away he reached for a napkin to wipe his mouth of the mayonnaise he sensed was there.

"The kitchen looks real good," Brandon said, ignoring Marissa's glare. "How much longer you figure?"

"Two days. I'll start putting the floor down tomorrow. Everything else goes back in place Thursday."

"That's fine. I won't be here the rest of the week. Should I write you a check for the balance before I leave?"

"If you're satisfied with the work, you can pay me today. If you find that something needs to be straightened out, when you get back, call me, and I'll take care of it right away."

"Good enough."

Marissa looked from one to the other. They were carrying on business like it was a normal thing for her to be sitting on the bed in the middle of the day with her face swollen, her hair in disarray, and her skirt halfway up her thighs.

"What should I do with your keys?" Levi asked.

"Do you fellas mind?" she asked irritably. Brandon looked at her. She gestured toward the door.

"Oh, sure," he said, though he stayed seated. "Marissa, Thursday afternoon, would you stop by and pick up the keys from Levi?"

She looked at him pointedly. Brandon's eyes twinkled mischievously. She didn't like it one bit. "I'm busy."

Brandon smiled. "Please."

Levi watched the two of them stare each other down. He started to tell Brandon that the keys were safe with him, but decided that he wanted to see how this battle of wills played out. Seeing Marissa again might irk her, but for some strange reason, it intrigued him.

"Well, if you can't, no problem. Levi, do you mind dropping the keys off at Marissa's apartment?"

"That's all right," she said quickly. "I'll pick them up."

Levi chuckled behind his napkin. He knew darn well what Brandon was trying to do. Charmaine had dared, now Brandon was doing the same. What he couldn't figure out was why they both were so intent on setting Marissa up with him. It wasn't like she was a hard-luck case and couldn't get a man. In fact, it seemed she had too many men. She didn't need him, and he sure as hell didn't need her. However, looking at her shapely legs and the sensual thighs they were connected to, the idea was intriguing to say the least, but damn, she seemed to be in the nastiest mood all the time.

"Marissa, you are my dearest friend," Brandon said, reaching for her hand.

She slapped his hand away.

"Temper, temper."

She sucked her teeth. "Brandon, cut it out."

"You two are funny," Levi said.

"Marissa is my girl. I can always count on her."

"Anything for you, dear," she said, feigning a smile. She started shifting her body forward to the edge of the bed so that she could stand up like a lady.

"Where are you going?"

"I am going into the other room to call the dealer."

"I already have," Brandon said, taking another bite of his sandwich. He took a quick swig of his soda. "Your windshield is a special order. They should have it by Thursday afternoon."

"I hate the subway."

"Personally, I don't know how you drive into the city every day anyway. There's a traffic jam around every corner, and it must cost you a fortune to park."

"Not when your employer discounts your parking in its own building."

"Excuse me."

Levi washed down the last of his sandwich with his soda. "Were you in an accident?"

She looked guardedly, unblinkingly into Brandon's eyes.

"No, a prankster," he answered for her.

"Too bad, nice car. If you need a lift home, I'll be leaving soon."

Her eyes never left Brandon's. This was his fault. No way did she need dirty-nailed Levi sniffing behind her. She had enough to deal with as it was. Besides, she didn't want to go home anyway. "No thank you," she said, refusing to look at Levi.

"Nonsense," Brandon said. "Paying for a cab is a waste of money if someone is willing to give you a lift for free."

"For your information, Dr. Wallace, I am not going back to my apartment."

"Where are you going?"

That was a good question. Where could she go?

"Oh," Brandon said, realizing that she might be afraid to go home. "Why don't you stay with me tonight?"

"I don't want to put you out."

"You know better than that. You can sleep on the sofa bed, you've done it before."

Levi's eyes leapt from one to the other. He knew they couldn't be lovers because Charmaine had told him that Brandon was gay, supposedly warning him, but at this point in his life, it made no difference. If he were twenty years old, he would not have come within a mile of Brandon much less sit in his bedroom. Up until then, he used to think that gay people weren't normal and what they did together was repulsive and sick. That is, until AIDS forced his favorite uncle, his father's much younger brother, to come out of the closet. It was a devastating blow to the family to find out that Joseph was gay and, worse, that he was dying.

His father never forgave his brother and when he died, a few years after Joseph, the last word out of his mouth was Joseph's name. Maybe if Joseph hadn't moved to California sixteen years ago, they might have guessed that he was gay, and the news would not have been so shocking. For a while, Levi felt betrayed and wouldn't speak to Joseph himself. It took six months of missing their monthly hour-long telephone conversations before he realized that death was going to end those conversations permanently. For that reason, he had to let go of his anger; and it was Joseph who helped him with that anger, enlightening him to a lifestyle he had misunderstood.

"My relationship with my partner," Joseph had said, "has absolutely nothing to do with you, like I have nothing whatsoever to do with what you and your woman do. I don't base how I feel about you on who you make love to."

When Joseph took his last breath, Levi was at his bedside, and to this day he still missed him. Too bad he wasn't here now to help him figure out Marissa. As Levi saw it, something had to be wrong if she didn't want to go back to her apartment. Whatever she was afraid of was waiting there for her.

"Marissa," Levi heard himself say, "it's really not a problem for me to give you a lift. No strings."

Levi and Brandon both waited for her answer.

She finally dared to look at Levi. If he'd had a smirk or a grin on his lips, or a twinkle in his eyes, she would have seen that he was playing with her. He had neither.

Brandon prompted, "I'd take you myself, Marissa, but I could use the time to pack while you're gone."

Any other time the suggestion that Levi take her home would have upset her, but the truth was, she was afraid to go home alone—no telling what was waiting for her there. But Levi? Who would have guessed that she'd have to accept his help?

"Well?" Brandon asked.

"I guess I could use the ride."

"Levi, she lives on Plaza Street near Vanderbilt. Why don't you two get going? I'll take care of this," he said, looking at the sandwich and a half left on the serving tray.

Carefully sliding off the bed, Marissa held onto her skirt until she stood up. Brandon picked up the serving tray and left the room.

Levi continued to sit, his long legs spread far apart, his hands hanging limply between his thighs. He watched her slip her bare feet into her black, open-back heels. He watched her comb through her hair with her fingers. He watched her steal glances at him in the mirror. He watched her as she turned and faced him, her eyes angry. Yet, behind that anger, for a fleeting second, he saw her fear. When Marissa sauntered past him out of the room, he caught a faint whiff of her perfume. Inhaling her sweetness, he slowly closed his eyes and opened them again. In that moment, somehow he knew that he would have her.

Chapter 16

As Levi expected, when Marissa saw his beat-up old Buick, she turned up her nose like she caught a whiff of rotten garbage. Still, he played the gentleman to the hilt; he opened the car door with a flourish and held it open for her to get in.

"Why is the rear so low?" she asked. "Can't you afford springs and shocks?"

"My tools are in the trunk, they're heavy," he explained, still holding the door open.

"Excuse me, but isn't that what pickup trucks and vans are for?"

He leaned on the open door. "How do you know that I don't have a pickup or a van?"

"I could care less," she said, stepping off the curb into the street. She looked up toward the corner. "You can leave, I'll take a cab."

He walked slowly to the back of the car. She turned to look at him just as he bent down and picked up a penny out of the gutter.

"You would pick up a nasty penny, wouldn't you?"

"Why not? It's no nastier than the pennies in your purse. For all you know, they were once in the gutter, too."

"Hey, as long as I don't know about it, who cares," she said,

screwing up her face in disgust when he dropped the penny into his pants pocket.

He ignored the look on her face. "My car isn't fancy enough for you?"

"It's not fancy enough to be a garbage truck."

He chuckled. "Looks are deceiving; it runs."

"I don't know how, it's as old as Methuselah."

Again he chuckled. "Not quite," he said, enjoying her sarcasm. "The old girl still got a bit of *varoom* in her engine."

"It ought to, it probably burns the garbage you got on the dashboard and on the floor for gas."

"Then environmentalists will love me," he said, beginning to lose patience with her insulting attitude. "Is it gonna hurt you to let me take you home?"

"Yes," she replied, still looking up the street for a cab. She hadn't noticed that he had stepped right up behind her.

"Woman, get in the car," Levi suddenly ordered, no longer amused with her sarcasm.

Marissa turned to face him, her hand on her hip. "Excuse me?"

"You heard me, get in the car."

"I will not."

"Yes, you will, with or without my help. Take your pick."

"Look, mister, I don't know who you—"

He reached for her arm. She pulled away, but he latched onto her anyway and pulled her to the open car door.

"Hey!" she exclaimed, yanking her arm free.

He placed one hand on the door frame and the other on the door, sandwiching her between his body and the car.

She tried to put some space between them by pushing on his chest. It was like pushing on a brick wall. She gave up. "Are you crazy?"

"I'm beginning to think so," he said, puzzled by his own behavior, yet standing his ground. "Get in the damn car . . . please."

"You can't make me get in your car."

"No, I can't, but I figure if I put two and two together, you don't wanna go home alone, either. Whatever or whoever is waiting for

you there is making you afraid. I'm willing to help you, whether you want me to or not, but you keep this up, lady, you're on your own."

Marissa hated him. She stared at him bitterly. Brandon had to have told him something. How else would he have surmised that she was afraid to go home? And where did he get the nerve to manhandle her and order her around like she was his woman? He was a bully. She didn't like him from day one, but standing so close to him, although he wasn't pressed up against her, was very disconcerting and somewhat unnerving. Only because she couldn't move him or get around him, she flopped down into the passenger seat.

"Pull your legs in."

Sucking her teeth, she yanked her legs in and sat stiff as a board staring straight ahead. She could feel the garbage under her feet. She cringed.

Slamming the car door shut, Levi walked around the back to the driver's side, all the while wondering why he was wasting his time on a woman who didn't seem to have a redeeming bone in her body. Using his key, he unlocked his door; it would have been too much to expect that she would have reached over and opened it for him. Sliding under the steering wheel, he looked at her. "Lady, I'm not the one. You need to save the venom for someone else."

"What the hell do you know?"

"Enough."

"That big-mouth—"

"Brandon didn't tell me a thing. As I said before, I saw and heard enough to put two and two together. Do you wanna talk about it?"

"With who? You?" she asked, eyeballing him. "I don't think so." She looked straight ahead again with her arms folded across her chest.

"Just an offer," he said, starting the car.

Humph. She'd have to be caught in the jaws of a grizzly before she'd even think about crying on his shoulders.

It wasn't like Levi didn't know that by talking to her he was irritating her more, but then that was part of the pushy nature he inherited from his mother. However, for the sake of peace, he was going to leave her alone. He drove on.

She was surprised that the engine ran as smoothly and as quietly as it did. Maybe burning garbage was good for it.

Stopping at red lights gave him the opportunity to study her profile. Maybe it was her pride, maybe it was her energy, there was something about her that reminded him of Janice. Not that she looked like Janice, but it was Janice's spirit she had. Marissa knew what she wanted—right or wrong—like Janice. Even when Janice was twenty-two and had been his one and only true love, she had been as strongwilled as Marissa, though not as much of a bitch. When she wanted something from him, she didn't browbeat him, she stroked him, she loved him into submission. That's how she got him to drive her up to Albany to attend a junior caucus at the state capital, making him miss out on his first big independent contracting job. It was a month before another job that size came his way, but Janice had made the wait well worth it.

Janice had dreams of being the first female governor of New York. She had asked him if he had a problem with her wearing the political pants in the family. He had said no. He never felt threatened by her. Not even when she said that "great men had great women behind them—why couldn't great women be out front for a change?" If Janice had lived to fulfill her dreams, she would have been an awesome woman. The night a drunk driver's car on the Long Island Expressway jumped the divider and hit her head-on, taking her dreams, taking her life, took a part of him, too. He hadn't let himself be with another woman in the same way since. It was years before he could get himself to a place where he didn't think about Janice all the time; a place where he didn't compare all the women he met to her. That is, until Marissa. Since meeting her, his weakness for strong, gutsy women was reawakened. Though she might be going after what she wanted the wrong way, she certainly wasn't sitting back and whining for her piece of the pie.

"Stop! You're passing my building!" Marissa yelled.

Levi jammed on the brake. "All you had to do was tell me," he said, putting the car in reverse and backing up. Maybe she wasn't whiney, but her nastiness was tiring. Before he could finish parking, she had opened the car door and leapt out.

"Woman, you crazy?"

"You don't need to come in," she said, slamming the door.

She sprinted toward the building. To her relief, it was Jim who opened the door for her. If it had been Maury, he would have been questioning her about why she was in such a hurry.

"Thanks," she said, rushing into the lobby.

"Miss Jenkins," Jim called behind her. "Just a minute."

She turned around but continued stepping backward, toward the elevator. "I'll be back."

"A note was left here for you," he said, picking up a piece of folded paper off the desk.

"I'm in a hurry. I'll pick it up on my way out in about twenty minutes," she said, looking past him through the glass door at Levi barreling up the walkway. She jabbed at the elevator button.

Jim began walking toward her with the note in his hand.

Levi rushed into the lobby.

The elevator door opened. She jumped inside and jabbed the eighth-floor button repeatedly. The door started to close. It suddenly stopped. So did her breathing.

It was Jim. He held his finger on the button on the outside panel, and stuck his foot against the open door so it wouldn't close. Handing the note out to her, he smiled.

Levi came up behind him.

She snatched the note out of Jim's hand and stepped to the back of the elevator. Her "thank you" was brusque.

" 'Scuse me," Levi said, stepping around Jim.

Jim's arm shot out to bar Levi from getting on the elevator. "You can't go up without being announced."

"I'm with the lady," he said coolly, pushing Jim's arm out of his way. Glaring at Marissa, in one long stride he stepped into the elevator and stood along the side wall.

The door was trying to close against Jim's foot.

Fingering the taped note in her hand, she fixed her eyes on the floor numbers above the door.

"Is he with you?" Jim asked.

She dropped her eyes and looked over at Levi. His eyes were

frozen in an angry glare and his jaw was rigid. She could feel the heat of his anger.

He needed to get his head checked. Fuming, Levi was angry with himself for trying to be a nice guy to this 'itch. Her thanks was a kick in the teeth for the effort.

"Should I call the police?"

"No," she said, hesitating. "He's with me."

"Oh."

Towering above the doorman, Levi looked down at him. "Move," he snarled.

Jim stepped back. He let the door close.

Levi glowered intently at Marissa.

A glimpse of his face told her that she had gone a little too far. His eyes were blazing, yet his dimples were deeper than ever—a strange combination of anger and sensuality. The same little quirky flutter that hit her the first time she met him hit her now. She shook her head in disbelief; she couldn't possibly be attracted to this man whose jeans were speckled and smeared with paints of every color, and who thought nothing of being seen in public like that.

The elevator stopped smoothly. Levi stood aside for her to step off ahead of him. She led the way down the hall to her apartment.

He didn't have to be told to take a seat. He went directly into the living room, flipped on the light, and sat down on the sofa.

She was bowled over by his boldness but she said nothing. In her hand she still carried the note when she went into the bedroom to pack a bag. She could only hope that it wasn't from that woman. Her fingers trembled a little as she carefully peeled back the tape.

"If my wife, Florence, should call you, tell her that you are just a friend—purely platonic. Keep it simple. Tell her you have not seen me in well over six months, that we talk on the phone. She believed me when I told her that we were not involved sexually, but the person who contacted her also told her that I spend a lot of money on you. Tell her that it is not so. I'll be in touch. Wayne."

She sat down on the bed. She could just see Wayne trying to explain about them. Of course, his wife believed there was no sex, he probably hadn't gotten it up for her in years, but in her eyes he had

cheated on her and his giving up money was akin to committing a sexual act. Feeling like crap, she opened the top drawer of the nightstand and dropped the note inside. Wayne had been good to her; she'd help him put his wife at ease and she'd tell her he never gave her a cent. Terrence, however, was another matter. She couldn't say that she'd do the same for him, not after what he said to her. Just thinking about his ugliness made her tear up. She didn't know how she fooled herself into thinking that he loved her. Her eyes swam in tears. How could she have been so naive?

Riiiing!

She jumped.

Quickly wiping her face dry, she glanced over at the telephone and immediately decided to not answer it.

Riiiing!

"Hi . . ."

"Oh my God," she said, bolting for the door.

". . . this is Marissa. If you leave a message, I'll call you back. 'Bye."

She ran headlong toward the answering machine to shut it off.

"Girl, if you don't return my call—"

She switched off the machine.

Levi looked at her questioningly. Clearly, the fear that he had seen earlier in her eyes was there again.

"That was just my sister."

"The light was blinking. You have other messages."

"I don't have time to listen to them," she said, angry that she bothered to explain herself to him at all. When he didn't bat an eye, she jerked her head and shoulders around and walked out of the room back into her bedroom, slamming the door. She certainly wasn't going to talk to Denise with him there. Grabbing an overnight bag from the shelf in her closet, she began tossing underwear, a nightgown, panty hose, whatever she needed into it.

Levi didn't know a woman alive who didn't have time to check her messages. Standing up, he looked over at the answering machine. The red blinking light was blinking no more. Whatever was scaring her was probably there. Moseying over to stand in front of

the answering machine, he stared down at it. He really wanted to know what messages awaited her. For a minute he stood listening for sounds of her moving around in the other room. He heard what sounded like a drawer being closed. If she opened the door, he was sure he'd hear her, at least he hoped he would. Switching the machine back on, he turned down the volume, rewound the tape, then pushed the Play button. The voice was low, but he could hear every word.

"Hey, slut. You like the present I left for you this morning? Next time I'll destroy the whole damn car. You didn't pay for it anyway. Got the message yet? Stay away from my man. Don't make me have to tell you again."

Beeep!

He listened out for her again.

"Rissa, why didn't you go to work today? If someone is threatening you, we have to go to the police. But you can't blame nobody but yourself for this mess. I told you to stay away from married men, but, oh no, you wouldn't listen. Not you. I bet you'll listen now. And by the way, if you ever hang up on me again, I'm gonna kick your ass."

Beeep!

"Marissa, Wayne. My wife got a call today from a woman who told her about us. We need to talk. Call me at work."

Beeep!

"Rissa, if you're there, pick up the damn phone. Don't make me come over there, I got too much to do. I called Momma. She said you have not called her in weeks. I didn't tell her what was going on with you, she'd only worry. Would you please call me?"

Beeep!

"Hi, Marissa. Why didn't you come into the office today? Call me when you get in."

Beeep!

"Hey, lady. You're a hard person to catch up with. I wanna see you."

Beeep!

"Marissa, I'm gonna have to stop seeing you for a while, like we

agreed. My wife's pretty angry, she's threatening divorce. I'll call you tomorrow."

Beeep.

"Girl, if you don't return my call. . . ."

Click.

Sliding the volume switch back up, Levi reached to the other side and switched off the machine. The red light went black again. Again, he listened for Marissa before easing backward over to the sofa to sit down.

"Whoa," he said softly. Those messages more than explained what was going on. Every male voice on that machine was different. He couldn't say that he was surprised, not after that argument she and Charmaine had. No wonder someone was after her. She *should* be scared. Whomever was on her tail meant business. Damn. She might as well be sitting in quicksand; at least she'd know the danger was under her ass.

"I'm ready," Marissa announced, standing in the doorway holding onto a bulging overnight bag and a garment bag.

He looked at her, taking her all in. She had changed into a short-sleeve, fitted red blouse and a pair of fitted black pants, there was no mistaking her small waist and shapely round hips. Any man pumping blood through his veins, including himself, would be attracted to her.

"How long do you plan on sitting there staring at me?" she quipped, although she was strangely flattered by the way he was looking at her body.

Pushing himself up off the sofa, he walked right up to her with the intention of taking her bag. He looked down into her eyes. She did not look away nor did she back away, and neither did he. In that instant, he had a sudden urge to kiss her, but this was the wrong woman at the wrong time. Another time, he would have followed through, but even then only when he was sure the woman wanted him to, and there was nothing in the way Marissa was looking at him that said she wanted him to. Damn. How could he even be thinking about wanting to kiss her?

Marissa felt strange. She felt herself flush. She sensed that Levi

was about to kiss her, but that was impossible. She tried to show that she could be just as bold, and looked back into his eyes just as intently, but her bravado faded quickly. Finally, she lowered her eyes and stepped back.

It surprised him that she didn't have the staying power. She was trying to go for bad, but she wasn't as tough as she wanted him to think; that's why she was running back to Brandon. He expected that she would resist when he reached for her bag, so he snatched it out of her hand and turned toward the door.

"Hey!"

He didn't bother to turn around.

She flipped him the finger behind his back as he walked out of the apartment. That's when she noticed her broken nail. "Idiot," she said. For someone she didn't even know or like, he was working her last nerve, and she didn't even know how he wormed his way into her life in the first place. She was going to have to tell him to stay the hell away from her; that is, after they got back to Brandon's. She began digging down in her shoulderbag for her emery board.

"What else can go wrong?" she asked.

Riiiing!

Grabbing her keys off the hall table, she darted out of the apartment and quickly pulled the door closed on the ringing phone. She knew what else could go wrong.

Chapter 17

THE CLICK OF the key turning in the lock broke through her vacuum of sleep. Instantly, though groggy, she lifted her head up off the pillow to listen to make sure she heard what she thought she heard. The door opened. She started to sit up.

"Take my card," Levi was saying to someone out in the hallway. "Give me a call when you're ready."

She quickly lay back down and snatched the covers up over her head. The last thing she wanted was to be caught in the apartment when he got there—much less still in bed. She had asked Brandon to wake her before he left this morning at 6:30, but obviously he saw fit not to. She could kill him. He had told her that Levi would be coming around nine o'clock, which meant that if he was here, she had overslept. She heard the door close.

From the doorway he saw her yank the covers up over her head. "If you were a fox, you'd be caught."

"Go away."

"Can't. I work here."

"I could use some privacy," she said, her head still covered.

"No problem, I'll be in the kitchen."

When she thought she heard him leave, she pulled the covers

down off her head. Her eyes popped wide open—he was standing in the doorway looking right at her. Smiling.

Whoosh! She yanked the covers back up over her head. "You bastard! Get out!"

"I'd kinda like to hear you say 'please.' "

"Drop dead."

"Say 'please.' "

"I hate you."

"Tell me something I don't know."

"Get out!"

"For the life of me, I don't know why you're covering up your head, you look the same as you did yesterday afternoon."

She snatched the covers down. "No one asked you," she said, looking at him contemptuously. "You're as irritating as a hangnail. Would you please leave me alone!"

"That's better. Did you sleep well?"

"Is English your second language? Get out!"

Leaning against the doorjamb, he crossed his ankles and folded his arms across his chest. "I didn't think you were the shy type."

"Screw you," she said, feeling the vein in her neck pulse.

"Would your boyfriend mind?"

"I hate you. Why don't you get a haircut? Afros went out with dashikis and platform shoes twenty-five years ago."

"Yeah, but I hear they're back now," he retorted.

"Oh, please."

The truth was, he didn't like his hair, either; he usually wore it closer to his head, but he hadn't found time to get to a barber. Most days he didn't have time to shave, but this morning he took the time and when he turned away from his mirror, he didn't think he looked all that bad. He patted his hair. "Don't tell me you don't like it," he said, pretending to be surprised.

"I bet you wear a dashiki when you call yourself 'dressing up.' "

"Seem to me, for your age, you don't have a problem wearing miniskirts. You like showing off those big, pretty thighs, don't you?"

That did it. She threw back the covers and pushed herself up off

the sofa bed. She stood boldly before him with her hands on her hips, glaring at him. "I hate you," she said, sneering.

He smiled. "You're being redundant."

Although she was glaring at him, she could not help but notice the twinkle in his eyes and the deepening of his dimples. He was enjoying this, while his dimples were killing her determination to hate him. She dared to continue standing in front of him with her nightgown on because she wasn't about to let him think that he was capable of making her feel ashamed or intimidated. The problem was, she was enjoying the look in his brown eyes as they glided slowly down her body. It was like watching chocolate syrup flow smoothly over vanilla ice cream. His eyes seemed to caress her body like a gentle embrace; she tingled shamefully.

Levi's heart thumped. He could not have been more pleased at the sight before him. She was wearing a long, slinky, red nightgown with thin shoulder straps. A plunging neckline exposed a succulent cleavage, while the silky fabric revealed erect nipples—she certainly had more than a mouthful. He almost licked his lips but caught himself; being lewd wasn't him nor was it necessary. Yet he wasn't the least bit bashful about letting his eyes linger on her soft curves. She was everything he had dreamed.

"I hope you got a good look," Marissa said, pushing past him to run into Brandon's bedroom, "it's probably the first time you've ever seen a woman."

He turned quickly. He saw enough of her butt before she closed the door to know that it was lusciously shaped. He brought his hand to his chest. "Heart be still," he said, smiling to himself as he went into the kitchen to start his workday. The woman was lethal, and he knew it. Gregory knew it, too. He had warned him the day he met her. His bitterness toward her was probably because he was attracted to her himself. It wouldn't be the first time a man was attracted to his woman's best friend. He could definitely understand it if he was, Marissa was certainly worth looking at.

As for himself, no matter how much he resisted last night, he fell asleep thinking about her and awakened this morning with her

still on his mind. He tried to tell himself that she was a tramp; a woman with no morals—it didn't work. The truth is, he secretly liked women with a little spice—not too much—just enough to keep the blood flowing. Mousy women with no fight in them did nothing for his imagination. Without a doubt, there was a lot of spice in Marissa to begin with, and now that she was being threatened, she was determined to put on a strong face by being cantankerous. She had been nothing but nasty to him, which went beyond being spicy. Yet he could see himself making love to her. In his dream last night and wide awake this morning, he more than saw it, he could almost feel it. Weak attempts to erase her from his mind served to only intensify his thoughts of her. And now, after seeing her sensually dressed or undressed, it would be a miracle if he ever slept again without thoughts of her. It had been a long time since a woman had consumed his imagination.

His last relationship had lasted eight months and as much as he cared for Diane, he could not give her what she wanted—time and commitment. He was so busy that if night didn't fall every day, he'd probably work around the clock remodeling and renovating houses. Because of his exhausting days, after work he was always beat—he had neither time nor energy for anyone or anything. If it wasn't for his mother, he'd wear dirty clothes and be a fast-food junkie. No matter what time he got home, she had a hot meal waiting for him every evening.

When Diane left him, he wondered if he had been in love with her, would he have cut his work hours in half for her? Somehow he doubted it. He hadn't gone with a women yet who'd gotten him to slow down. It was Diane who had asked him what was driving him. Until she asked, he hadn't thought about it. Now that he had, he had to say that it was probably the ghost of his father. He didn't want to end up like him—broke with nothing tangible to show for sixty-two years of getting up out of his bed every day.

Most of his working life his father worked as a butcher, but he was never able to save a dime, much less buy a house for his wife and son. He never earned much more than minimum wage, yet when his whisky was talking, he talked about one day owning a silver

Mercedes. He thought that was the epitome of success. The problem was, he was never successful. Beyond his day job, he never did anything to make an extra nickel, which was the bone of contention between him and his mother whenever they argued. His mother would tell him to get up off his ass, stop talking trash, and go get a better job. His father might have wanted to do just that, but he couldn't. He had no education beyond the tenth grade, and no real skills other than throwing back a bottle of whisky, which eventually killed him.

Levi probably worked as hard as he did because he wasn't going to be his father's son in any sense of the word. He finished high school, even had two years of college, but his knack for working with his hands kept him so busy, he didn't have time to study. When he saw that the money was plentiful and willingly paid by people who wanted to live in nice homes, he dropped out of college, worked under a master carpenter for three years, and then struck out on his own. He never looked back.

Marissa dashed past the kitchen door, hoping to get out of the apartment before Levi saw her.

"You leaving?" he asked, darting out of the kitchen into the foyer.

"Good guess," she answered, pulling the door open.

"I have the key, remember? Are you coming back here?"

Stepping outside the apartment, she turned. "None of your damn business. Why don't you get back to your one-man business."

"Hey! I don't give a rat's ass if you never come back."

Bang! He slammed the door in her face.

Dumbfounded, she stood staring at the closed door only inches from her face. Where did he get off slamming the door in her face? She struck the door with the palm of her hand. "You stupid jerk!"

Not a peep came from the other side.

She hit the door again—harder. "Open this door!"

Dead silence.

Jabbing at the bell, she laid on it until it squawked like a scalded goose. The second he opened the door she was going to curse him until he cried for mercy.

Levi ignored the ringing bell as he angrily screwed the door handles onto the cabinets. He'd had about all he could take of her nasty

mouth. No wonder she didn't have a man all her own—who would want to put up with such a shrew?

He made her blood boil. "I hate you!" she shouted, kicking at the bottom of the door.

"Are you looking for Brandon?"

Marissa stopped cold.

"Is that you, Marissa? What in the world is wrong?"

"Miss Jessie. Good . . . good morning," she stammered. She wanted to be sucked into the floor as she slowly turned around to look into the face of Brandon's neighbor.

"I can't believe you're fighting with Brandon."

"No . . . no. I'm not fighting with Brandon, he's not home. I—"

"Then why you carrying on like that, child?"

Her face flushed. "I'm sorry," she said, starting off down the hall. "I didn't mean to make so much noise. I'm sorry." She didn't bother waiting for the elevator, she thrust the door to the stairwell open and ran down the five flights of stairs.

Chapter 18

MARISSA'S DAY HAD gotten off to a bad start when Levi was the first face she had seen upon opening her eyes, not to mention the humiliation she felt in front of Miss Jessie, Brandon's favorite neighbor. Though in her eighty-three years—judging from the tales she told Brandon about her glory days as a dancer in clubs up in Harlem—she'd done quite a bit more than bang on doors. Miss Jessie claimed she shot one of her lovers for cheating on her with one of the other girls from the chorus line. Looking at her now, old and bent, who would guess the life she once had?

Adding to Marissa's anguish, she had to ride standing up on the train all the way to work, crushed up against droopy-eyed beings whose swaying, jerking bodies stole the newly cleaned freshness from her suit. Thankfully, most of their breath smelled of mint.

Long after she had her first meeting, long after she cursed Levi's name for the hundredth time, she still couldn't get past her anger with him. If she'd had Brandon's key, she'd probably still be in his apartment cursing Levi, instead of sitting behind her desk shuffling half-read papers from one side of her desk to the other. Nothing much made sense, and nothing at all was getting done because too much was clogging her mind that had nothing to do with her work.

Until she found out who was stalking her, nothing would ever get done.

She knew that Denise was at work. She called her house anyway, knowing that she'd get her answering machine. "Denise, sorry for hanging up on you. My life is a little tense right now, I need a little breathing room. I'll call you later." A whole lot later when she could weather the preaching.

Charmaine called to remind her that she needed to try on her dress to make sure the fit was right. For the third time she mentioned that she did not want a bridal shower, which was just as good as saying that she did. Her reason was that she would rather wait and have a housewarming. Obviously, she had better gifts in mind. Either way, it would probably hurt her feelings if she knew that Marissa had never thought of giving her a bridal shower. She turned down lunch with Charmaine so that she could call and catch up with Wayne.

"My wife isn't speaking to me," he said right off.

"Did you explain that we were just friends?"

"I did and she said if our relationship was so platonic, why is it she didn't know about it."

"Do you want me to speak to her?"

"No!"

"Wayne, please don't shout in my ear."

"Sorry, but talking to you might make things worse."

"I bet," she said, no longer feeling that she liked him all that much anymore.

"Marissa, I have to take a call."

"Me, too," she said. " 'Bye." She hung up. Again, it was obvious to her that he did not consider their relationship to be all that innocent. Again, she felt like she was being put down. What was clear was that he, Terrence, and Louis were not willing to risk their marriages for her. Brandon was right. She had been delusional all along. She had never been put before any one of their wives. Was it so far-fetched for her to have hoped that at least one, Terrence, would willingly tell his wife that she was truly important to him? Was it too much to ask for?

While Wayne and Terrence were running scared that their wives might divorce them, Louis seem to be taking it all in stride and wanted to see her again once his wife cooled down. Even he was not putting her before his marriage; and from him she could accept that. Then why did she feel so hurt? So low?

She wanted desperately to go home and crawl under her bed, but she couldn't go home, could she? If Brandon had left her a set of keys like he said he would, she would have gone back to his place. Of course, long after Levi was gone.

Buzz!

"Yes."

"Line two."

"Thanks," she said, pressing the button for her private line. "Hello."

"Hello yourself."

"Eric, hi."

"I can't wait to see you tonight, I miss you."

She didn't know what to say.

"Marissa? Are you there?"

"Yes. How are you?"

"Tired, but liking it."

"That good kind of tired, huh?"

"You know it. I can't get a minute to myself, someone's beckoning to me now. I'll see you tonight."

He was gone before she could ask him if everything was all right at home. Since he didn't say anything about his wife receiving a call, maybe she didn't need to ask. Then again, what if it was his wife, and he just didn't know what was going on? She had only been seeing him about two months. Maybe his wife didn't know, maybe the caller didn't know, either. Now that she thought about it, the calls had started coming after she met Eric. Of course, if it were his wife, she would have said something to him by now, unless she was a closet lunatic.

Seeing Eric tonight might be risky, but Marissa had to get to the bottom of this nightmare. She was tired of being scared, it was draining. She didn't know how far this woman was willing to go to

get her out of her man's life and she didn't want to find out. Damage to her car was one thing; however, an entity coming out of the shadows and stabbing or shooting her was something else entirely, something to worry about. It would kill her mother if there was a headline splashed across the newspapers that her daughter lost her life over a married man. It wasn't worth it.

Chapter 19

ONCE MARISSA SAW that her dress fit, she wanted to leave. Charmaine, however, wouldn't let her. She wanted to talk about her wedding plans, something Marissa could care less about. Thank goodness Charmaine's sister Lisa and her cousin Gail came over to try on their bridesmaids' dresses also, lending their voices to different conversations. Lisa and Gail were both pretty in light dusty rose chiffon dresses, while her own dress was a putrid shocking pink. The fit was good, but what Charmaine was thinking when she chose that color for her, Marissa didn't know. Maybe she was trying to tell her something. Whatever it was, suffice it to say, she didn't like it, but she zipped her lips and smiled. They hung their dresses back up on the borrowed dress rack in Charmaine's bedroom, which is where they would dress on the day of the wedding.

Charmaine didn't have her gown yet, so she paraded around in her long, lacy white veil. It was pretty. It flowed down from a sparkling silver-and-pearl tiara to her waist. Still wearing it, she set out cheddar, brie, and crackers on a platter, while Gail refilled their glasses with champagne. Even before they emptied the first bottle,

they giggled like silly schoolgirls; not that anything they said was especially funny. First Charmaine got the giggles and then one after the other, they all did.

Marissa gave in and let a wave of giggles wash over the fear that sat heavily in her chest all day. She figured it wouldn't hurt to hang out with them for a little while, especially since the wedding was three days away. She pulled Charmaine aside. "I can stay till seven-thirty. Then I have to run."

"Great!" Charmaine said, hugging her.

"Don't you think you should take off your veil before you soil it by mistake."

Charmaine fluffed her veil around her shoulders. "I feel like a princess with it on."

"You do look pretty."

"I do, don't I?" she asked, preening. "Now I understand why bridal gowns are so elaborate. The wedding by itself is special, but the minute a woman puts on a wedding gown and veil, no matter how rich, no matter how poor, no matter how plain she is, she feels as regal as a queen."

"That's what I hear," Marissa agreed, though she didn't need a wedding gown to feel like a queen; any new expensive outfit would do. She picked up a cracker and a small piece of brie.

"Marissa, you have got to get yourself a man and get married."

She froze as she was raising the brie and cracker to her mouth and looked intently at Charmaine.

Carefully lifting her veil off her head, Charmaine timidly stepped closer to Marissa and whispered, "I'm sorry. I didn't mean anything by that."

"Yeah, right," Marissa said, pressing the soft cheese into the cracker.

"What are you two talking about?" Lisa asked.

"Nothing," Charmaine replied.

"We were talking about getting married and being queen for a day," Marissa said. "See, I think that's all a wedding day is—a day. Once the honeymoon is over, the rude awakening hits pretty hard when the queen has to cook, clean, wash the king's dirty underwear,

and hold down a full-time job to boot. Let's not even mention the kiddies."

"Please don't spoil this for me," Charmaine said, laying her veil over the back of the sofa. "I know you don't respect the sanctity of marriage, but—"

"It's not that I don't respect the sanctity of marriage, it's just that the rules haven't changed since Eve was given to Adam as his companion."

"Pardon me," Gail said, "you mean as his servant, don't you?"

Charmaine sat down on the arm of the sofa. She gave her cousin a jab in the arm.

"I stand corrected," Marissa said. "Eve was the one who had to tend the garden, harvest the food, put it on a leaf, and then serve it to Adam, wasn't she?"

"That's right," Gail agreed, "she started the whole mess."

"Sure did. And all the while she served, Adam sat under a tree pondering the why of the universe. He did absolutely nothing to tickle Eve's fancy, that's why she was so easily persuaded by the serpent to take that apple."

"That's right," Gail agreed again. "When she offered that apple to Adam and he took it, she thought it was the least he could do for her. She had nothing else to look forward to."

Lisa laughed. "The girl didn't know she was digging a bigger hole for herself."

Charmaine sat stone-faced. None of this was funny to her.

"I bet she found out real quick though," Marissa said. "After Adam took that apple, she gave herself more chores. She had to shop for his fig leaves, then once the kids came, she had to suckle them along with Adam; fig them, and baby-sit them all by herself while Adam went house hunting amongst the elms and spruces. Most of the time he sat around watching the fruit fall off the trees into the baskets she wove for him."

"That's probably the real way basketball got started," Gail said, she and Lisa high-fiving each other.

"And wouldn't you know that she'd have boys?" Lisa asked. "If Eve had girls, they would have helped her out."

"She did have girls," Gail said, "us, and all of our foremothers. Some legacy she left us."

Feeling pleased with herself, Marissa tossed the cheese and cracker into her mouth. She chewed smugly.

Charmaine screwed up her face. "Must I be subjected to blasphemous putdowns of Adam and Eve's marriage only days before my wedding?"

Lisa laughed. "Oh, lighten up. It was funny."

"It was not."

"Funny but true," Gail said.

"That's right," Lisa agreed. "It didn't help my marriage that Joe watched football and basketball games on television while I cooked, cleaned, and raised our kids. While we were married, he acted like his hands were broke when it came to helping me out around the house."

"Just like a man," Gail said. "As long as he had a wife, his hand was broke."

"That's what I'm talking about," Lisa said. "After we divorced, he ate out or cooked his own food. When the kids are with him, he makes them pancakes for breakfast. Sometimes, he even cooks dinner for them. Go figure."

"Oooh!" Gail said, raising her hand. "That's because somebody, and I don't know who, tells men that once they marry, their wives are responsible for preparing the food and for doing all the chores; that all they have to do is go to work. They forget that wives are working just as hard, if not harder, inside the house and out."

Charmaine folded her arms across her chest. "What are you all trying to do, ruin my marriage before it even starts?"

"No," Lisa said, "we are trying to tell you to start out on the right foot. I didn't, and you know the problems I had. I was eager to please J.T. I wanted to cook the best homemade meals he'd ever eaten; even better than his mother's. I wanted to show him that I could keep a clean house, and that I could launder the whitest whites. I created that monster for myself. I see that now. If, from the

very beginning, I had gotten J.T. to share the cooking and the house-keeping, he would have known that it was partly his responsibility, too."

"That's what I say," Marissa said, picking up another cracker. "My mother slaved for my father. There were days when I thought she might drop."

"I've had plenty days like that," Lisa said.

"Most wives and mothers have," Marissa agreed, continuing. "My mother came home after working all day to cook dinner for my father. He didn't ever want to hear about her being too tired or about going out to dinner. And my father didn't like leftovers—period. Nor did he eat pizza, or franks and beans. He liked meat and pota-toes or rice, fresh vegetables and hot cornbread or biscuits—every day. My mother didn't dare put a store-bought loaf of bread on his dinner table."

"I know what you mean," Gail agreed. "My grandfather was like that. My grandmother baked biscuits and cornbread and cakes and pies with a smile on her face. She was about pleasing her man."

"I know that's right," Lisa said. "Granddaddy didn't play, he wanted the best."

"Neither did my father," Marissa said. "When we got older, Niecy and I tried to help out by cleaning the house and cooking, but my fa-ther didn't like our cooking, just our mother's. And you know what he did every day after he got in from work?"

"Sit in front of the television," Gail answered.

"That or go to sleep until dinner was ready."

"Like a lot of men," Lisa said.

"Like most men," she said. "He took my mother for granted. Not once did he compliment her on being a good wife and mother."

"All men aren't like that," Charmaine said.

"Maybe not all, but most," Marissa said. "But I think—"

"Gregory's not like that."

"Charmaine, I said maybe not all. Don't be so thin-skinned."

"I'm not being thin-skinned. I just don't think it's fair for you to brand all men as chauvinistic."

"Marissa, she's getting married," Lisa reminded her. "She's a little sensitive."

"I am not."

"Yes, you are," Lisa said, biting into a piece of cheese.

"Well, you guys are supposed to be making me feel good—I feel miserable," Charmaine said, pouting.

"Then ignore us," Marissa said, "and forget what I said about my mother and father, they are the past. As for me, in my next life, I wanna come back as a man."

Lisa drew back and gaped at Marissa. "You're not . . . ?"

"Watch your mouth, I'm not that way."

"Then why do you wanna come back as a man?"

"Because men have it made in this world."

"That's true," Gail agreed. "But I like being a woman."

"Ain't that the truth," Charmaine said, high-fiving Gail.

"Believe me, I love being a woman," Marissa confirmed, "but men get to have wives."

"Ha!" Lisa said, laughing. "I gotcha. I want me a wife, too. I can use the help."

"I know that's right," Gail agreed.

For a minute they all laughed, including Charmaine, who laughed behind her hand.

"Hold up," Gail said, no longer laughing. "I have to stick up for my father. To tell the truth, he wasn't all that bad."

"Yeah, Uncle James was kinda cool," Charmaine said.

"He was," Gail agreed. "He didn't mind taking my mother out once in a while, and he ate leftovers. Now, he didn't do kitchen chores, but he did do lots of things around the house. He died when I was fifteen, broke my mother's heart. Took her a little while, but she got herself together and got herself a little boyfriend, whom she won't let move in with her, because she said she'd never get married again."

"Can't say I blame her," Marissa said glibly. "My father died six years ago, and my mother took his pension, her pension, and the insurance money and retired to Florida. She rarely cooks, eats out

most of the time, and her boyfriend treats her like a queen every day."

Charmaine popped her fingers. "Is the way your father treated your mother why you're so against marriage? Are you . . . ?"

"Am I what?"

"Well, are you trying to . . . ah, I mean, are you afraid to have your own . . . ah . . . ?"

Marissa eyeballed Charmaine, warning her to tread lightly.

Heeding the warning, Charmaine shrugged. "Forget it."

She knew what Charmaine was about to ask—in front of Lisa and Gail, at that. Did the woman never learn?

"Okay, girls, give," Gail said. "What's going on?"

"Nothing," Marissa said. "We don't see eye to eye on some things. Charmaine, I know what my mother went through and I know that's not the life I want for myself. In fact, my mother was the one who told me that I didn't have to get married to get what I wanted. She told me to make my own money, make my own rules, and not to ever let any man make me his servant. In essence, she said, 'Do as I say, not as I did.' "

"I wish my mother had lived to school me," Lisa said.

"We had Daddy," Charmaine said, "he raised us the best he could."

"And I love him for being there for us, but he was a man raising girls to be subservient."

"Don't say that. Daddy worked hard for us. We were lucky to have a father who kept four girls and raised them himself."

"Charmaine, there is no denying that Daddy was good to us, but he was still a man."

Gail looked over at her cousin and saw that she was tearing. "Aww, Charmaine, we didn't mean to make you cry."

"Charmaine," Marissa said, going over to stand next to her. "Don't take what we said personally. You don't have to go through what my mother went through. From the minute you say 'I do,' make your marriage what you want it to be."

"But you all are so bitter about marriage."

"Yeah, but that has nothing to do with you. I'd get married to-morrow if the guy I married didn't sit on his ass and expect for me to do all the work. And on top of that, he'd have to wine, dine, and romance me like I was still his girlfriend. A marriage license doesn't give a man the right to write *servant* or *housewife* behind a woman's name. When he does that, he doesn't see the woman he romanced, he sees his mother."

Lisa applauded. "Preach, sister!"

"But you haven't given yourself the opportunity to meet the right man, Marissa."

"Let's not go there, Charmaine. I live my life the way I want. To you it's wrong, but I've had my fringe benefits."

"But what about your future?"

"I don't want you to worry about me, Charmaine, but I will tell you this. I do see where I might have to make some changes in my life."

"Really?"

"You two are doing it again," Gail protested. "What are you talking about?"

"I think I know," Lisa said. "It's a man."

Marissa fixed her gaze on Charmaine.

"No, Lisa," Charmaine said quickly, "you don't know."

"Then tell us already."

"It's personal, nosy," Charmaine said.

"Don't you think you two are being rude?"

"Yes, with reason," Marissa said.

"And the reason is?"

"Nosy," Charmaine said, laughing.

"Lisa," Marissa said, annoyed that she was again put on the spot, "let's just say that my love affairs of tomorrow will be nothing like my love affairs of yesterday. Cryptic, but that's all I'm saying."

Charmaine's eyes widened. "Wow."

Lisa picked up the champagne bottle. "What the hell does that mean?" she asked, shaking the empty bottle.

"Can't you take a hint?" Charmaine said, going over to the table.

She lifted a new bottle of champagne out of the ice bucket. "The girl does not want to discuss her love life."

"Fine, keep your damn secrets. I don't care."

Charmaine popped the cork.

"You'll get over it," Gail said, holding her glass out for Charmaine to fill after she poured for Lisa.

"Let's make a toast," Charmaine said cheerfully. "Champagne, Marissa?"

"No, I'm fine," she said, joining the three women in a circle. She meant what she said about not dating married men anymore. For a while, she might not date any man. It was time for a much-needed hiatus.

They stood with their glasses raised.

"Me, first," Charmaine said.

"That's bad luck," Gail said. "We're supposed to toast you."

"Please! I don't believe in superstition. I want to toast to the sanctity of marriage."

"If something bad happens at your wedding, don't blame nobody but yourself."

"Girl, please," Charmaine said, waving Gail off but looking at Marissa. "Isn't anyone going to raise her glass to the sanctity of marriage."

Although she groaned, Marissa touched her glass to the others and daintily sipped her champagne.

"To the divorce court, when all else fails," Gail said gleefully.

"Thanks a lot, cuz."

"I just want you to know that there is a way out."

"Greg is good to me. I won't need a way out."

"Then you'll be counted in the lucky percentage of marriages that last a lifetime. Instead, I'll say, till death do you part."

"Thank you," Charmaine said, taking a sip of her champagne.

Lisa raised her glass. "Sister, dear, what I wanted for myself, I want for you. Lots of babies, lots of laughter, and lots of loving. Not necessarily in that order."

"Thank you," Charmaine said, hugging Lisa.

They all took a quick sip and lowered their glasses. All eyes were on Marissa. She smirked.

"Let's not be cynical," Charmaine advised.

"I won't," Marissa said, raising her glass higher. "To a wedding day that you'll always remember. May love be your beacon through the toughest times, and your smile in the happiest of times."

"Oh, that's nice," Charmaine gushed, hugging her.

Together they emptied their glasses.

Marissa looked at her watch. "I have to get going."

"Can't you stay a little longer?" Gail asked. "We could play a few hands of spades."

"I'd like to," Marissa said, finally feeling comfortable. "But I have a date. I'll see you all Friday evening."

Charmaine walked her to the door. "What changed your mind about the men you were dating?" she asked out in the hallway, out of earshot of Gail and Lisa.

"Let's just say I've seen the light. I'll see you Friday night at the church."

"Okay. Drive carefully."

If Charmaine had not left work early, she would have known that Marissa didn't have her car. At least Marissa knew that Charmaine wasn't the one who vandalized it.

Chapter 20

LEVI WIPED AWAY the steam from the bathroom mirror with a wad of balled-up toilet paper. Like he always did after work, he had taken a long, hot shower. The day's sweat and grime had washed away, but the agitation he'd felt inside all day after Marissa wagged her nasty tongue at him had not. It didn't make any damn sense that ten hours had passed, and yet he was still seething. All day she had him talking to himself. Because of her, it took him longer to lay the floor in Brandon's kitchen. He messed up two squares of linoleum tile by cutting them wrong. Several squares were mislaid and had to be pulled up, which wasn't easy; the glue had bonded the tile to the floor right away. Every time he messed up, he cursed her name, and that aggravated him more. Marissa wasn't his woman, they hadn't even shared ten minutes of mutual admiration. Yet he felt like he did that one time a year before Janice died, when she broke up with him for taking Big Butt Betty to the movies. Janice's cousin saw him with his arm around Big Butt Betty and snitched. No matter how much he explained that it wasn't a date but just friends hanging out, Janice wasn't buying it. And she was right not to. The truth was, he was lying. He thought he could play around, like everyone else, and not get caught. Well, he was wrong. It was the first and only time he

cheated on Janice. He had to beg like a cross-eyed fool to get her to take him back. They were apart for just a week, but it was, at that time, the most miserable week of his life. On the outside, he was cool. Inside, he was messed up. He had all these feelings coming at him at once—sadness, irritability, anger, guilt, and loneliness. He felt even worse when Janice was killed, but thought no one could make him feel that way again. He was wrong. Marissa, just being around her, had awakened all those feelings and more.

Studying his face in the mirror, Levi rubbed his chin. He was never very hairy and often went days without shaving. Still, he was glad he had shaved this morning; it was one less thing for Marissa to insult him about. His hair was another matter. Yes, it had been more than a month since his last haircut, but he didn't think it looked all that bad. An afro? Forget her. He didn't care what she thought, although he had planned on getting it cut Friday before going to the wedding rehearsal. Her pointing out how long his hair had gotten didn't bother him as much as her shooting him down when he thought he was being charming. She treated him like he was a country bumpkin with no finesse, no cool.

The woman was downright insulting when she called him a "one-man business." He could have told her that he had five men working for him on another job. For a small job like Brandon's kitchen, it wasn't cost effective to have a plumber, an electrician, a carpenter, and a tile layer, all crowded up in that eight-by-ten space. Not when he could do it all himself and see more profit.

Pensively, he went about getting dressed. Like Gregory said, Marissa was an 'itch. Most likely, she was a selective 'itch. All those guys weren't calling her because she had a pretty smile, and she certainly must not have been browbeating them. They could get that at home. She gave them what they wanted and much of that giving had to be pleasurable for them or they wouldn't keep coming back. The question was, how pleasurable was the giving? Damn. Why the hell should he care? He wasn't interested. He needed to stop harping on Marissa and her life. He was going to drive himself crazy thinking about her. Overhead, he could hear his mother, Freda, moving about the kitchen. Any minute now.

"Lee!" Freda called from the top of the basement stairs. "Your dinner's getting cold."

"I'll be right up, Ma."

"If you need more time, I'll keep the oven on a little while longer; of course the gas bill will be higher."

"I'm coming up," he said, shaking his leg so that his jeans would fall down over his sneakers.

"Okay, if you're ready."

Knowing that she meant for him to hurry up, he started up the stairs. Once his plate was on the table, his mother expected him to be there with his mouth open ready to inhale her food. Looking after him had become her raison d'être since his father died. That's probably why she refused to use the microwave oven he bought for her. The speed at which it cooked or warmed up food would leave her with too much free time on her hands. Whether she cooked from scratch or pulled out leftovers, she put his dinner into the oven on low until he got out of the shower and she stayed in the kitchen herself until the food was hot. She did nothing to occupy herself outside of the house. The few times he tried to get her involved in senior citizen activities at her church, she accused him of not needing her, of calling her old.

"You're moving mighty slow tonight," Freda said, sitting a glass of iced tea on the table next to his aluminum-foil-covered plate. She carefully removed the foil. "You been taking your vitamins?"

Sitting down at the table, Levi picked up his fork. "I'll take them after dinner," he said, suddenly hungry for the smothered pork chops, fluffy mashed potatoes, and cut green string beans in front of him. "Looks good."

"Then eat it before it gets cold," she said, sliding a large square of buttery corn bread on a saucer over to him.

He dug into the mashed potatoes. They were his mother's usual—they melted in his mouth.

Freda busily wiped down the already spotless table. "You didn't take your mail today or yesterday."

"I'll go through it on Sunday."

Freda stopped wiping. "What about the bills?"

Jabbing his fork into one of the pork chops, Levi sliced off a size-able chunk and stuffed it into his mouth. It was tender and seasoned with a lot of black pepper—the way he liked it. He looked across at his mother; she was frowning. He'd seen that worried look on her face all of his life. She was always worried about whether or not the bills would be paid on time. When his father was alive, past due notices every month on everything from the rent to the telephone bill were the norm. He paid his bills when he felt like it, and often said that the companies had more money than he did and should be glad that he paid at all. That screwed-up attitude is another reason why his father never got any further than he did.

"What about the mortgage payment for May? You don't wanna lose your house."

He wiped his mouth with a napkin before taking a big gulp of iced tea. He sat the glass down firmly. "Ma, relax. The mortgage is covered."

"But . . ."

"Stop worrying so much. We're more than okay."

Pulling the chair out from the table, she sat down and leaned forward, folding her arms on top of the table. "I wouldn't worry so much if you slowed down and took better care of yourself; I'm not gonna be around forever."

He stopped chewing. His left cheek bulged with food as he looked at her. She had been saying that as far back as he could remember and way back then, as it is now, her not being around was unimaginable. He swallowed his food in one big gulp. He hated when she started talking like she was about to check out at any minute. She'd been to the doctor more frequently lately about her rheumatoid arthritis, but she'd probably outlive him.

"Lee, you need to settle down and get yourself a wife who can make you want to come home at a decent hour."

"I don't wanna talk about this," he said, dropping his fork onto his plate.

"You never do, but it would be nice if you could find a wife before I'm called home to glory. I'd like to meet her."

He sat back from the table. "I don't need this tonight, Ma, I had a

hard day. Can we talk about something else? What about you? What did you do today?"

"Enough to keep me busy. It was a woman that gave you a hard time today, wasn't it?"

Amazed at the woman's audacity, he stared at her, though he couldn't help but wonder how she came to that conclusion.

"Well?"

"I worked today. I wasn't hanging out at a club."

"Was it a customer? Is she single?"

"Ma, let it go," he said, pushing his plate away.

"Lee, I don't mean to pester you, I just want you to be happy."

"I am."

"You think you are."

He got up from the table and took his plate to the sink. He dumped the uneaten food down the garbage disposal. The loud churning, however, didn't stop Freda from talking.

"Lee, I raised you, I know when you're happy. You were happy when your business grew; and you were happy when you bought this house. If you ask me—"

"I didn't."

"You need a woman in your life."

He ran hot water onto his plate. "I got a busy day tomorrow," he said, shutting off the water. He started out of the kitchen.

"Lee."

"Ma, I'll see you in—"

"I am talking to you," she said, pushing her glasses up on her nose and peering at him.

Dropping his head to his chest, he stopped walking. Damn.

"You know I don't like to get in your business, Lee, but I been worrying about you."

He hated when she called herself worrying about him. Once she started harping on him to find a wife, there was no stopping her.

"Lee."

The respect he had for her kept him from going on, but he didn't go back to the table. He went instead to sit on the stool at the center island he'd built for her.

"I've been watching you," she said, turning sideways in her chair so that she could face him. "For the last few days, you've been mighty irritable."

"Ma, can't I have a tough day at work without your maternal radar kicking in?"

"No. I know when it's business and I know when it's personal. You just dumped your dinner, that's why I know what's bothering you is personal. It's a woman."

"You're a psychic now?"

"When it comes to you, I am. Are you seeing her?"

"You don't quit, do you?"

"You are, aren't you?"

"You know everything," he said, annoyed that she wouldn't let up, "you tell me."

"You don't have to tell me if you don't want to, but if this woman can get to you like this, then she must be something."

"Like what?"

"For one thing, you're eating less."

"Aww, c'mon. I'm eating 'bout the same as I always do."

"That's what you think. Plus, you're impatient all of a sudden. Like now."

"I'm tired. I worked—"

"It has nothing whatsoever to do with work. Nobody's more thorough, more detailed, more patient than you when it comes to your work. Matter of fact, the more difficult the job, the more patient and the more excited you are. No, it's a woman that's got you all worked up."

He chuckled and shook his head. When he was a teenager, she used to get him to tell her intimate details about his girlfriends by wearing him down with persistent questions about them. What little he knew about Marissa, who wasn't even his woman, he could never tell. "Give it up, Ma, there is no woman."

"There is, whether you admit it or not. Whoever she is, she's gotten under your skin, and knowing you, you don't like that one bit. You like to be in control of your emotions because you're scared

that some woman might see that all that muscle is hiding a big, sentimental softie."

"You know, Ma, I think you missed your calling. I'm working for a guy now who happens to be a psychiatrist, maybe he's looking for a partner."

"He couldn't be my partner," she said lifting her chin slightly, "he's not qualified."

"Oh?"

"He'd have to get a degree in motherhood first. We mothers know what we're talking about."

"Not this time."

"Well, I know this much. If this woman is calling the shots, you're either intrigued or annoyed or both. Plus, you like strong women. So if she's strong and got you guessing, too, you're a goner."

"I hate to burst your bubble, but you're wrong," he said, wishing that he could talk to her about Marissa, but he knew better. She had a definite opinion about any woman who slept with married men. She called her Jade; a name her own mother called the single young thing that took his grandfather from her, leaving her very bitter. His grandmother never trusted any man again enough to remarry and warned his mother to trust no woman around her man. Likewise, she told him to never trust any man around his woman. He never did meet his grandfather and his mother never talked about him. That's why, if he ever did tell her about Marissa, he could never tell her everything. She would waste no time gathering wood to make a blazing fire to torch her at the stake. She took to heart the phrase "Let no man or woman put asunder." Still, he was interested in how she thought he was acting. So he continued to sit.

"Lee, after thirty-seven years, I'd say I know everything there is to know about you that counts. So, let's cut to the chase. Is she pretty? Is she nice?"

At that he chuckled. "That's a good question."

"I knew it was a woman!" Freda exclaimed, clapping her hands.

"What if it is? I'm not involved with her."

"Whether you know it or not, you are."

"Nah," he said, shaking his head.

"She's not married, is she?"

"Nope."

"Good. Lee, I've seen you with your women. Not one has ever made you doe-eyed."

"Doe-eyed?"

"I'm telling you, you should see yourself in the morning. I have never seen you look like that over a woman."

"Doe-eyed?"

"You look like she's on your mind."

"Awww," he said, waving his hand at her. He stood up and stretched. "I don't know why I listen to you."

"Because you know I'm right."

"I'm going to bed."

"And that's another thing. You haven't sat and listened to me this long since that boy called you a momma's boy back in fifth grade because I called you to come in the house."

"I had no choice. I was grounded for beating him up."

"You had no business fighting, but ever since then, you've gone out of your way to be independent. I know that's the reason you took the basement apartment in your own house when you got fifteen rooms upstairs. I bet people think I own this house and not you."

"So. Nobody needs to know my business. I took the basement because it's private; away from prying eyes."

"I'm not nosy."

"Says you."

"I am not," she said indignantly. "I think you live downstairs because you try to convince yourself that you don't live with your mother. That's why you won't let me come down there."

He bent down and kissed her on the forehead. "Same old argument, same old song. Good night."

"Do me a favor."

"What?"

"I can't wait forever for grandchildren. Bring your woman over here, I wanna meet her."

Frowning, he looked down at her. "My woman? Grandchildren?

That's why I don't tell you anything. You done made the girl my woman and started planning grandchildren. I'm outta here."

"Good night," Freda called to her son as he headed for the basement stairs. Standing up slowly, she supported her lower back with her hands as she walked gingerly over to the sink. "We'll see who's right," she said to herself as Levi escaped to his sanctum.

Chapter 21

THE DOZEN RED ROSES Eric brought Marissa sat in a tall, slender crystal vase on the bedroom dresser. Their fragrance filled the room. She lay across the bottom of the bed while he slowly and sensually massaged her shoulders, her back, her buttocks, and the back of her thighs. He had never touched her so intimately, and she let him only after a minute-long feeble attempt at dissuading him failed. It was beginning to feel like foreplay and that was the last thing she needed. Through her long, black silk lounging pajamas, she could feel how hot his hands were. The warmth felt good; she purred shamelessly under his touch, and he, too, seemed to be enjoying himself. She could hear a low rumble in his throat.

As good as his hands felt, every time she sensed that he wanted to do more than therapeutically massage her backside, she tightened up and complained about her aching back, forcing him to retreat. She really didn't want to go all the way. She didn't want Eric. It wasn't that he wasn't sexually appealing, he was that and more. Months ago when he gave her his business card in a restaurant in Manhattan, she had no intention of ever calling him, but as luck would have it, she had bumped into him again at the same restaurant a week later. That's when she decided to call him. It had been easy

to be platonic with him; he was always so tired. And now, with everything that was going on, starting a sexual relationship with him at this point was dangerous and stupid.

"You feeling better?" Eric asked, his voice husky.

Hearing the way his breathing was getting deeper and feeling the way his hot hands, again on her behind, were beginning to inch their way down between her thighs, Marissa knew she had better get up before it got to be uncomfortable for both of them. She began to roll away from his hands.

"I feel a lot better," she answered softly. His massage had truly done wonders—she no longer felt tense. This was the most relaxed she had been in days. The telephones were unplugged; the messages she didn't listen to were erased; her car was safe in the dealer's hands; and hopefully, she was no longer on the mind of the phantom wife. She sat up.

Eric lay his hand on the middle of her back. "You smell good," he said, slowly sliding his hand up and down her back.

"Thank you."

He leaned in closer, kissing her tenderly on her earlobe. "You like this?"

"It tickles," she replied, shrinking away from his butterfly kisses. Oh, yes, she had better stop him before he couldn't be stopped. She pulled back. "Eric, let's talk."

"I've been wanting to talk to you, too," he said, gently squeezing her waist.

Her heart jumped. "About what?"

"You and me."

Looking at him anxiously, she waited for the left shoe to drop.

"Don't look so terrorized, I'm not about to propose a root canal."

"That's good to know," Marissa said, though she'd take a root canal over her present situation any day.

"What I do propose, however, is that we spend more time together, perhaps a weekend away. Maybe we could even think along the lines of having a more serious relationship."

That was the last thing she expected to hear from him. What about his wife?

"My practice has been very demanding. It has taken up much of my time. However, things are running a lot smoother now. You and I need to decide what we want. Our future . . ."

"Wait a minute," she said, getting up off the bed. "What future?"

"Ours."

"Wait," Marissa said, touching her fingertips to her head as she tried to get her thoughts together. "What about your wife? Are you getting a divorce?"

"Who told you I was married?"

"What?"

"I'm not."

"Wait . . . wait," she said, holding her hand up like a traffic cop to stop him from talking. She closed her eyes. He did say that he was not married. That is what she heard, but that could not be.

He waited.

"Eric, let me understand this," she said, opening her eyes again. "You are not married?"

"No."

"Wait a minute. Didn't you tell me that you were married when we first met?"

"I might have said that I was once married for nine years, but I've been divorced for the past three."

She pointed an accusatory finger at him. "Eric, that is not what you told me."

He got up off the bed and stood in front of her. He scratched his head. "Why the third degree? Why are you so upset about me not being married? I'd think you'd be happy that I'm not."

Turning away from his scrutiny, she marched angrily out of the bedroom into the living room. She felt like a fool.

For a confusing moment, Eric stood where she left him. He tucked his shirttail into his pants before going into the living room where Marissa had wrapped herself up in her afghan and was sitting in a tight ball on the far end of the sofa.

"Okay, Marissa. What the hell is this about?"

She felt stupid. She had no sane explanation for why she was so

angry, other than she felt that he had lied to her. Part of it, she knew, had to do with not wanting to be involved with any single men.

Eric sat down next to her. He reached for her hand. She was about to pull away, but then she glimpsed his left hand. He was wearing a diamond-cut wedding band on his ring finger. She took his hand. She studied the ring. She let go of him.

"What?" he asked.

"If you're not married, why are you wearing a wedding band?"

He looked at his ring. "It was my grandfather's, he wanted me to have it. I've worn it for the past thirteen years."

"Don't you think wearing a wedding band will make people think you're married?"

"I don't wear this ring for people, I wear it for me. That's why I know I never told you that I was married."

She cut her eyes at him. "In a way, you did. In addition to the wedding band, you told me that you could only see me Wednesday evenings and even then, you always left before eleven; you never spent the night; you never invited me to your place; and you never gave me a home number. Need I say more?"

"So from that you deduced that I was married?"

"Anyone would."

"Not if they knew that Wednesday night was the only night I had free. The other nights I work. My practice is less than a year old. I've had no time for socializing beyond seeing you once a week."

She pursed her lips and looked at him suspiciously. She wasn't buying it.

"You don't believe me, do you?"

"Not really."

"Well, believe this. In the last few weeks, my partner and I have hired an additional dental assistant and an office manager, freeing up a considerable amount of time for ourselves. I always left you early because I needed my rest. If I had stayed overnight with you, I would have never slept, and I didn't give you my home number because I was rarely there."

He had mentioned his new dental practice, but she assumed that

he also had a wife and family. Had she known, she would have left him alone. "You're not seeing anyone else besides me?"

"I won't lie. I do have a friend that I've known for several years who has a more serious relationship with someone else."

"And you can deal with that?"

"Yes, I can. I didn't have time for the relationship. It would have been selfish on my part to expect for her to wait for me. That's why I never pressured you, but you act like my being single is a bad thing. I would think you'd be pleased about it."

Hugging her knees close to her chest, she rested her chin on top of her knees and stared down at the floor. Isn't this a bitch?

"Marissa."

Sighing, she lifted her head and looked at him. Confusion was written all over his face.

"If you thought I was married, why didn't you ask me about it?"

She shrugged her shoulders.

"A better question, why did you see me if you thought I was married?"

How was she supposed to tell him that she had only been going out with married men? It was hard enough trying to come to grips with this revelation. Anyone else would have jumped all over Eric—his practice was thriving; he drove a nice car; he dressed well. She didn't know where he lived, but it was most likely in a good neighborhood. Yet he was a catch she didn't want for herself.

"Marissa?"

"I was attracted to you, okay? It didn't matter that you were supposedly married."

"Then I don't understand why you're so upset now that you know that I am not."

Again she shrugged her shoulders. "This is too much for me to handle right now."

"Then tell me, what can you handle?"

"Not much. My life is so complicated right now, I need to take a break from this relationship. I need to think about what I want before I can think about making commitments."

"Are you saying that I should back off?"

"Well, yes. I need space and time."

"How much space and how much time?"

Twisting her bracelet around her wrist, she looked at him like he was stupid. This is exactly what she didn't want—questions. Single men demanded what she was not willing to give—deadlines and commitments. Already he was questioning her, pushing her. Trying her best to remain calm, she continued to twist her bracelet.

"Tell me something, Marissa," he demanded.

"Eric, we're friends. Can't we just keep it that way for the time being?"

For a second he peered into her eyes. "I have plenty of friends. I need a woman. I need someone in my corner. If you can't be that woman, then I need to find someone who can," he said, standing up. He stood over her looking down into her eyes, and not once did she blink.

If he was waiting for her to fall down at his feet and suddenly proclaim a great love for him, he'd be waiting a long time. As far as she was concerned, he was a liar. He had to know that she thought he was married; his wearing that ring was not just for sentimental reasons. If it were, he could have worn it on his right hand.

"I'll get my jacket," he said, though he continued looking down at her.

Marissa looked away.

Eric stood a minute longer looking at her.

Still, she wouldn't look at him. She wanted him to leave.

He walked off abruptly. He went to the hall closet and plucked his jacket off the doorknob. He opened the apartment door.

She could not see him, but she knew that he was standing in the open doorway, probably hoping that she would run after him. She would not.

"Marissa, I suggest you keep this in mind: I won't wait long."

She heard the door close. She could not have been more relieved. There it was, the ultimatum. That Eric could keep. If he said another stupid thing, she would have given him his answer before he walked out of the door. He was not for her. In the little time she spent with him, bits of his smugness and arrogance had reared their ugly heads.

He could be very tender and attentive, but when they discussed politics or current events, he came off as a know-it-all. A few times, she had to tell him that none of those issues were important enough for her to argue or debate over. Besides, if he was willing to argue in the little time they spent together, no telling what kind of arguments they'd have if they were together more. No, she would not be seeing him again.

Chapter 22

No SOONER HAD she locked the door behind Eric, gone back into the living room and sat down when the intercom buzzer sounded. Thinking that Eric had forgotten something, she answered right away, "Yes?"

"Miss Jenkins, there's an envelope down here for you."

"I picked up my mail."

"This was left here by a lady maybe twenty minutes ago."

"What's her name?"

"She wouldn't say."

"Have you seen her before?"

"No."

Closing her eyes, she shook her head. As nosy as Maury was, this would be the one time he didn't give a visitor the third degree.

"Maury, why didn't you buzz me while she was here?"

"She didn't want me to."

"And why not?"

"She said to give it to you after your visitor left."

Her heart skipped a beat. "How did she know I had a visitor?"

"She asked."

"You told her?" she asked incredulously. "You . . . !" She caught

herself. She angrily released the Talk button and hit the intercom box with the side of her fist. "You stupid, nosy-ass bastard!"

Buzzz!

She stabbed the button with her finger. "What?"

"Miss Jenkins. I didn't tell the lady you had a visitor," Maury defended. "She said that she knew that Dr. Grayson was up there and not to disturb you."

That certainly didn't make her feel any better. "Did she actually say his name?"

"No, she said, your 'guest.' "

That didn't make her breathe any easier, either. Whether Eric's name had been mentioned or not, this woman knew that he was with her. But how? Did she know him? "What did she look like?" she asked.

"If you're coming down, I'll tell you then," he said, disconnecting them.

She threw the afghan back off her shoulders and flung it into the living room onto the arm of the love seat. Hopefully, there would be some answers in that envelope. Within minutes she had slipped her feet into a pair of black mules and pulled a trench coat on over her pajamas, tying it snugly at her waist. Grabbing her keys, she rushed down the hall to the elevator. The doors opened at once. She practically leapt onto the elevator.

Maury was standing outside the door, talking with an elderly man she'd seen before. She checked the top of his desk—there was no envelope, though she did glimpse Eric's name on the sign-in book. Her apartment was listed next to his name. The book was wide open for prying eyes. Maybe the woman had seen the same thing. She could have read every name in the book if she wanted to.

Going over and standing in front of the door, Marissa tapped on the glass. Maury turned around. He lifted a single finger, indicating "one minute" to her. He continued to talk. Folding her arms across her chest, she stood in place, tapping her foot on the carpeted runner. He kept talking. She pushed open the door.

"Excuse me," she said to the older man. "Maury, if I may speak to you for just a minute?"

"Let me get to the store," the man said.

"I'll see you when you get back."

She wanted to grab him. "Well?"

He pulled the envelope from inside his uniform jacket. It was large like the envelopes in which greeting cards are mailed. She took it from him and inspected it. It was stiff like a card. She turned it over to see if it was sealed. It was. Her first and last name were printed in big block letters across the front.

"Who left it?"

"Like I said, she wouldn't leave her name. She said you'd know."

Again, she looked at the envelope, but she had no intention of opening it anywhere near Maury.

"What did she look like?"

"Let me see," he began, sidling past her into the lobby. He sat down on top of his desk. "She was an attractive black woman with long black hair; kinda slim; tall . . ."

"How tall?"

"A little taller than you, a little shorter than me; and she was wearing a really short, tight red dress."

"What did her face look like?"

Glancing past Marissa to the outside, Maury stood up and stepped quickly over to the door.

The lights from the front of the building shone only halfway down the path. Until the woman emerged from the darkness and was halfway up the walkway, Marissa had not seen her. This woman, however, was nothing like Maury described. She was white.

Maury kept his eyes on the woman coming up the walkway. "Like I said, she was pretty, but she wore a little too much makeup for my taste. Oh, and she had one of those moles painted on her cheek near her mouth. That, I liked."

"I bet you did," she said softly.

"Huh?"

"Nothing. I don't know anyone like that. Did she say anything else besides 'wait for my guest to leave'?"

"Just a minute," he said, pulling open the door. "Evening, Mrs. Volpe."

"Good evening, Maury."

He nodded once. "How's your mother?"

"She's doing fine now that she's able to get back to her weekly mah-jongg game."

"Bet she's happy as a tick in a dog pound."

Mrs. Volpe's smile was wide and toothy. "That she is."

"That's wonderful. Tell her I asked about her."

"I sure will," Mrs. Volpe said, glancing over at Marissa. "Evening."

"Evening," Marissa replied, before turning her back on both of them. She studied the sign-in book. As many times as she and Mrs. Volpe had seen each other, they had never exchanged more than a nod. It would be interesting to know if they shared the same opinion of each other—snooty. She waited until Mrs. Volpe had checked her mailbox and gotten on the elevator before she turned back to Maury.

She was about to burst. "Did the woman say anything else?"

"She said something like, 'lovely evening.' That's it. She left."

"Do me a favor, will you? Next time someone comes looking for me, whether they simply ask for me, leave a note, or go up to my apartment, make them sign in."

"But that's only for visitors who go to tenant's apartments."

"This is a special request," she said. "If I need to pay for that service, I will."

"I'll have everyone asking for you to sign in."

"Thank you," she said, walking quickly toward the elevator. She was itching to open the envelope, yet she was afraid of what it might say. It was apparent that the card was left because the person couldn't get through on her unplugged telephone line.

"There she is!" Maury said suddenly, pointing out the door at a woman standing midway down the walkway.

Rushing back to the door, Marissa had to peer intently into the night with her hands cuffed around her face against the glass in order to see who Maury was pointing at. Sure enough, there was a woman in a short, tight red dress. Trashy. She couldn't imagine the wife of either Wayne, Terrence, or Louis dressing like that.

The woman was standing too far down the walkway away from the light for her face to be clearly visible. The building cast a shadow from her face to her shoulders, but Marissa could see that she looked much like Maury described. She stood with one hand on her slim hip, the other hung at her side. Her long, slender brown legs dropped down from under her short skirt like pillars under a pier. She stood even taller in the red spikes she wore.

Even in the shadow of darkness, there was no question at whom the woman was looking—her. Marissa could not see her eyes, but she felt that they beamed through her like a laser. A heavy, foreboding feeling washed over her.

"How come she's standing there like that?" Maury asked, reaching around Marissa to pull open the door.

Continuing to stare at the woman, Marissa automatically stepped out of the way of the opening door. Nothing about her was familiar.

"Miss!" Maury called to the woman. "You wanted to see Miss Jenkins?"

Clasping her hands together, the woman steadily raised both arms straight out, high up in front of her chest. She pointed her forefingers at Marissa like she was pointing a gun. She recoiled three times.

Marissa's eyes widened. A chill seized her heart.

Still holding onto the door, Maury stepped outside the building onto the walkway. "Hey! Hey!"

Marissa could feel goose bumps sprout up on her arms. Completely mesmerized, she could not tear her eyes away from the woman.

The woman blew the tips of her fingers. Then she extended one arm and pointed threateningly at Marissa again.

"She's crazy," Maury said.

The rapid pounding of her heart scared her, but she was more angry than she was scared. She jetted outside and stood in front of Maury. "Who the hell are you?" she shouted.

Without uttering a single word, the woman turned casually and started walking away.

"You got something to say to me? I'm here. Say it to my face."

The woman kept walking.

Marissa started down the walkway. "Hey! I'm talking to you. Don't leave. Say what you have to say."

"Miss Jenkins!" Maury called anxiously.

The woman walked faster.

Marissa started running.

"Miss Jenkins, where you going?"

The woman started running. Her dress slid up higher on her thighs.

Marissa shouted behind her, "You had so much to say over the telephone!"

"Miss Jenkins!"

The woman ran faster.

Marissa tried to run faster, too, but her two-inch-high satin mules kept her from running as fast as she could have. She had to grip them with her toes to keep them from falling off.

The woman hit the corner of Vanderbilt Avenue and rounded it like a hundred-meter sprinter.

Marissa didn't know how the woman could run so fast with spikes on. By the time she got to the corner, the woman was halfway down the next block. The night was swallowing her up the farther away she got. Marissa stopped running. It was just as well that the race was lost. She felt stupid anyway, chasing behind some fool she didn't even know. Suppose she had caught her? She might have run smack dab into trouble; the kind of trouble she might not have been able to get herself out of. Breathing deeply, trying to catch her breath, she brought her hand to her chest. Her keys rattled, letting her know that she didn't have the envelope in her hand. Instinctively, she began patting the pockets of her trench.

From behind, someone came up and touched her on the shoulder. *"Eeeek!"* Marissa screeched, turning quickly and bumping into Maury. His eyes darted down the street and then back to her. In his left hand, she saw that he was carrying a baseball bat.

"Where did she go?"

Out of breath, she pointed down the street.

"That was the craziest thing I ever seen."

"Me, too," she said, looking down and searching the sidewalk around her. "Did you see that envelope you gave me?"

"You dropped it," he said, taking it from his jacket pocket and handing it to her. "Who was that?"

Taking the envelope, she shook her head. This was one conversation she was not going to have. She started trudging back toward the building.

Maury quickly got in step alongside her. "Why did . . . ?"

"I don't have any answers."

"But—"

"Maury, I—"

Screech!

They both turned to see three police cars stop at the curb.

She looked at Maury.

"I called the police," he said.

"What for?"

"That lady threatened you."

She looked back as the policemen were leaping from their cars. "Did I ask you to call the police?"

"I thought—"

"You the doorman?" one of the officers asked, rushing up the walkway toward them.

"Yes, sir."

"What's the problem?"

"There is no problem," Marissa answered, slipping the card into the pocket of her trench.

Three more policemen rushed up and stood alongside the first officer.

"We got a call saying that a woman was threatening a resident of this building."

"She was," Maury said, nodding. "She—"

"There was a woman here," Marissa said, pushing open the door. "She left. I'm fine."

The four officers exchanged glances and then they all looked at Maury, who shrugged his shoulders and, in turn, they all looked at Marissa.

"The report said there was a weapon. What was it, a gun, a knife?"

"There was no weapon, except her fingers," she said.

"What? Did she assault you?"

"No, she pointed her fingers at me like a gun."

"There was no gun?"

"No."

"She didn't touch you? She didn't have a weapon?"

"No. Thank you for coming," Marissa said, going into the building.

"We're outta here," the first officer said, wasting no time retreating.

Maury halfheartedly saluted the officers before he, too, went back into the building.

"How come you didn't tell the police what happened?"

"Because nothing happened," she said, too angry to feel embarrassed anymore. "There was nothing to report."

"But that woman woulda shot you if she had a real gun."

It looked that way to her, too. "Maury, you know how the police work. They won't do anything until a person is actually hurt, which I wasn't. I don't know who that woman is. I've never seen her before. Therefore, I'd appreciate it if you'd forget about what happened."

"If that's what you want."

"It is," she said, knowing full well that he would never let her forget, because he'd be asking her about it every time he saw her.

"You should be careful."

Getting on the elevator, she nodded. As soon as the door slid closed, she pulled the envelope from her pocket and tore it open. Her breath caught in her throat. Her skin drew tightly around her eyes. Her heart thumped. "In Sympathy" was written above an arrangement of purple and white orchids. Her fingers trembled as she opened the card.

"When a loved one passes, many hearts are broken." The next three lines were whited out and handprinted in their stead was, *"When Marissa passes, many hearts will cheer. It will be said, that a slut was sent to her maker. She'll burn in hell for ever and ever."*

Her hands began to shake; tears stung her eyes.

The card was unsigned.

The elevator door opened on eight. She bolted. At her door, she fumbled with her keys before she could find the right one to unlock it. Rushing inside, she slammed the door and double-bolted it. Falling back against the door, she let herself breathe, she let herself cry. Even while she cried, she felt the pounding of her heart. Terrence might not want to hear from her, and she certainly did not want to speak to him again, but she had to ask him about his wife. She had to know. Wayne and Louis, too, were going to hear from her. Maybe they lied about the way their wives looked. Somebody was going to have to tell her something. She couldn't keep living this way.

Chapter 23

No one told Marissa a thing, at least not anything she wanted to hear. Wayne was away on business, according to his secretary, and no one answered the telephone at his house. Which meant that if he was out of town, maybe his wife was with him. She could only hope that he and his wife both were out of town last night.

Her two calls to Terrence, thus far, had not been returned. It wouldn't surprise her if he had told his secretary to say that he was permanently unavailable. That wasn't going to stop her though. She'd keep trying. If she had to leave a message that might embarrass him, then so be it. If anything, he owed her an explanation for his drastic change of heart about her, unless everything he had ever said about loving her had been a lie. A lie she had readily believed. Terrence was everything she would have wanted in a husband if she had wanted to marry. He was devoted to his children, and, in spite of his cheating on his wife, he was, at the same time, considerate of her in that he always stole a minute to call her to let her know what time he'd be getting in. That used to bother Marissa but she got used to it. The truth was, she liked that about him. If he were her husband, she might be able to live with him having a mistress because he was taking care of home, too.

Knowing all of this, she could only blame herself for daring to dream that he cared just as much for her. That, too, Brandon had been right about. Talking to Terrence again would hurt, but she had to know if his wife was her nightmare. Looking at her watch, she decided that she would give him until three o'clock to return her call. In the meantime, she needed to speak to Louis. Although that woman had called his wife, which meant that she was not the one in the beginning harassing her, who's to say that she wasn't doing it now.

As usual, Louis returned her call within minutes of beeping him. She broached the subject of his wife cautiously. "Is your wife still very upset?"

"She's mellowing. It'll take a while, but she'll be okay."

"That's good. Uh ... do you think she's harboring a grudge against me?"

"If she is, she hasn't said anything to me."

"Good. By the way, Louis, I was thinking. In all this time, you have never told me what your wife looks like."

"You never asked."

"No, I didn't, but I always pictured you married to a tall, dark, willowy model type."

"Ha, I wish. My wife is light-skinned; five feet high to a giraffe's shin; and rounder than a steel drum. She didn't always look like that, but she sure as hell looks like that now."

That was a weight off her mind. "But she's still the woman you love, right?"

"To be brutally frank, no, and she knows that. That's probably why she called you, she doesn't want anyone else to know it. But don't worry, I told her that she's to leave you alone. Anything she has to say, she'll have to say it to me."

"Was she all right with that?"

"She has no choice."

"She could divorce you."

"I doubt it, she has too much to lose."

"You mean financially?"

"She has nothing to lose financially, I'd give her the house, and

the court will give her a hefty alimony check. See, my wife thrives on being Mrs. LaSalle, she likes the fringe benefits, socially."

"Oh, I see."

"Our children are grown, she has nothing to do with her time other than plan our social schedule. I won't flaunt my affair in her face, I don't want my children to know," he said, lowering his voice, "but I won't stop seeing you."

She rubbed her forehead. Unlike Mrs. LaSalle, she did have a choice. She was going to stop seeing Louis. The complications of seeing him and the others was more than she had bargained for. When it came to men, her life was supposed to be simple—no commitments meant no headaches, no heartaches, no subservient obligations on her part, no arguments, and no lies that she had to live with that bothered her. And it did bother her that Wayne and Louis's wives now knew about her and were possibly upset enough to hurt her.

"For the time being, I'll stay at home until she's more relaxed, I don't wanna hear her mouth. But I was thinking; since I can't see you in the evenings for a while, how about during the day?"

It was clear to her what he had in mind. "We both work during the day."

"You can take a long lunch hour once in a while, can't you?"

"Not really," she lied.

"Sure you can. Say you have a meeting somewhere. We could meet at a hotel here in the city."

"Louis, you work on Wall Street, I work in midtown. It'll take an hour just to get through traffic."

"Not if we use a limo service and meet around eleven or twelve."

"I don't know."

"C'mon. There are plenty of good hotels between Twenty-third and Forty-fifth Street, and, actually, you'll have a shorter distance to travel than I."

She switched the telephone to her right ear. "I don't think this is such a good idea."

"Why not? No one will know."

"Suppose your wife tries to reach you."

"That's what beepers and secretaries are for," he answered coolly.

"My hair will look a mess. People will know."

"Not if you wear it pulled back in that twist you wear sometimes."

Feeling pressured, she began to drum on the desk with her fingertips. He had an answer for everything. Again, it was her own fault. From the first time their eyes met, their relationship had been about sex for him, and about money for her. She had made it her business to do whatever it took to keep him wanting more because she got more. Why wouldn't he want to keep it going? He was satisfied, and, admittedly, so was she, that is until this craziness began.

"Baby love, c'mon. I need you. I'll make it worth your while. Name your price."

Marissa felt cheap. What leapt to her mind was that old saying, "A girl can't do what the boys are doing and still be a lady." She couldn't blame Levi for treating her like a prostitute when she had never hesitated to take his money or his gifts.

"Baby love, please don't let me down. I'm getting hard just thinking about your sweet thighs wrapped around my body," he whispered.

She didn't think she could feel any lower. "What about your wife?"

"If my wife had your passion, I'd be begging her to meet me at a hotel."

"Louis, I can't. I'll have to come back to work afterward. I won't feel fresh."

"Take a shower at the hotel."

She grimaced. He wasn't going to let her get out of this. "But what if your wife should find out? Suppose she wants to hurt me?"

"Don't be ridiculous, my wife wouldn't hurt you."

"But suppose she finds out somehow and calls me again?"

"She won't, I'll use cash to pay for the room. Look, it's almost eleven. We could meet today."

Every inch of her being screamed, *"Don't!"* She had to listen. "I can't."

"Marissa, baby, please."

"I'm sorry, I can't."

"Aww, damn!"

"I'm sorry."

"Don't be sorry, just meet me tomorrow," he said, suddenly sounding very businesslike. "I'll pay you whatever you want. Just give me your price."

There it was again—prostitute. Louis had called it as he saw it, and Marissa was ashamed. "Regardless of what you think, Louis, I am not a prostitute," she said, her voice shaky.

"Marissa, baby love, I didn't mean anything by that. You know how I feel about you."

"I know now."

"Baby, please. I have the highest regard for you."

"I can't see you anymore, Louis."

"Marissa, baby, don't do this."

"I have to, I don't feel good about myself anymore. I'll never forget you."

"Goddamnit, all of a sudden you don't feel good about yourself? You been taking my money all these years and just like that, it's over because you say so. You're a whore and—"

She put the receiver down softly. Just as quickly as the tears welled up in her eyes, she angrily wiped them away. She would not allow herself the luxury of crying. She had put a price on her body and Louis was just offering to pay for a service. It wasn't him she was angry with, it was herself. She had done this to herself. No, she would not cry.

Buzzz!

Pressing the intercom button on her telephone she asked, "Yes?"

"Marissa," Vivian said, "Brandon Wallace, on one."

"Thank you," she said, releasing the button. She took a deep breath. Picking up the receiver, she pressed the lit button. "Hi."

"How are you?"

"Don't ask. How's the conference?"

"I'll get my money's worth. How about you? Any more problems?"

Beginning to feel weepy again, she sniffled. It touched her that

Brandon always thought of her. His was the one solid relationship she had that wasn't based on what he could do for her, or on what she could do for him.

"What's wrong? Are you still being harassed?"

"Yes."

"What happened?"

"Last night a woman left me an ugly condolence card, and then—"

"Who died?"

"I think I did."

"Oh, God."

"Believe me, it's ugly."

"What did it say?"

"It's at home. I don't remember verbatim," she said, not wanting to repeat the words.

"Don't throw it away, I want to see it."

"Sure, why not. Anyway, she showed up outside the building while I was down in the lobby picking up the card from Maury."

"So you saw her, who is she?"

"It was too dark, I didn't get a good look at her face."

"Damn!"

"Wanna hear something weird? She pointed her finger at me like she was shooting me."

"Marissa, catch this clue—call the police."

"I can't."

"Yes, you can. Technically, this is a stalking. The card is tangible proof. I asked you before, what else needs to happen before you report this?"

"Brandon, before I can report anyone, I have to know who I'm reporting. The police are not going to be of any help to me if I don't know who to point a finger at."

"They could put a trace on your telephone calls. Did you apply for the Caller ID box yet?"

"No, I actually forgot."

"Do it when you get off the phone with me."

"I will."

"By the way, I called you last night at your place and at mine. Where did you stay?"

"In my apartment. I unplugged the phone."

"Marissa, God, I can't believe that you don't get it. This woman called you at home and at work; and when she couldn't get you by phone, she showed up at your building. Hence, unplugging your phone won't stop her. If you're not going to call the police, then stay at my place. Yours isn't safe."

"I know. When I left home this morning, I was looking around like a fugitive. I used a car service to get to work, and I have Vivian screening my calls. In fact, I think the witch called here this morning. Vivian said some woman wanted to speak to me but wouldn't give her name. I refused the call because if it was her, I didn't need to hear more stupid threats."

"Smart move," he said. "If you had taken her call, you would have given credence to the importance of her harassing you. On the other hand, ignoring her might frustrate her because she's not getting the needed anticipated response."

"So what am I supposed to do? Lie down and die for her?"

"Go to the police."

"I told you, I can't."

"Marissa, those men are big boys; if they have to answer to their wives, let them. They knew what they were doing. I suggest you forget about being concerned about anyone other than yourself."

"I *am* thinking about myself. I don't want anyone to know my business."

"You're not thinking about yourself if you're more concerned about your reputation than your life. So what if you have to reveal the number of married men you're involved with; you think you're the only person, man or woman, who has ever done that?"

She closed her eyes and rubbed her forehead.

"If you're worried about what the police will think of you, get over it. They're not gods."

"No, but I don't wanna be looked down on."

"Marissa, listen to me. You are going to have to face up to the choices you've made and the consequences of those choices."

"I know that."

"Then I hope you also know that one of the consequences is this crazy woman who could do one of two things to you: she might continue to harass you just to make your life miserable; or she might try to kill you. Neither is acceptable."

"If she was such a threat to me, why did she run from me last night when I tried to confront her?"

"What? Were you alone?"

"Yes . . . no. That nosy-ass Maury was right behind me with his old self."

"Be grateful that he was, that's probably why she ran. Look, this is getting uglier. Stay at my place. I'm sorry I didn't leave you the keys, I was being naughty."

"I figured that."

"I'm sorry. Levi should be finished today. When you get the keys from him, you don't have to worry about him coming back."

She sucked her teeth loudly. "That Levi person is the least of my worries, even though he did pop up in my dreams last night."

"The subconscious at work, huh? Tell the doctor."

"It was stupid."

"Tell me anyway."

"Well, it seems that I was walking in the rain. I had an umbrella but the rain was getting through anyway. I checked it, and it didn't have any holes. I was cold, wet, and annoyed because I couldn't figure out why the damn thing wasn't keeping the rain off of me."

"That's interesting. It could mean that the shell, the defenses you've built up for yourself, is no longer doing the job."

"What defenses?"

"Think about it, Marissa. You used to be able to defend your decision to go out with married men. Can you defend that decision now?"

"Oh, come on, that's not what the dream meant."

"Why not? We all build up defenses for ourselves to protect our

fragile egos from the outside world. Your defenses could be weak, more penetrable at this point. You could have doubts about those very same choices you were once very adamant about."

"Says you," she said, not wanting to admit that he was right.

"Well, look at what you're going through. You have to be rethinking your choices. I'd be surprised if you weren't."

Feeling that she was always susceptible to Brandon's psychiatric meddling, Marissa said, "I can't go back and relive my past, Brandon; therefore, for sanity's sake, I have no regrets. However, I did tell Charmaine, in so many words, that I wouldn't be going out with married men in the future."

"That's what I'm talking about. Subconsciously, you had to realize that there were 'holes' in your reasoning to come to that decision. Hence the umbrella."

"Brandon, that's your interpretation."

"Yes, and I could be wrong, but I doubt it. Where did Levi come into it?"

She frowned. "That's just it. He came out of nowhere with a gigantic umbrella, which he held above my umbrella."

"Did you still get wet?"

Again she frowned. She had played right into his hands. "No, but that could mean . . ."

"That could mean that he could be your protector."

"No way, Sigmund."

"Perhaps I should take that as a compliment, smarty. Anything else happen in your dream?"

"Nothing," she answered, annoyed because he was seldom wrong. "Your contractor disappeared into thin air. Then the dream changed and I was driving my car down a highway and suddenly my car turned into a scooter. What does that mean, Sigmund?"

He chuckled. "It could mean that you crave a simpler lifestyle."

"And how did you come to that conclusion?"

"It's simple. A car is mechanical, complicated. A scooter has two wheels and a handle bar. How simple can you get?"

"That's too simple for me. I'll take my car any day over a scooter."

"Yes, but dreams are subjective—they're part of your subconscious reality," he explained. "But what do I know? No telling about dreams, they could mean something or nothing at all."

"Well, neither dream meant a thing to me," she said. "I can buy a bigger umbrella and a new car if I have to. I can also stay in my own apartment, thank you very much. I am not going to let this crazy woman dictate my living arrangements."

"Okay, you're brave. You've convinced me, but please do it for me. Until I get back home, I'll be worrying myself silly about you, and worry is bad for my skin. You know how vain I am. Besides, my building is a lot more secure than yours."

"I have a doorman," she defended.

"Be for real, Marissa. After watching ten minutes of the *Ninja Turtles,* most toddlers can take out any one of your doormen, especially Maury."

She chuckled. "That's true."

"Listen," Brandon continued, "my doormen are trained by a security firm, they know how to disarm an intruder. Please stay at my place. I'll be home Saturday morning in time to make the wedding. You're still part of the wedding party, aren't you?"

"As of last night I was."

"Good. Are you going to my place?"

"Maybe. I don't know yet."

"What time should I call you there?"

Again she chuckled. It was truly too bad that Brandon was gay. He would have been easy to be in love with—he was so caring. "You can call me," she said, giving in, "around nine. I have to go home first to get a change of clothes."

"Okay. I left my number for you in case you needed to call me. It's on my nightstand."

"I saw it, thanks."

"Is your car ready?"

"I didn't check on it. I want to leave it as long as I can, at least until that fool has crawled back into her hole. I'm thinking about garaging it elsewhere."

"It's probably best for the time being. So, I'll talk to you later."

"Fine."

"Oh, and Marissa, when I get back, I want to talk more about your dreams."

"You would," she said, "but by then, I will have dreamt that I climbed the Matterhorn and swam the English Channel."

"We can talk about that, too."

"Boy, I'm not one of your patients, you better stop psychoanalyzing me. Don't you have a pet rock to play with?"

"No, I have you. You're great for fine-tuning my skills."

" 'Bye," she said, hanging up on him. Her throat tightened a little, but she inhaled deeply and it went away. She had to do something special for Brandon, he was the sweetest person. Cooking dinner for him Sunday would be nice if only she cooked better than he, which she didn't. And since she didn't want to make him gag, she'd take him out to his favorite restaurant. It was more palatable.

Beeep!

"Yes?"

"Your sister, Denise."

Without a second thought, she said, "Please tell her that I'm in a meeting. I'll call her this evening. Thank you."

"Okay."

"Oh, and Vivian, if Charmaine should call, tell her I'll call her this evening, also."

"Okay."

Clicking off, she looked at the pile of mail in her in-box and the pile of work yet to be done on the corner of her desk. She sighed. She wasn't going out to lunch so maybe, if she forced herself, she'd get some of it done. Right now, she had to try Terrence again. Picking up the receiver, she punched in his job number. The ringing felt ominous.

Chapter 24

IT WAS 3:45 by his watch, and Levi had asked himself for the second time in the fifteen minutes since he got off the telephone with Brandon, "What have I gotten myself into?" He was still sitting in the living room trying to figure out why Brandon would ask him, in fact beg him, of all people, to look after Marissa. There had to be someone else he could have asked who knew her a whole lot longer and, possibly, even liked her a little bit.

Gregory came to mind, being that he was a correction officer. He might not like her, but he had known her a whole lot longer than he did. Of course, Gregory might say that he ought to be guarding Marissa behind bars because what she was doing with other women's husbands was criminal. No, he'd never go out of his way for her, and she'd be the last person he'd want to protect from some irate wife.

Brandon put him on the spot when he asked him to find an excuse to hang around the apartment longer. All day he had been pushing to finish the job on time so that when Marissa showed up to pick up the keys, he could drop them in her hand and say, "See ya, wouldn't wanna be ya." He had never been a glutton for punishment and staying around her longer than he had to was like asking to be abused.

His mother was right about him liking strong women, but he didn't consider Marissa's nasty attitude a show of strength. If anything, it was more likely a show of weakness. She probably acts tough, he thought, so that people won't think they can walk all over her, but obviously, she was wrong. Because whoever was after her was not impressed with her show of strength. If she was, she would not have left threatening messages on her answering machine, nor would she have brought a condolence card in person to her building and then waited outside to be seen.

When Brandon told him about those things, he thought he might be exaggerating a bit, but Marissa was coming to spend another night in his apartment, and knowing women, they do not like to be inconvenienced; and living out of an overnight bag is a big inconvenience for a woman like Marissa. She had to be scared. Yet he would bet that she was going to show up acting like she was tough as nails by aggravating him with her snide remarks; and all the while pretending that she was there to watch the apartment. It's easy to save a drowning man when he lets you, but hard as hell when he fights you all the way. Marissa wasn't going to be easy to save. No way did he want the aggravation, but the threats were real. He couldn't walk away. He let Brandon talk him into staying at least until ten o'clock, and he promised to come back Friday morning.

The problem was, this job was finished. Besides the cleanup, after he put the refrigerator in place and the microwave oven on its shelf above the counter, his job was done. Even if he worked at a snail's pace, two hours at most would do it—just in time for Marissa to get there. If he stayed, he'd have to be working. There was no way he was going to be able to convince her, or himself for that matter, that he wanted to sit around and keep her company because he liked her. And he'd die of boredom if he had to pretend to be working. What excuse he would use to pull this off was where Brandon was of no help. He had said to create work if Levi had to; the cost of his time and labor wasn't a problem. See, that's what confused him. As much of an 'itch as Marissa seemed to be, she had loyal friends like Brandon, who was willing to spend money to protect her, and Charmaine, who, according to Gregory, went out of her way to make up

with her. Damned if he knew why they liked her so much. He didn't see it.

"Oh, well," he said to himself as he got up to go back into the kitchen. Standing in the doorway, he surveyed his work. If he had to say so himself, he did good work. The grout work was smooth; the backsplash and counter were aligned; the cabinets were hung plumb; the floor tile was finally laid right. If he could, he would pat himself on the back. He'd be lying if he didn't admit that he always felt good after he finished a job and his skill was proved once more. Unexpectedly, he yawned. Because of Marissa, he hadn't slept too well. Despite her nastiness, her woeful eyes and the memory of her in that red nightgown haunted him throughout the night. Again he awakened feeling her, wanting her. Could his mother be right? And if she was, did he want to do anything about it? Or a better question: Would Marissa let him do anything about it?

Since he had to stay longer, he could use a nap. In fact, he'd nap until she got there, but first, he had to create some work for himself for after she got there.

Chapter 25

"THE DOORMAN RANG you three times," Marissa said, an edge to her voice. "What took you so long?"

Not that Levi expected anything else from her; "Hey, dog" would have been generous. Now wide awake, he turned away from her and went into the kitchen to wipe the grout film off the tile, leaving her at the door to close it for herself.

Behind his back, she screwed up her face; he could have at least taken her bag. No surprise that he didn't—he was a classless oaf, after all. Stepping inside the apartment, she started to slam the door but thought better of it. This was Brandon's door, not Levi's. She slowly pushed the door closed and locked it. Going by the kitchen, she did not look in. He would be gone soon and she could relax.

From the corner of his eye, he saw her pass. He looked at his watch—three hours to go. Rubbing harder, he grunted angrily. Already she had ticked him off, one minute seemed an eternity. If she kept it up, he might hand her over to the stalker himself. He rubbed harder still at the white film on the tile.

Until he leaves, she decided to hole up in Brandon's bedroom. The chicken and broccoli dinner she brought in with her would have to wait until then, as she had lost her appetite. After unpacking and

hanging up the suit she would wear to work tomorrow, she looked around for the remote control. She found it under the folded newspaper on the chair. For an hour, she sat, she laid, she reclined on the bed watching the news. As much as she wanted to peel out of her work clothes, she dared not; for any minute, she was hoping that he'd knock on the door and say that he was leaving. She waited. By 8:30, the knock still had not come.

Picking up the receiver, she dialed Charmaine. "Hi."

"I just called your house."

"I'm not home, I'm at Brandon's."

"I thought he was out of town."

"He is. I'm . . . ah . . . sorta house-sitting."

"Why? Who's gonna get past the security in his lobby?"

She knew that she might be asked why she had to house-sit for Brandon and she was ready. "He has a contractor redoing his kitchen and he's still here."

"Oh, you mean Levi? I referred him to Brandon."

"I know."

"How's the kitchen coming?"

"I wouldn't know, I haven't seen it."

"Why not?" she asked, then quickly said, "Forget it. Anyway, I had called you earlier because I wanted to know if you wanted to stay with me tomorrow night. Gail and Lisa are planning to stay."

"I'll have to let you know in the morning, I'm not sure of my plans yet."

"It'll be like an old-fashioned sleepover. We could rent a movie, or—"

"Charmaine, I have to go."

"Oh. Okay. 'Bye."

Hanging up the telephone, she huffed. Why is it that Charmaine wouldn't leave her alone? The woman was smothering her. Sometimes Marissa felt like moving to another state and starting over. Where? She didn't know, but if she did relocate, she'd have no close female friends. It was just too hard to deal with the neediness and jealousies of women; and men, too, for that matter. In fact, it might not be such a bad idea to swear off men for a while, and even if she

got involved again, before her emotions blinded her, she might hire a private detective to follow the guy for a month to see if he was married or if he had a girlfriend. The lesson had been hard and long in coming, but she did learn it. No married men ever again.

Right now, however, she had to go to the bathroom. Getting up, she tiptoed over to the door. With her ear to the wood, she listened for Levi. She heard nothing. Hopefully, he had gone home. Opening the door a few inches, she listened again. A soft clanking sound came from the kitchen. He was still working. She eased the door open, and walking softly, went in the opposite direction of the kitchen to the bathroom. As a precaution, so that she wouldn't be caught with her panties down, she pushed the button on the door-knob and locked the door, something she hadn't done in her own apartment for as long as she had been there, even when she had company. As soon as she sat down on the toilet, she turned on the water in the sink, full force. She would be too embarrassed if he heard her tinkling.

That done, she flushed the toilet. She washed her hands and dried them on the thick, fluffy green towel she had used two days before. She had started out of the bathroom when she realized that water was still running into the toilet bowl. Instinctively, she jiggled the handle. She waited a minute. The water still didn't sound like it usually did when a tank was filling up. She jiggled the handle again. That didn't work. She lifted the top off of the tank and saw that it was empty of water other than the water that rushed out through the hole on the bottom. The metal ball that was supposed to float to the top had dropped to the bottom, and while the rubber stopper appeared to be in place, it didn't stop the water from rushing out.

Placing the top carefully down on the toilet seat, she jiggled the handle repeatedly. The stopper went up and down, but in the down position it did not keep the water inside the tank. Beginning to feel anxious, she rolled the sleeve of her blouse up past her elbow and stuck her right hand down into the rust-stained tank. Pressing down on the rubber stopper with her fingers, she held it in place. As the tank started to fill up, the ball began to rise. The cold water crept up

over her hand. That was okay, until it eased up her arm toward her elbow. It felt clammy, reminding her that it was toilet water, after all. Pulling her arm out slowly to keep from splashing water all over the floor, she held it over the tank while she reached for the towel. It took longer to dry her arm than it took for the water to gush out of the tank. The ball dropped to the bottom like it was made out of lead.

This she was not going to be able to sleep with. Not knowing what else to do, and as much as she hated to, she was going to have to ask Levi to fix it. No doubt he'd think that she broke the toilet, but she could care less. Then again, she did care about giving him the satisfaction of having to do something else for her. She could do without his smugness.

Rather than ask him to fix the toilet, she left the bathroom door open and sneaked back into the bedroom to wait. She left the door open about an inch so that she could hear the running water. If Levi wasn't deaf, he should hear it also and investigate.

In the kitchen, he had just slid the stove partway back into its space when he thought he heard water running. Walking softly, he went to the kitchen door and peeked down toward the bathroom. The door was open. The water was running as he had expected it would. He crept back over to the stove and continued maneuvering it in place.

She waited. Five minutes. Ten minutes—the water continued to run. Growing tired of waiting and growing increasingly irritable from the sound of the running water, she bounded off the bed and strode out of the bedroom to the kitchen. Levi was bent over the stove hooking its hose up to the gas line in the back.

"Don't you hear that water?"

Levi didn't straighten up or turn to look at her.

Marissa stomped her foot. "Would you please go look at the toilet? It sounds like Niagara Falls back there."

Giving the bolt a final turn with the monkey wrench for good measure, Levi straightened up. He turned his head slowly and looked at her. "Is there a problem?"

Glaring at him, Marissa had to remind herself to bite her tongue.

He might pack up and leave her with a broken toilet, just to spite her. She hated that she even had to talk to him. She took a deep breath and then exhaled loudly. "The toilet is broken."

"It was fine earlier. What happened?"

"How should I know? I didn't break it."

"I didn't say that you did. What's it doing?"

"The water keeps running."

"Why?"

"Because it keeps going out the bottom."

"Why?"

"Look, damnit, I am not a plumber. I simply flushed the damn thing. It never stopped running."

Seeing the tight lines around her mouth and the tense, angry glint in her eyes, he decided to stop taunting her. "Soon as I check the gas line for leaks, I'll check the toilet."

"Fine," she said curtly, pivoting on her heels and strutting out of the kitchen.

He stared at the empty doorway. That was one woman he wouldn't waste another second trying to figure out. It wasn't the kind of challenge he wanted, after all. He turned back to the gas line.

This time she closed the bedroom door all the way. There was an empty, achy feeling in her stomach. Maybe she was hungry. She glanced over at the bag of Chinese food on the dresser. It was probably too cold to eat. After Levi left, she'd use the microwave to reheat it. That is, if he ever did leave.

With his hand, he dripped soapy water on the connections of the gas line. No new bubbles formed. He watched for a few minutes more before he was satisfied. All that was left to do now was to put the refrigerator back. He'd do that before going to "fix" the toilet. He could do that in one minute.

Riiing!

She looked down at her watch. It was nine o'clock.

Riiing!

"Hi, Brandon," she said, answering the telephone.

"Hey, slut!"

She froze in sheer terror.

"Bitch, why don't you come outside and chase me tonight. I got something for you."

"Leave me alone!" she screamed, slamming the receiver back down onto the cradle. She couldn't take it anymore. It was all too much. "Just leave me alone," she cried.

Chapter 26

LEVI HEARD Marissa scream.

In the living room, he carefully but quickly lowered the hand truck until the refrigerator rested solidly on the floor. He rushed into the bedroom. Marissa was sitting on the bed with her hands covering her face.

"What happened?"

She immediately lowered her hands, but she turned away from Levi when she answered, "Nothing."

"Then why did you scream, 'Leave me alone'?"

She began to shake her legs nervously as she stared at the wall. "I do not want to talk about it."

He had heard the telephone ring. He could about guess that she had gotten another one of those calls.

Riiing!

She jumped. Her eyes darted to the telephone. Her lips began to quiver.

Riiing!

Levi bounded across the room and snatched up the telephone. "Hello!"

Her heart froze.

"Levi?"

He relaxed. "Yeah."

"It's me—Brandon. What's happening? Where's Marissa?"

"It's Brandon," he said to her.

She felt herself deflate.

"She's sitting right here. I think she just got one of those calls."

Looking at him, she was startled that he seemed to know about the calls, about the threats, about her. Ashamed, she dropped her eyes. She wanted to cry.

"When?"

"A minute ago."

"She called my house?" Brandon asked incredulously. "How did she get my number? How did she know that Marissa was at my house?"

"I don't know," he answered, looking at Marissa. "You wanna talk to her?"

"Put her on."

Levi held the telephone out to her. "Marissa."

While she didn't raise her head or her eyes, she reached out and took the telephone. "Hi," she said meekly.

"Are you all right?"

"No," she said, feeling defeated.

"Marissa, this has gone from bad to worse. You have to call the police."

"Maybe."

"Maybe, my ass. Marissa, do you have a death wish?"

"Of course not," she said, her eyes resting on Levi's hard-looking brown work boots. There was obviously more to him than she thought. While she was being flip with him, he had ammunition that could have blown her out of the water. He could have easily humiliated her. Yet not one time had he thrown what he knew about her in her face. Why didn't he?

"Then call the police, Marissa."

"I will, but not just yet."

Levi did not move away, he stood only inches from her. The same faint scent of flowers he'd smelled before surrounded her. He inhaled her sweetness. It was nice.

"Think, Marissa. That woman got my telephone number, you're not safe there alone."

"You said that I was safe here."

"I'm not so sure about that anymore. I'm really worried about you."

She glanced up at Levi; he was looking down at her. She could not read his face. "I'll be fine."

"Marissa, ask Levi to stay with you."

"No."

"Since you won't call the police, and since this woman has tracked you to my apartment, I would think you'd welcome the company; men aren't the only ones who kill, you know."

"I know that."

"Do you, Marissa? This woman is psychotic. You don't stand a chance up against her alone."

"I can take care of myself, Brandon. Besides, you claim that the security in this building is better than mine. I shouldn't have to worry about anyone coming upstairs," she said, refusing to look again at Levi.

Buzzzz!

Her heart stopped.

"I'll get that," Levi said, rushing out of the room to answer the intercom.

"What did he say?" Brandon asked.

"He went to answer the intercom."

"Are you expecting someone?"

She turned to look at the door. Her hands began to shake. "No."

"Marissa, let Levi stay with you."

Levi walked over to the foyer.

"Yes," Levi said, answering the intercom.

"There's a note down here for Miss Jenkins."

"I'll be right down," he said, releasing the button. He saw no need

to ask Marissa if he should go for it. Taking the keys off the counter in the kitchen he rushed out of the apartment.

Brandon would not let Marissa off the phone. "Forget your damn pride, Marissa. Let the man help you. When I told him about last night, he was as angry as I was. Believe me, he'll stay with you."

"Brandon, I don't like him," she whispered.

"I'm not asking you to sleep with him, just to let him stay with you."

She sucked her teeth. "If I didn't know better, I'd swear someone was trying to set me up with this man."

"This is no time to play games."

"But suppose he doesn't want to stay?" she asked, watching the door, wondering what was taking Levi so long to come back.

"He will," Brandon said confidently. "Who was at the door?"

"I don't know, he hasn't come back yet."

"I don't feel good about this."

"How do you think I feel? Whoever she is, she must be following me to know that I was here."

"Yes, but that doesn't explain how she got my telephone number."

"Your doorman wouldn't tell anyone who I was visiting, would he?"

"He'd better not."

"Maybe she got a look at the sign-in book like she might have in my building the other night."

"Maybe."

"It's a note for you," Levi said, coming into the room with a piece of folded white paper in his hand.

She shook her head. "I don't want it."

"Give me the phone," he said, taking the telephone from Marissa's hand. "Brandon, a woman left a note downstairs with security."

"What does it say?"

"Do you want me to read it?" he asked Marissa.

"Tear it up," she said, getting up off the bed and walking over to

the window. The curtains were drawn, she left them that way. She stared into their satin folds.

"Don't tear it up!" Brandon said quickly. "Read it to me."

He looked over at Marissa. "I don't think you should destroy it," he said. "You might need it if you have to go to the police. Should I read it?"

"Yes," Brandon said in Levi's ear.

"Marissa?" he asked, waiting for her to tell him herself.

Without turning around, she said softly, "I don't care. You seem to know everything anyway."

He looked at the back of her head as he unfolded the note. He read it silently to himself.

She turned around and looked at him. His eyes had dulled.

"What does it say?" Brandon asked.

"It says," he began, looking at Marissa, " 'I can taste your death.' "

"Oh, God," Brandon said.

Marissa hugged herself tightly as she turned away from Levi's pitying gaze.

He had seen that fear again in her eyes before she turned away. If there had not been that wall between them, he would have gone to her and taken her into his arms.

"Levi. Levi."

He couldn't tear his eyes away from Marissa's bowed head. "Yes."

"Call the police. Don't let Marissa talk you out of it. This is more than a stalking. Someone wants her dead."

"I'll take care of it," he said, suddenly feeling that he had to help her. "I have your number, I'll let you know what happens."

"I had planned to leave here Saturday morning, but I'm going to check out Friday afternoon. Call me no matter what. And Levi, please, do me a favor."

Anticipating Brandon's question, he said, "I'll stay here all night if I have to." Hearing that, he knew that she would turn around, and she did. It didn't surprise him that the light in her eyes was now smothered by the fear that consumed her.

Chapter 27

MARISSA DIDN'T HAVE the energy to protest when Levi started dialing the police.

It didn't take long for him to explain the threatening calls and notes. It also didn't take long for the police officer to tell him that there was really nothing they could do if they didn't know who the perpetrator was. The officer suggested that Marissa come into the precinct and file an aggravated harassment report. Although the perpetrator would be listed as unknown, it would be on record in case she did make herself known.

"Thank you," he said, hanging up the telephone.

"Don't tell me, I know. They can't do anything until I'm dead."

Placing the note on the nightstand, Levi folded his arms across his broad chest. To her, he looked powerful. His biceps bulged under his T-shirt. For an uncomfortable minute, they stared at each other. She wondered if he was thinking that she deserved this.

He wondered if she was still seeing the woman's husband. "You don't have a clue who this woman is, do you?"

She trudged over to the door. "No."

"Did you get what was said about filing an aggravated harassment report?"

Her urge to cry grew stronger. "What good is that going to do?" she asked, leaving the bedroom.

Walking out behind her, he answered, "When this woman makes herself known, it'll be easier to charge her if there is a record of the threats."

"I'll think about it," she said, going over to the living room window and peeking timorously through a slit in the blinds. She struggled hard to keep from crying in front of Levi.

Because he knew why she was being threatened, he didn't have to embarrass her by asking her about it. He'd stay like he promised. He started to turn away.

"You don't like me very much, do you?" she asked.

"I could ask you that same question."

"Well, at least it's mutual," she said, rubbing her hands together, trying to rid herself of the chill she had since sticking her arm down into the tank; a chill that had grown worse since the phone call and the note. "You don't have to stay with me, I'll be fine."

"I promised Brandon that I would," he said, going over to the refrigerator strapped to the hand truck. "Don't worry, I'll stay out of your way."

Putting his foot on the base of the hand truck, he steadily pulled the large refrigerator back toward his body until the weight of it rested on the two wheels and on his right shoulder. Before he took a step, he glanced over his left shoulder. His path was clear.

She watched him, stepping backward, effortlessly pull the refrigerator out of the living room; smoothly pivot it around in the hallway; and, finally, push it into the kitchen. Left alone, the feeling of dread grew more intense. She went to stand in the doorway just as Levi was attempting to maneuver the refrigerator into its narrow space between the counter and the wall. It seemed to be stuck.

"Do you need help?"

Like she could help him. He almost laughed.

"What are you looking at me like that for? Do you want my help or not?"

"Uh . . . sure. If you want."

She entered eagerly. "What do you want me to do?"

He wanted to laugh. He didn't believe for a minute that she'd ever done more than maybe push a vacuum cleaner. If anything, she'd be in the way, but if she wanted to think that she was helping him, he'd let her.

"You could take the cord off the handle and hold it out to the side so that it won't get caught between the refrigerator and counter."

"Okay," she said, reaching for the cord.

Holding up the weight of the refrigerator against his shoulder while Marissa busily unwrapped the cord—like she was really doing something—he wondered if she was trying to be nice to him because that note shook her up and now she needed a friend.

She held the cord out to the side. "Okay."

Using his shoulder, he started shifting and pushing the refrigerator, trying hard to get it to turn into its snug slot between the wall and the counter. He pushed harder, scraping the wall. For a minute he wondered if the new counter was longer than the old, when suddenly the refrigerator cleared the wall. The wheels on the hand truck slipped away from him; the weight of the refrigerator started falling backward against him.

Marissa, quickly sidling up next to Levi, threw her hands up to catch the falling refrigerator. She braced her feet against the base of the counter behind her and pushed. The side of her body was pressed up against Levi. Astonished, he glanced at her. Her softness, her sweet scent, made his heart flutter. He never would have imagined that she'd get this close to him. Then again, he never would have thought she'd help him with anything, much less do something that required brute strength. She was perplexing.

Together they pushed the refrigerator back upright, while he, using his chest and thigh, regained control of the hand truck and lowered the refrigerator to the floor with a *thump*. There was not an inch to spare on either side.

"Thanks," he said, releasing the lock on the support strap. Then pulling the strap from around the refrigerator, he rewrapped it around the hand truck and wheeled it out into the entrance foyer. He'd take it with him when he left.

"Should I plug it in?"

"Just a minute," he answered, turning and putting his back up against the refrigerator door. Digging his heels into the floor, he pushed it back up against the wall. "Okay."

Plugging it in, she stepped back. "I don't hear anything."

"It's on Off inside on the climate control," he said, opening the door. Reaching inside, he turned the knob around and stopped on four. The motor started. He closed the door. "That should do it."

"There's nothing in there. Maybe it's a waste to leave it running."

"Nah, it's okay."

"Oh," she said, holding her folded hands genteelly at her waist. She couldn't look at Levi, so she looked at the refrigerator. She felt good helping out. It was the least she could do; he was doing more for her by staying.

"Thanks," he said.

She nodded slightly as she turned.

He watched her leave. There might be some substance to her after all.

"The water's still running in the bathroom," she called to him from the hallway.

"No problem. I'll have it fixed in no time," he said, walking past her to the bathroom.

It didn't take but a minute for him to adjust the chain that was connected to the rubber stopper. If he had to pretend to fix it, he would have shut off the water and gone out to his van and sat to make her think that he was looking for a part. Standing astride the bowl, he watched as the tank filled with water.

"It stopped," she said behind him. "What did you do?"

"The chain was caught on the hook. That happens sometimes."

"Oh."

Replacing the top, he turned to face her. For the third time, he noticed that she would not meet his gaze. She was looking down at the water inside the bowl.

"If a licensed plumber had come in here," he said, "he would have charged seventy-five dollars to cross the threshold, and probably one hundred dollars to unhook the chain."

"I saw a report on that on television," she said. "That's nothing but greed."

"Nothing but."

"Can't trust anyone."

"Nope."

There they stood, both looking down into the toilet bowl, both at a loss for words, neither seeing in the water a way to break the ice between them.

What in the world is wrong with me, she wondered. Just hours ago she couldn't stand to be in the same room with him with his dirty nails and his dirty work boots. Now, all of a sudden, she didn't mind being in the bathroom with him.

Tired of looking down into the bowl, he started out of the bathroom. "I'm starving. How 'bout you?"

She looked up. "I could eat a little something."

"Your friend, Brandon, don't have much of anything I'd want to eat in here. I'm thinking about going out to grab a bite."

She looked at him through the mirror over the sink.

"I could bring you something back or you could come with me if you like."

"I don't think so. That maniac could be lurking out there somewhere."

"Then I'll bring something back, and we can eat in?"

"Well, I . . ."

"You don't have to eat with me if you don't want."

Sighing softly, she said, "Believe it or not, I do act grown up sometimes. We can eat together."

"No doubt. Pizza or Chinese?"

She was about to tell him that she had food, but looking at his dimples, she changed her mind.

"Pizza?" he asked.

"Extra cheese?"

"Yes. A ginger ale, too."

"Okay. I'll be right back," he said, starting to turn away.

"Wait a minute. I have to get my wallet."

"My treat."

"Thank you."

"Lock the door behind me," he said, walking away. At the door, he put on his flannel shirt. Leaving it unbuttoned, he stepped out into the hallway. "If the phone rings, don't answer it."

"I didn't plan to," she said, closing the door. Locking it, she about-faced and sprinted into the bedroom and picked up the small pink, plastic bag, feeling it to see if the container was still warm. It was cold. She opened first the plastic bag, and then the brown bag inside. The tangy smell of broccoli in soy sauce sprang out at her. She quickly closed it. She didn't know why she didn't just tell Levi that she already had her dinner. It wasn't like she had a hidden agenda or anything, but not telling him put her in a predicament.

If she put the bag in the refrigerator, he might see it if he happened to go back in there. Then he might think her conniving and, in a way, she was. Wasn't saying that she had to get her wallet just a gesture? She knew that he would, like most men, offer to pay for her dinner. The right man, she usually accepted. That, too, was strange. Just an hour ago he could have offered her a seven-course meal fit for a gourmand, and she would have turned him down. Three weeks ago she couldn't even sit down at the same table with him. Maybe she was more frightened than she realized, even his presence was preferable to being alone. What a difference a day makes.

Yet she could not see a man like Levi in her life. Imagine him taking her to the theater in those clunky work boots and a flannel shirt over a T-shirt; or to a social gathering where everyone else talked literature and politics, while he talked wrenches and toilet bowls. She didn't know why she was wasting her time thinking about him, it wasn't like it was remotely possible that she'd ever go anywhere with him beyond this apartment. No way. Then why did she care if he saw that she had already bought her food? Because, she knew, no matter how she felt about him, she didn't need to look any worse than she already did. Sighing deeply, she held the bag in the palm of her hand, weighing it. Why explain anything when she could throw the food away? Her mother's tale about starving chil-

dren in Africa might haunt her for half a second, but tossing the bag down the compactor shoot before Levi got back would save her a little embarrassment.

Careful to not let the door close all the way, she went out to the small compactor room two-thirds of the way down the hall. She dropped the bag down the shoot and started back to the apartment, passing the two elevator doors. She was steps away from Brandon's door when behind her, she heard one of the doors slide open. She didn't bother to look back because it was too soon for Levi to be back and most likely it was someone who lived on that floor.

Suddenly, she heard the *clickety clack* of heels moving quickly behind her. They were coming closer. She turned around. Sucking in a gulp of air, her eyes bulged in disbelief. Running at her like a charging bull, her teeth bared, her face twisted up in a vile mask of hate, was the woman who had stood outside her building shooting blanks at her.

Her heart leapt into her throat. Her brain screamed at her to run, but her feet would not move.

The woman seemed to be growling. Her hair was flying behind her as she was trying to dig down in her pocketbook for something. The distance between them was closing fast.

"Eeeck!" she screeched. Her legs felt rubbery, but she forced them to move. She could almost reach out and touch Brandon's door, yet it seemed like it was pulling away from her. Her lungs burned as she struggled to breathe.

"Bitch! U'm gonna kill you!"

A burst of adrenaline shot through her body, propelling her into the apartment door, throwing it open. With all her might, she grabbed the door along the side and slammed it shut just as the woman came into view. Quickly double-bolting the locks, she screamed, "Noooo!"

"You bitch!" the woman screamed, ramming the door.

Although the walls shook, the door did not give in its metal frame. Jumping back away from the door, her hands covering her mouth, Marissa muffled her scream. Whatever the woman had been digging for down in her pocketbook, she now had in her hand. She

used it to bang on the door. It sounded like it was metal. Supposing that it might be a gun, Marissa leapt into the corner alongside the door.

"Bitch! I warned you!"

Marissa began to shake violently. Her knees buckled under her, making her drop to the floor.

Bang! Bang! Bang!

The banging was earsplitting. She covered her ears with her hands.

"Stop that! Get away from that door!"

"Old bitch, mind your goddamn business before I shoot you!"

Across the hall, a door slammed.

Then, *bang!* at the door.

"Next time, bitch, you're mine."

Marissa held her breath.

A deafening silence echoed behind her. Marissa's breath burst from her lungs, relieving the pain in her chest.

Buzzz . . . buzzz . . . buzzz!

Again her heart leaped. "Leave me alone! Go away!"

"Marissa! It's me—Levi. Open the door!"

Marissa clambered to open the door and get to her feet at the same time. Throwing open the door, she threw herself into Levi's arms, clinging to him desperately.

Chapter 28

"MISS, WHO DO YOU know would wanna hurt you?"

Marissa slowly shook her head. She might have been able to tell one officer that she was being harassed by the wife of one of her lovers, but certainly not seven male and two female officers, all of whom were standing stoically staring down at her. She continued to clutch Levi's hand. She had not been able to let go of him from the moment she opened the door to let him in. Nestled in his arms, she had cried like a baby. She cried all the harder when he told her that he had hurried upstairs when he returned with their dinner and found that the medics had just revived the security guard, who had been knocked unconscious by a woman who had started off seducing him in the mail alcove. The police came upstairs minutes after Levi got into the apartment. They had been called by Miss Jessie. That's who Marissa had heard the woman yell at to get back into her apartment.

Levi sensed that Marissa was too embarrassed to tell them about her affairs with married men. "Officer Karras, this woman seems to come out of nowhere. She's been stalking Marissa for about—"

"A few weeks," she said.

"She has no idea who this woman is. Until last night, she had never seen her before."

"Sir, did you see her?"

"When I got off the elevator, the other elevator door was closing. I just caught a glimpse of a woman with all black on. I couldn't begin to tell you what she looked like."

"Then we have nothing to go on," Officer Karras said. "The best we can do is take your statement and file an aggravated harassment report. We'll have to take the note you got earlier. Hopefully, we can lift a fingerprint. To eliminate you and the security guard, you may have to come in to the precinct to be printed."

"No problem," Levi said, "just let me know when."

"Miss, do you know of any possible reason why this woman is stalking you?"

She lowered her head and covered her face with her free hand.

Levi felt the trembling of her hand in his. He knew that no matter how many times that question was put to her, she'd never answer it. "You've asked that question; she doesn't know."

"Sir, according to the lady across the hall, the perp was brandishing a gun," Officer Karras said, flipping the page he had written on over in his notepad. "Until we get an answer as to why, that question will be asked ten more times."

Lowering her hand, Marissa glared up at the pale, freckle-faced, pudgy officer. "I am not the perpetrator, I am the victim."

"Lady, if the perp had fired through the door, you could have been the murder victim. That's why I'll ask you again, do . . . ?"

"Hold up," Levi said, standing. He still held on to Marissa's hand. "I think you need to back down."

Officer Karras took a step toward Levi, his hand on the butt of his gun.

"Wait a minute," Officer Perlman said, stepping in between the two men. Facing his partner, he put a hand on his shoulder. "Matt."

Although he had never been arrested, Levi knew all too well that there was always at least one officer with a short fuse who thought

that his badge and gun made him all-powerful. He suspected that Officer Karras was the kind of cop who shot first and asked questions later, but he had no fear in his heart. He returned Officer Karras's threatening glare.

"Mr. Bronson, maybe you could wait in another room?" Officer Perlman said.

"No!" Marissa said, standing up. She grabbed Levi's arm and held on to him tightly.

Levi laid his hand atop hers. "Unless either one of us is under arrest, I think we'll stay together."

The two officers looked from one to another. Officer Perlman nudged Office Karras back several paces. "It's for your own good, miss," Officer Perlman said. "You might recall that you do know this woman."

She began to cry. "Don't you think if I knew who she was, I'd tell you?"

"Okay, miss, why don't you sit down?" Officer Perlman said, trying to wave her down with his hand.

"Just calm down," Officer Karras said, "no need to get upset, nothing happened to you."

"I can't calm down, I don't want to sit down, and I have every reason to be upset."

Levi was incensed. "Officer Karras, your attitude sucks."

Marissa buried her face against Levi's shoulder. Filled with regret, she closed her eyes and wished that she had never touched another woman's man.

Officer Perlman defended, "Mr. Bronson, we're just doing our job."

"Well, I don't like the way he's doing his job."

"Sir, I suggest you tread lightly," Officer Karras said, his threat clear.

Two feet stood between them. "Or what? You gonna do something to me?"

Officer Karras squared his shoulders.

She felt the stiffness of Levi's body. She stopped crying. The silence around them was static. "Levi, it's all right."

"Okay," Officer Perlman said, getting between them again. "Let's all calm down here. Karras, go down and check on the security guard."

Officer Karras's steady gaze at Levi was menacing.

Levi was unflinching.

"Now, Karras."

Marissa squeezed Levi's arm and, in turn, his hold on her grew firmer. She saw that his jaw was rigid and his body was ramrod straight. Clearly, he was not intimidated by the badge before him. She was impressed.

Officer Karras tipped his hat to Levi. He sauntered out of the apartment like he didn't have a care in the world.

Levi stroked Marissa's hand. "That man should not be a cop. Are you all right?"

"Yes," she lied.

"Sir, I apologize for Officer Karras. However, we should concern ourselves with the safety of Miss Jenkins."

"That's why we called you."

"Our hands are tied, sir. Until we know who we're dealing with or even why the threat was made, we can't do much. A patrol car will sit outside for a few hours just in case she comes back, though I doubt if she will. You're gonna have to be very watchful."

Levi nodded. "I will not let anything happen to her."

Tears slid down Marissa's cheeks.

"Meanwhile, we'll file the aggravated harassment report. Tonight, you should stay in. Keep the door locked."

"I'm not staying here," she said. "I'm no safer here than in my own apartment."

"Miss, wherever you go, try not to be alone."

Levi squeezed her hand. "She won't be."

Officer Perlman started for the door. As an afterthought, he turned back. "Mr. Bronson, Miss Jenkins, please excuse my partner; he's had a few problems of his own this past year."

Marissa slumped down onto the sofa.

"That's too bad," Levi said, going to the door. "He needs to leave

his problems at home. His job is too sensitive for him to be acting like that."

"I understand. We'll be in touch."

Levi locked the door and returned to the living room. He felt sorry for Marissa. She looked tired, she looked beaten, she looked scared. He didn't blame her. What if the woman had shot through the door? He went back to the sofa and sat down next to her.

"Do you wanna talk about it?" he asked, hoping that this time she did. He wanted to know himself if she knew whose wife it might be.

Crossing her legs, she asked softly, "Can I have something to drink?"

"You want your soda?"

"I could use something stronger, but I'll take the soda."

Rushing into the kitchen, he took a can of ginger ale from the bag he'd brought in earlier. He popped it open and stuck a straw down in the hole.

"It might be a little warm."

"That's okay," Marissa said, taking the soda. She took a sip.

Levi sat down again.

The soda was warm. It had a flat, sweet taste. But it was wet. She took another sip. Softly belching into her hand, she sipped again. She knew Levi was watching her, waiting for her to tell him something. She owed him an explanation. He had stuck by her, he had protected her. She wanted him to understand. Sitting the soda down on the end table next to her, it was now or never. "I really don't know who she is."

"Not even a clue?"

"No," she said, suddenly standing up. Folding her arms across her chest, she began to pace.

He suppressed his urge to question her. Whatever she was going to tell him was going to be of her own free will.

She stopped in front of him. He wasn't smiling and his dimples were barely there. He was the one and same Levi whom she would not confide in yesterday, whom she was about to confide in now. It was all so boggling. She almost couldn't face him, but she

was compelled to. "I was seeing four men," she began, "all married." She waited for his reaction but there was nary a twitch from him. He was an enigma. If he judged her at all, he didn't show it. He didn't bat an eye.

"When I got the first threat, I was with one of them, but we weren't lovers, ever. We were just . . . just friends," she said, feeling that she had to make that clear.

None of this surprised him, and he waited for her to continue.

"I described the woman's voice to my friend. He said it was definitely not his wife. In fact, he said his wife was petite, and, we both know, this woman is no amazon, but she's far from petite."

"That eliminates one," he concluded.

"Another woman called me at my job. She said she wasn't going to put herself in the gutter to deal with me. She said that if her husband left her for me, she would make sure that he was penniless. I spoke to her husband and he said that he had convinced her that it was over between us."

"Is it?"

"He wants to keep it going in the middle of the day when his wife won't suspect."

"Will you?"

Shaking her head, she said, "It's over."

Sitting back, he quietly clasped his hands and rested them on his lap. "It doesn't sound like this guy's wife is crazy enough to come after you. She'd get more satisfaction from bankrupting him."

"That's what I was thinking," she conceded. "Oh, and I forgot. After she called me, later that night, the stalker called and asked me if Mrs. LaSalle had given me a piece of her mind. So it couldn't be her. Plus her husband's description of her doesn't fit."

"That eliminates Mrs. LaSalle. Have you spoken to anyone else's wife?"

"No."

"Do the other two men know about the threats?"

Thinking of Terrence, she turned away from Levi.

"Are you all right?"

She turned back to face him. "Yes," she said, mustering the

courage to continue. "I told the third guy and he was highly insulted that I would even think that his wife would sink so low. I don't know if his wife knows, I haven't heard from him. We will never see each other again."

"Do you know what his wife looks like?"

"No."

"I wouldn't eliminate her. What about the fourth guy?"

She shook her head. She would have laughed if she wasn't so scared. "Well, the joke turned out to be on me. I just found out last night that he's not married."

"What about a girlfriend? They can be just as obsessive as wives."

"That's true, but he says that his friend is involved more seriously with someone else. I figure, if she's more involved with someone else, then she wouldn't be coming after me."

"That's what I would think. So, the only one who it could be is the third guy's wife."

"Terrence's wife?" she asked, surprised. "I don't know. He never gave a hint that she might know about us."

Hearing one of her lover's names sent an unexpected pang of jealousy through Levi. It surprised him. He cleared his throat.

"Should I tell the police about Terrence?" Marissa asked. "I didn't want to involve anyone in this if I wasn't sure, and I'm not. His wife could be innocent."

"The only way to find out is to either tell the police about Terrence, or confront him yourself and ask him what his wife looks like."

"I really don't want to speak to him again."

"You don't have a choice," he said, standing up himself. "This situation has come dangerously close to you losing your life. If you're trying to protect him, don't. I think he'd appreciate it if you called him instead of the police, especially if his wife is innocent."

"Perhaps," she said, beginning to pace again.

He followed her with his eyes. "Can I ask you a question?"

She stopped and looked at him. She prayed that his question wouldn't embarrass her.

"You don't have to answer if you don't want," he said quickly, sensing her wariness.

"Go ahead."

"You're a beautiful woman."

She felt her face grow warm.

"You're intelligent and, I gather, quite independent. You can get any man you want. Why would you saddle yourself with married men?"

It was not the question that surprised her, it was the realization that the pat answer she used to give about having it all without any obligations no longer worked. It wasn't as simple as that anymore and, what's more, it had never been that simple. What she hadn't realized was that she had been trying to protect herself from being hurt again.

"When I was twenty-three," Marissa began, "I was engaged to get married. His name was Wyatt. I really loved this guy, and I was even a little obsessive about him. What was bad about him, though, was that he was obnoxiously vain; he was a stud who knew his hold over me. I believed every lie he told me about loving me. Even when I suspected he had other lovers, I never questioned him because I didn't want confirmation. Of course, getting gonorrhea confirmed it for me, but I let him lie his way out of that, too."

"How did you do that?"

"I accepted that he had a one-night stand when he was drunk."

She stopped talking to see if Levi's face would show disgust, but his face was again unreadable.

Levi was thinking, Is that what "stupid in love" meant? The guy used her. It was too bad that she had let that long-ago betrayal from one man take her trust.

"Looking back, I know now that he had no intention of ever marrying me. You see, I was the one that was in love, not him. He didn't introduce me to his family, he didn't take me out; he didn't spend money on me. In fact, I spent money on him. You have no idea how funny that is," she said, feeling the heaviness of her heart. "It's so ironic that I'd want a man that didn't do a thing for me."

"You were young."

"I was stupid. My sister tried to warn me; I wouldn't listen. It was my life, I knew what I was doing, but Wyatt showed me that I didn't."

"What did he do?"

"He devastated me. I left him in my apartment one day when I went to work. When I got home later, he wasn't there but I figured he'd be back. I went into my bedroom to change and immediately sensed that something was different. I looked around and realized that my perfumes were rearranged on my dresser. None of my personal things were where I had left them, which was suspicious; and then I noticed this huge wet spot in the center of my bedspread. Even before I stripped the bed, I knew."

"Dog."

"He had changed the sheets but he couldn't wash the stain out of the mattress."

"Damn."

"In his arrogance, he called only minutes after I uncovered his dirty lie. He had the gall to apologize for spilling tomato juice on my bed. Can you believe that?"

"Damn. You didn't . . . ?"

"No, I hung up on him," she said sadly, "but I couldn't stop crying. I never told anyone about this. For a long time, I stayed to myself; I refused to go out with anyone."

"Did you ever see him again?"

"A year later in the subway. I asked him why; he asked, 'Why not?' "

"A real bastard."

"After I stopped crying, my first date was a married man. I didn't know it at the start because he lied, but he treated me well. He gave me money, he bought me things, he took me out. When he finally told me he was married, I didn't care. It was easy, it was comfortable, it was safe. Right from the start, he spent more time with me than Wyatt ever had. Then, when he had to spend less time with me because his wife was suspicious, I started seeing the second guy. By then, I didn't like being alone. I saw more men to try and occupy my time, yet no matter how many men I saw, I was never really satis-

fied. And I thought I had everything I wanted from those relationships, but I was empty inside. I was lonely."

"Could it be because there was just time enough with each of
them for you to satisfy their needs but no time for them to take care
of you?"

"Levi, I can't blame anyone but myself for the void in my soul. I
should have learned how to take better care of me. Then, maybe, I
would not have needed all those men, certainly not married men.
I've been so stupid."

"Don't be so hard on yourself, Marissa. With each of these men,
you went with what you thought was right for you at the time."

"Yeah, well, apparently I was wrong. My sister and Charmaine
tried to tell me so."

"It wasn't for them to judge. It was your life, like you said; but tell
me, is the first guy one of the men you were seeing recently?"

"Terrence," she answered with a nod. Feeling drained, she began
rubbing her eyes.

Going to stand in front of her, he asked, "Do you want to call him
tonight? I'll talk to him for you."

She knew that he was only inches from her even before she lowered her hands and opened her eyes. She didn't shy away, she didn't
want to. "You would do that for me?"

He said nothing, he took her hands.

She flushed from the warmth she saw in his eyes. He was real.
He really cared. No other man, besides Brandon, had ever been
so concerned for her. She looked deep into his eyes, unblinkingly,
unwaveringly, unafraid.

He returned her gaze. Brandon was right, she wasn't a bad person; she was a wounded person. The more time he spent with her,
the more he saw the different shades of Jade. The sadness he saw in
her eyes made him want to reach out and take her into his arms.
When he held her earlier, it felt good, it felt right. Instinctively, he
opened his arms, and she, without hesitation, stepped right into his
embrace. Their eyes closed and their lips met; the kiss was soft, un-
hurried, and tender, yet it belied the passion that erupted in both
their hearts.

Chapter 29

THE CEILING FAN above Marissa's head was unfamiliar. The feeling in her body was unfamiliar, too. She was satisfied. She smiled as she turned onto her back and stretched her body out long and hard, feeling every muscle awaken and come alive. Levi had left her while she slept; she hoped that he wouldn't stay gone long.

It didn't take much for him to convince her last night to come home with him since she was scared to be in her own apartment and Brandon's. The minute it had taken to repack her bag was too long. They didn't bother to call Brandon because he'd only worry once he heard that the woman had come after her in his building.

Strange, it didn't seem at all unnatural for her to climb into Levi's bed. She felt right at home. He had planned to sleep upstairs in another bedroom, but he said he'd wait until she fell asleep. An hour later he was still waiting, sitting in a straight chair next to the bed. She couldn't sleep. Her heart was pumping both from fear and the discovery of a yearning that she could not suppress. After their kiss, the yearning not only consumed her mind, but her body ached to be touched by him. She was completely stumped.

"I know you're tired," she had said to him. "Go on to bed, I'll be all right."

"I'm not sleepy," he said, looking at the thin, red straps of her nightgown on her bare shoulders peeking from under the sheet. He remembered how she looked in that gown; the way the silky fabric hugged her hips and kissed her behind while revealing her nipples. His blood was hot. No, he was not sleepy.

"It was nice of you to bring me here."

"You'll be safe here. Try to sleep."

"I can't."

"Do you want me to turn out the light?" he asked, reaching for the lamp on the nightstand.

"Then you'll be sitting in the dark," she said. Then she dared to say, "You should at least be resting and not sitting on that hard chair. You can turn off the light if you lay down next to me."

Surprised, he asked, "Are you sure?"

Easily scooting over to make room for him, she answered, "It's your bed." She loosened the sheet around her body so that she wouldn't feel penned down once he laid on top of it.

He switched off the light. The room was instantly bathed in darkness. A ray of light from the street lamp outside the window seeped through a crack in the curtains. As he lay down, stretching out his body alongside hers, his heart beat faster. Laying on his back, he listened to her breathing softly.

Completely relaxed, she thought about his arms around her; about how good his lips felt on hers. She yearned to be in his arms again. Turning onto her side to face him, she whispered, "You did a lot for me today. Thank you."

"It was my pleasure," he said, glad that the light was off. Laying next to her had stimulated him more.

Hoping that she wasn't assuming too much, she lay her head on his chest and lay her arm across his stomach.

He held his breath. His chin rested on her head. He wondered if she was making a move on him, or if she was just holding on to him as she had done since she was frightened out of her mind.

Raising her head, she asked, "Do you mind?"

He could feel her breath on his face. He swallowed to wet his throat before he whispered, "No." He could see the outline of her

face, but not her expression. He raised his head. His lips touched her nose.

She moved her head back so that her lips touched his. Again, the kiss was tender. He let the tip of his tongue touch her lips, but then like a baby sucking on a pacifier, she took his lower lip into her mouth and gently sucked on it. Every nerve in his body tingled like they had been charged. Sighing deeply, he took her into his arms and crushing her to him, pulled her on top of his body. When she opened her mouth to let his tongue in, they tasted each other timidly at first, then deeply and passionately.

While still kissing her, he rolled her onto her back and lay on top of her. He felt like he would explode if he couldn't have all of her. He stopped kissing her. Breathing deeply, he said hoarsely, "I want you."

"I want you, too," she said breathlessly.

At the same time, they both started pulling his T-shirt over his head. Then, pushing himself up off of her, he sat up on the side of the bed, untied and yanked off his work boots, and then standing, he pulled off his jeans.

She reached over and turned on the lamp; she wanted to not just feel him, she wanted to see him. She clicked the switch three times until it was on the lowest wattage, the softest glow. Levi stood in his black athletic boxers. He looked down at her. She was serenely looking back up at him. He held his hand out to her. Taking it, she let him help her up off the bed. Again, he took her into his arms. They kissed hungrily while he pulled the straps off her shoulders and together they pushed her gown down off her body, letting it drop to the floor. Their lips never did part. With her soft warm body pressed up against his, for him, it was a dream come true. He wasn't about to rush it. He let his hands savor every inch of her softness.

The feel of his hands caressing and gliding all over her body stimulated and heightened her desire to be with him. Wanting more of him, she slid her hands down his back to the waistband of his boxers and slowly began to push them down. He eased up on his hold on her long enough to let her push them down all the way. When they embraced again, he held her with powerful arms that

never wanted to let her go. With his tongue dancing passionately with hers, he tried to draw out all of her fear. In that moment, while he felt that he was her protector, he also felt like a man who had long thirsted for the succulence of her body alone.

She clung to him as they fell back onto the bed. When they became one, fire surged between her thighs, while every thirsty muscle in his body drank of her intoxicating nectar. They took each other to an ecstasy that neither had ever experienced. For her, the sweetness that first seemed to start from a tiny little core swelled to a mighty crescendo and then exploded from her body time and time again, bringing tears to her eyes. Now she knew what it was to reach the summit and go over.

For him, she pulled from his being a force so powerful his eyes rolled back in his head and he had to bite his lip to keep from crying out. Completely spent, he fell atop her, breathing like a man who'd run a marathon. Even before they could catch their breath, they kissed, and then she did what she'd been wanting to do all evening. She tongued his dimples one by one. He giggled like a little boy.

They made love again; more slowly and more indulgently. When sleep claimed them, locked in each other's arms, only a whisper of a breath was between them.

Chapter 30

"YOU'RE AWAKE."

With the phone to her ear, Marissa glanced over at the door. She smiled. "Okay, Vivian, I'll see you first thing Monday morning. You have a good weekend." She hung up. Levi came in carrying a tray of food. She was pleased with the way he was dressed. He was wearing a pair of charcoal gray slacks, a white polo shirt, and looking down at his feet, she smiled again. He had exchanged his work boots for a pair of casual loafers, but she realized he had looked just as good last night in his work clothes.

"You never did get a chance to eat last night," he said, sitting the tray on the chair. He sat down on the bed and bent down to her. They clung to each other, kissing and enjoying being kissed by each other. He stroked her face. "Embraced we lay; legs and arms entwined; whispered words brushing our brows; we lay thus for hours; sweetness lingering, fragrant on the air; our hearts beat a tender serenade."

His words stirred her. "Oh, Levi, that was so nice."

They kissed tenderly. "You taste good," he said to her, enjoying the sparkle in her eyes.

She covered her mouth. "I need to brush my teeth."

He gently pulled her hand from her mouth and kissed her again. "You taste real good."

She returned the kiss. "So do you."

"I hope you like grits," he said, reaching for the tray.

"They're not my favorite," she admitted, glimpsing his nails. They were clean. This was not the man she met at Charmaine's.

"No problem. We also have eggs, bacon, toast, orange juice, and coffee."

She sat up, pulling the sheet tightly around her body. "Did you cook all this?"

He sat the tray on her lap. "My mother did. She lives upstairs, remember?"

"Does she mind that I'm down here?"

He chuckled.

"Well, does she?"

"Marissa, I'm well past the age of consent," he said, handing her the glass of orange juice. "Besides, this is my house."

"Really?" she asked, surprised. "Then why do you live in the basement?"

He looked around. "Is it that bad?"

"No . . . not really," she said, looking over the traditionally furnished bedroom. "Actually, it's fixed up rather nice; it doesn't even feel like we're in a basement."

"Good."

"And it's clean, nothing like your car. Does your mother clean for you?"

"She'd like to, but I think I do just fine for myself."

She agreed with a nod. "You know, from what I could see last night when we drove up, it's a beautiful house, a big house. Why do you live in the basement?"

He sat sideways on the edge of the bed facing her. It felt good to be sitting next to her. "Other than privacy, this was all the space I needed. Of course, I'd have no problem moving my mother down here if I should find that I'm no longer a bachelor."

Was that a hint? "Your mother might have something to say about that."

"Not much. She's the one who told me that no two women can be the boss in the same space. After living with my father's mother for six years and hating it, she said she'd rather live in a cardboard box than live with a mother-in-law any day."

"That bad, huh?" Marissa asked, biting into a piece of toast. That was something she never had to think about. She wondered if she was supposed to be thinking about it now. "I can't eat all this. Are you eating?"

"I ate while you were sleeping. Did you sleep well?"

The thought of what made her sleep so well made her tingle all the way down to her toes. Marissa smiled bashfully.

"Mmm, me, too," Levi said, enjoying the glow that radiated from her.

She noticed that his dimples deepened, making her want to tongue them again. "Is your mother upstairs right now?"

He noticed that her eyes sparkled with mischief. "You have something, I hope, in mind?"

"Maybe. Is she?"

"She just left to go to the doctor. She wanted to cancel her appointment so that she could be here when you woke up."

"Do you think she heard us? You know. . . ."

"I doubt it, her bedroom's up on the second floor. And no, she didn't say anything. She'll be back around two, if you wanna meet her."

"Not just yet, okay? I'm not ready."

"No rush."

That pressure, she didn't need. "Your mother, is she sick?" she asked, forgetting about seducing him. A sick mother was a serious matter.

"She has rheumatoid arthritis. She manages. She's far from being an invalid."

"That's great," she said, relieved. It would be a little much to go from single and selfish to full-fledged involvement and nursemaid in twenty-four hours, but then she was getting a little ahead of herself where Levi and his mother were concerned. "Levi, what if your mother doesn't like me?"

"I wouldn't worry about it."

She picked up a forkful of eggs. "But suppose she doesn't?"

"Marissa, I told you, I'm well past the age of consent."

Looking down in her plate, she felt herself getting weepy. Never in her wildest dreams would she have imagined that she would be with Levi or anyone like him. "Where were you when I was twenty-three?" she finally asked.

"Probably wondering where you were."

That did bring the tears. She covered her face, but Levi again reached over and pulled her hands away. He tenderly kissed the tears on her cheeks and then he kissed her lips.

Marissa pulled away. "I'm so sorry I was so mean to you," she sobbed, dropping her head so that she didn't have to look at him.

"I've got broad shoulders."

His generosity didn't make her feel any better, but the tears stopped.

He took her chin in his hand and lifted her face. "If it'll make you feel better, you can make it up to me whenever you think about it. I'm not hard to please."

She gave him a weak smile, but she wondered. "Levi, you say that you're not hard to please. How is it you're not married?"

His hand slipped from Marissa's chin. The joy in his heart was, for a moment, replaced with sadness. He hadn't thought about Janice since Marissa fell into his arms; since her lips touched his. Taking care of her, falling in love with her, making love to her, had filled the huge void that Janice's death had left so long ago.

"Are you all right?" Marissa asked, concerned about the sadness she saw in his eyes.

"I am now," he answered softly, though he wasn't sure that he could talk about Janice.

Marissa had to know. "There was someone once, wasn't there?"

He nodded slowly. "Janice."

"Were you married to her?"

He shook his head. "I would have married her, if that drunk driver had not snatched her from me."

"Oh, Levi!" Marissa exclaimed, bringing her hand to her chest. "I'm so sorry. That must have been so painful for you."

"Yeah, it was pretty rough."

Levi said nothing more, but Marissa could see that he was pensive. "Janice must have been very special. You must have loved her very much."

He nodded. "I loved her. She was very special. She was a lot like you."

Marissa didn't expect that. She felt herself welling up again. "You think . . . ?"

"Yes, you are," he said, feeling the newness of his love for Marissa becoming one with the love that he had for Janice. His heart felt full. He kissed Marissa.

Kissing him back, she allowed herself to believe that it was possible that he could be true to her.

Levi ended the kiss. He wanted to be with Marissa, but they had some unfinished business to take care of. They looked into each other's eyes.

"Marissa, I'm not going to work today, either. Let's see if we can reach this Terrence and check out his wife. If it's his wife, we go to the police. If it's not, we still got some looking to do."

"I'll call him at his office at nine-thirty."

"We have an hour then," Levi said, looking down at his wristwatch. "That reminds me, I called Brandon while I was upstairs. The clerk said he checked out."

"He must be on his way home. If he tried to reach us last night and couldn't, he probably got worried."

"We'll catch up with him later. Charmaine's wedding rehearsal is at six this evening. We should—"

"How do you know about that?"

"I'm Greg's best man."

"Yes, Charmaine did tell me that. I forgot."

"That's why she made dinner for us. I was supposed to meet the maid of honor—you."

"And I thought it was a setup."

"I gathered."

"I am so sorry for the way I behaved."

"Don't be. I don't think you would have gotten my attention if you hadn't been upset. I wasn't interested in anything but eating, meeting you, and getting myself on home. After you left, I couldn't stop thinking about you. You made quite an impression."

"Levi, please forgive me."

"Like I said before, you can make it up to me. By the way, what do you think Charmaine and Gregory will say when they see us together?"

"What won't they say?"

Chapter 31

PERHAPS IF THEY had spent time together beyond the stolen hours, beyond the idyllic weekend trysts, she might have seen how ugly Terrence could get. The first two times she tried to reach him he would not take her calls; his secretary kept saying that he was not in. By one o'clock when he had not called her back, Levi prompted her to tell his secretary that she'd call his wife if she couldn't speak to him. Then he came on the line right away.

"If I have to take out an order of protection against you, I will," he blurted.

His hostility floored her. Her hand began to shake. She almost hung up the telephone herself, but this had to end. She gritted her teeth. "Terrence, would you just listen. I need to—"

"There is nothing that we have to say to each other. My wife—"

"Terrence, please. I don't understand your hostility. I have never done anything to you."

"My wife has never done anything to you. I'm telling you for the last time, don't—"

"Terrence—"

"Bitch," Terrence spat, "don't call me again!" He slammed the telephone in her ear.

Until he said it, she didn't know the word *bitch* could sound so nasty, so ugly. It was as if he reached down into the gutter to pronounce it because it cut through her heart like a jagged, rusty old blade. Dumbfounded, Marissa sat the receiver down quietly.

"He hung up?" Levi asked.

She sat stone-faced, thinking only that he called her a bitch. Anyone but Terrence. How could she be so wrong about a person?

Levi didn't know what was said, but he saw that she was stunned by whatever it was. He took her hand. "Since he won't talk to you, we have to go to his house."

"We can't do that."

"Yes, we can. We need to see his wife. Where does he live?"

She didn't want to go anywhere near Terrence's house, much less his wife. "She might not be home," she finally said. "Maybe we should wait till tonight."

"How's he doing financially?"

"Very well, I guess."

"Is he an older man?"

Turning her lips in and pressing them together, she nodded.

"She's home."

She felt a chill on her neck. "Terrence won't like me going to see his wife."

"Do you care?"

She thought about it for a second. He had called her a bitch. If he had spoken to her calmly, she might have cared. "No."

"Good," he said, pulling her to her feet. "Where does he live?"

"Queens. I took him home, several times, when he didn't have his car."

"Let's go."

What she expected Levi to drive out of his two-car garage was the ugly old car he'd taken her home in a few days ago. She had chided herself to hold her tongue. What rolled out of the garage was a sleek, sparkling emerald green Cadillac Eldorado, and hold her tongue she did—to keep from gawking stupidly.

"Is this more to your liking?" he asked.

"You're full of surprises," she said, settling down on the soft, creamy tan leather.

He looked at her and winked.

She certainly should not have judged this book by its cover. There was apparently a lot more yet to be discovered about Levi Bronson. Inside, he was intriguingly sensitive; outside, he was a beautiful chameleon.

As they glided their way to Jamaica Estates, they devised a plan wherein Levi would go up and ring the doorbell while she watched from the safety of the car, just in case Terrence's wife was the stalker. Despite the NO PEDDLERS sign on the wooden arch opening onto the exclusive community, Levi was going to say that he was a contractor seeking work. Five blocks in, they pulled up to Terrence's splendid English Tudor and parked. It was the first time she saw the house during the day. It was surrounded by a variety of colorful flower beds and a well-manicured lawn. When she was younger, she used to wonder about the people who lived behind the doors of such fabulous houses. After knowing Terrence, she wondered no more.

Unbuckling her seat belt, she slid down in her seat and peeked over the top edge of the car door as Levi ambled up the walkway. In his hand he had one of his business cards.

The name *Applecrumby* was on a brass plate over the bell. It was the right house. He rang the doorbell. He waited. He was about to ring again when the door opened. A young woman of about twenty stood on the other side of the screen door. He saw right away that she was not the stalker—too young, too short. He handed her his card.

"My name is Levi Bronson, I'm a local contractor. This is a beautiful house, but there's always something that needs to be done. Are you the lady of the house?"

"No. You need to speak to my father. He's not home."

He pressed on. "We both know that the man of the house pays the bills, but it's the lady of the house who decides to renovate. After all, it is her showplace; it reflects her style and taste."

"That's true," the young woman said. "My mother has always been the one to make changes."

"Then she's the lady I need to see. Is she home?"

The woman glanced back over her left shoulder to the inside of the house. "This isn't a good time to talk to my mother."

He saw the strained look on her young face. "I promise, I won't take up much of her time."

"You don't understand," she whispered. "My mother is very ill, she just got home from the hospital."

"I'm sorry to hear that," he said, relieved. "I hope she feels better soon."

The woman suddenly welled up with tears. "My mother has cancer. It's terminal."

The feeling of relief he felt was replaced by guilt. He felt like he was intruding. "I'm sorry," he said, slowly stepping back off the stoop. He didn't know what else to say.

The young woman closed the door.

Rushing back to the car, he wasted no time pulling off. Saying nothing, he concentrated on the road ahead.

She could see that he was upset, so she waited until they exited the Jamaica Estates compound and were driving along Hillside Avenue. "What happened?"

"His wife just got out of the hospital; she's dying of cancer."

Marissa's breath caught in her throat. She stared at Levi in disbelief.

He glanced at her. "He didn't tell you that his wife had cancer?"

"We never talked about his family."

Perplexed, again he glanced at her. "I don't understand that. How can you have an intimate relationship without sharing personal information?"

She avoided looking at him. To answer him truthfully meant telling him about how shallow she had been in her relationships. She couldn't tell him that. Only now did she fully understand that not knowing anything about the families of her men did not negate their existence. It had been pure selfishness on her part, but she thought it was the only way to keep herself guiltless of any wrongdoing. Feeling sick, she clutched her pocketbook to her stomach.

"Maybe that's why Terrence lashed out at you when you told him that his wife might be harassing you. He probably feels guilty."

"Yeah," she said softly, looking out at the passing cars. Her own guilt was stifling. She let the window down a few inches.

Controlling the steering with his left hand, Levi reached over and lay his right hand on Marissa's thigh. "His wife's illness is not your fault."

"No, but if I wasn't seeing her husband, she could have had more time with him."

"That's not your fault, either. Terrence is the one who took the vow to honor and cherish, not you."

Misty-eyed, she turned and looked at him. "You don't have to keep finding loopholes for me, I know what I did was wrong."

He squeezed her thigh. "Marissa, did you put Terrence in a head-lock to make him step out on his wife?"

She shook her head.

"Well, then," he said, putting both hands on the wheel as he accelerated to get onto the Grand Central Parkway heading back to Brooklyn.

"You're not real," she said, looking at him. "Don't tell me you can't be a little judgmental, a little bit accusatory even."

"Would you feel better if I was?"

"Yes . . . no . . . I don't know. Maybe."

"Why?"

"I don't know. It's just that you're trying to make me think that I'm blameless when I know I'm not. I wasn't a child when I got involved with Terrence. Even after I found out that he was married, I thought, Hurray for me and the hell with his family. I was getting everything I wanted. I didn't care. That's why that woman is after me; she knows I'm as much to blame as her man."

"That's just it, Marissa. I don't think she blames her man. It's you and you alone she blames, which isn't right. You could get killed. Look," he said, taking her hand and squeezing it. "I'm not about to let anyone take you from me. So, since it's not Terrence's wife we have to worry about, let's find out who we do have to worry about."

"I don't know where to begin," she said, thinking about what he had just said. It amazed her that he wanted her, knowing all that he knew about her.

"Let's take a look at the guy's wife who called you."

"Mrs. LaSalle? Louis described her to me, she doesn't fit the description."

Levi changed smoothly to the third lane. "What about the guy who isn't married? What about his girlfriend? We need to check her out."

"That might be kind of difficult, I may not be able to find out who she is."

"Why not? This guy won't speak to you, either?"

Feeling about the size of an ant, she slumped slightly in her seat.

"Marissa, I didn't mean anything by that."

"I know. I'm just a little sensitive."

"Why don't we make that call after we get something to eat."

"Maybe we can eat after we talk to him," she said, wanting to get it over with.

"That's fine," Levi said, squeezing her thigh. "Let's talk about something more pleasant. How do you like your steak?"

"I don't."

As soon as they got back to Brooklyn, they called Eric's dental practice but it was closed for the afternoon. According to his answering service, she had just missed him. She felt like screaming. Was this never going to end?

"So we call his house," Levi suggested.

Buckling herself in, she settled back. "I don't have his home number, and I don't know where he lives."

"You serious?"

She stiffened. "I never saw a reason to have his home number. Is that a crime? Was I wrong about that, too?"

"Take it easy, I'm not accusing you of anything," he defended. "It was just a question."

Closing her eyes, she let her head fall back onto the headrest. She was losing it.

"Marissa, it'll be all right."

She began to twist her bracelet around her wrist. She felt as if she was never going to wake up from this nightmare. How much more could she take before losing her mind?

"We'll get through this," Levi said, touching her hand, trying to reassure her.

He was too forgiving of her; she didn't deserve him; and he didn't deserve to be her whipping boy. Of all people, she did not want him to be upset with her. Besides Brandon, he was the only one in her corner. She was taking back what she said about him not criticizing her. She did not want him to judge her, after all; she couldn't handle it.

"Marissa," he said, gently shaking her hand.

She opened her eyes.

"I'm sorry if I upset you."

Her bracelet stopped moving. "You didn't. It was me. I'm sorry for snapping at you."

"You're going through a lot, Marissa; I understand. We both wanted to get to the bottom of this today."

"I don't have that kind of luck."

"I think you should stay with me this weekend."

Her first thought was of his mother. She wasn't up to meeting and schmoozing with her yet. "I don't want your mother to meet me like this."

"No problem, your place then."

She nodded. That she could live with.

"At the rehearsal tonight, don't leave my side."

Chapter 32

THEY HAD A LONG, leisurely dinner at a steak house two blocks from the church. Levi had eaten his steak and onions, two baked potatoes, salad, three rolls, and part of her chicken cordon bleu without a single belch. While she passed on dessert, he didn't—he had a generous slice of cheesecake. She got heartburn just watching him. And now as they sat in the back of the dimly lit church waiting for Charmaine and Gregory, she teased him about his huge appetite. "Where did it all go?" she asked, pressing on his hard, flat stomach.

He lay his right arm over the back of the pew behind her. "My body works like a new furnace—efficient."

"Lucky you. I would've barfed if I had eaten a third of what you ate."

"That's because you're a woman."

"Not that I'd want to eat as much as you, but what does being a woman have to do with it? I know women who can eat more than you."

"That's not the average woman. Check it out. If you had one hundred men, one hundred women, two hundred cheeseburgers, two hundred thick shakes, and a tub of green salad all in one room,

watch all the men and maybe ten percent of the women dive into the burgers and thick shakes."

"You said all that to say . . . ?"

"That ninety percent of the women will nibble on the salad and maybe drink half of their shakes. When it's all over, the men won't leave a crumb of bread, but I bet you half the salad will be left and half the women will complain about gaining weight. When the women get home, they'll eat a pint of ice cream."

"See, you don't understand women."

"I understand them well enough."

"Then you should understand that women nibble on salad because we don't look good stuffing our faces in public. Secondly, food sticks to us like Velcro. It's not our fault Mother Nature played a cruel joke on us and gave us more body fat to begin with."

"That's my point; most men can eat a cow and still have a good body, while women can munch on grass and grow fat."

"Now, that's the truth. I've—"

"Marissa. Hi," Charmaine called from the entryway on the other side of the church.

She waved while nudging Levi in the side. "Watch her face when she comes over here."

Leaving his right arm behind Marissa, Levi brought his fist up to his mouth and coughed. This was going to be funny. As Charmaine approached them, he saw the wide-eyed, open-mouth surprise on her face.

Marissa nudged Levi again. She didn't want to give Charmaine the satisfaction of thinking that she had brought them together, which she hadn't, but she certainly wasn't going to tell her about the nightmare that did bring them together.

Charmaine looked at Levi's arm behind Marissa. She cut her eyes from one to the other—once then twice. "Are you two together?"

"Uh-huh," she answered.

"When?" she asked excitedly, practically jumping up and down.

"*Shhh!* Charmaine, we're in church. It's no big deal."

"No big deal?" she asked even louder. "Levi's grinning from ear to ear; the two of you are up against each other like you're glued at the hip. You hated him! I wanna know what's going on."

There was a frantically funny expression on Charmaine's face. Marissa pressed her lips together—it was hard to keep from laughing. She glanced at Levi when he squeezed her shoulder. He was grinning so hard, his dimples were deeper than a pair of potholes. Again she nudged him, but that cracked him up. He threw his head back and roared with laughter. She lost it herself then, laughing so hard that she doubled over.

"Will somebody tell me something?" Charmaine pleaded.

Marissa couldn't stop laughing. Tears rolled down her cheeks as she buried her head against Levi's chest. She didn't know why she was laughing, it really wasn't all that funny, but it felt good to laugh.

"I don't believe this," Charmaine said irritably.

Forcing herself to sit up straight, Marissa wiped her face dry and tried with all her might to stop laughing.

Levi did get control of himself. He stopped laughing, but he couldn't stop smiling. "Seriously, Charmaine, where's the groom?"

"Forget the damn groom!" she said in a hushed yell. She sat down in the pew in front of them, then twisted around to face them.

"Yeah, Charmaine," Marissa said, "where's the groom?"

She glared at Marissa. "I want the details on how and when."

"There's nothing to tell," Marissa said.

"Don't lie in church."

"I told you, it's really no big deal. Where are the rest of the folks? Don't we have to get started? It's almost six."

Stomping her foot, Charmaine groaned.

"Hey!" Gail said, walking in with Lisa.

Smiling, Marissa said, "Hi."

"Hey, ladies," Levi said, standing up. "I think I'll go out and look for the men." Bending down, he kissed Marissa on the cheek.

"Chicken."

"*Chirp . . . chirp,*" he said, laughing as he slipped out of the church.

"He's cute," Gail said.

Charmaine peered into Marissa's eyes. "I don't believe this. You could have told me that you were seeing him."

"What's up?" Lisa asked, looking from Charmaine to Marissa.

"Not a thing," Marissa replied, ignoring Charmaine's unwavering gaze. "Shouldn't we get started?"

"I wish we would," Gail said. "I got my beautician coming over to Charmaine's house tonight at eight to do our hair."

Marissa touched her own hair. "Darn, I forgot to make an appointment with my stylist."

"My beautician can do your hair tonight, also."

"I wish. I'm gonna have to do it myself."

"Ladies, come down front please," the minister called from the front of the church, which was suddenly awash in bright lights.

"We're coming," Gail said, starting down the aisle.

"Are you ladies coming?" Lisa asked, waiting for them.

Marissa stood up. "I am."

Standing up quickly, Charmaine went and stood at the end of the pew in front of Marissa, blocking her. "Go ahead Lisa, we're coming," she said.

Lisa went on.

"You better tell me something," Charmaine said. "You had me abase myself to get you to forgive me for trying to set you up with that man."

"Do you want me to apologize to you? I'm sorry. Okay?"

"No, it's not okay. You owe me an explanation."

"I can't give you one."

"Why not?"

"I just can't"

"Stop playing with me, Marissa. You hated the very sight of the man. How is it that you're all of a sudden so lovey-dovey?"

"This is not the place to talk about it."

"Charmaine, the minister wants to talk to you," Lisa called from halfway down the aisle.

"In a minute."

"Charmaine, you don't have the church all night," Marissa reminded her. "Go on. I'll talk to you later."

At first hesitant, Charmaine finally relented. "You better," she said, hurrying down the aisle to the minister.

Blowing out one long, silent whistle, she flopped back down on the pew. As soon as rehearsals were over, she was going to fly out of there. The door behind her opened. In walked Gregory, Levi, and two men she didn't know. Going past her, Gregory did not speak.

It didn't bother her, but she clicked her teeth anyway.

Levi stopped. "Jerry, Scott, this is Marissa."

"How you doing?" Scott said, taking her hand.

"Hi," she said, shaking first his hand, then Jerry's.

"We'll be down in a minute," Levi said, crouching alongside her. "How did it go?"

"She wants answers."

"You don't have to tell her anything."

"It's not that simple. I do owe her."

"Why?"

"She's my friend," Marissa said simply. "I don't care that she knows about us, I want her to. I just don't want her to know about what brought us together. It's too ugly."

Taking her hand, Levi said, "Then tell her that I bugged you until you gave in."

"You're telling a fib in church."

"Forgive me, Lord," he said, looking up at the ceiling. Then he kissed her tenderly on the lips.

"Are you two in this wedding party?" Lisa asked.

They hadn't noticed that she had come back up the aisle. Levi stood up. "We're on our way."

Together, holding hands, they walked down the aisle behind Lisa. This time the one gawking at them was Gregory.

"Our friends don't seem to be too happy for us," Marissa whispered.

"Too bad."

Charmaine was eyeing them suspiciously, but she remembered her manners. "Reverend Simmons, Marissa Jenkins, my maid of honor, and Levi Bronson, the best man."

"Reverend Simmons," Levi said, extending his hand.

As Marissa was shaking the reverend's hand, she glimpsed Gregory staring at Levi's arm around her waist. The startled look on his face was so funny she had to put her hand to her mouth to stifle a giggle.

"Mrs. Simmons is our organist," Reverend Simmons announced, indicating his wife sitting behind the organ alongside the altar.

They all greeted her, most with a smile and a nod.

"The groom and the best man should stand here on my left."

Gregory didn't move.

"Too late, brother," Scott said, pulling Gregory backward into his place. "Can't back out now."

Levi whispered in her ear, "We won't hang around when this is over."

Marissa nodded.

"When Mrs. Simmons begins playing," Reverend Simmons began, "that's the cue for the bridesmaids and groomsmen to start their walk down the aisle. Miss Maid of Honor, you'll come in after them. Then the lovely bride will come in to the wedding march. Charmaine, where's your father?"

"He couldn't make the rehearsal, but he said to tell you that he has had enough experience walking three daughters down the aisle to know what to do."

"That he does. Well, since you've chosen the traditional ceremony, we don't have much to do. Ladies, if you'll all step outside in the vestibule with the groomsmen, we'll get started."

"Let's get this show on the road," Lisa said, locking arms with Charmaine, who didn't look too much like a happy bride-to-be.

"Can we put some spirit into this wedding party," Gail said, also starting up the aisle.

"I'm game," Marissa said, going off behind her. She glanced back at Levi. He winked at her.

Gregory poked Levi hard in the side with his elbow.

"Hey!" he said, grabbing his side.

"Man, what the hell you doing with her?"

"Greg, leave it alone," Levi said, massaging his side.

"What you say?"

"I said, leave it alone," Levi said, watching the minister who was looking at them.

Gregory didn't care. "Man, I warned you about her."

"Gentlemen, we're ready," Reverend Simmons said, silencing Gregory with a stern visual scolding.

Gregory left Levi alone.

"Ladies, are you ready?" Reverend Simmons called out.

"Yes," Charmaine said, stepping out into the vestibule.

Organ music suddenly filled the huge, cavernous hollowness of the church. The maids stepped; the groomsmen tried but were awkward; the groom stood at the front of the church ramrod straight, his eyes hard, his jaw clenched. Charmaine shook off her somberness once she started down the aisle. Laughingly, the maids teased the groomsmen for walking like stiffs. They tried again—twice more.

"We don't have to walk like lames, put a little bop in it," Jerry said.

"You guys better not be bopping in my wedding," Charmaine scolded.

They all laughed, except Gregory. "Man, do it right. I got things to do," he said.

"Grouchy," Lisa whispered to Charmaine.

"Baby, you all right?" Charmaine asked.

"He has wedding-day jitters," Gail remarked.

"He'll be just fine tomorrow," Reverend Simmons said to Charmaine. "Why don't you and Gregory come back to the office, we have to get the paperwork in order. Did you bring your license?"

"Yes."

"Are we done?" Jerry asked.

"Sure. Practice your walk a bit more and you'll do just fine."

"Thanks, Rev," Jerry said. "Hey, fellas, we down at the club?"

"We'll be right with you, Reverend Simmons," Charmaine said.

The minister and his wife left through a side door behind the organ.

"I'm down for the club," Scott said, looking at Gregory. "You coming? It's your party."

"I'll meet you there."

"Charmaine, give me your keys," Gail said. "My beautician is probably on the way to your apartment."

Taking them out of her pocketbook, she said, "I won't be too long."

Gail and Lisa walked out with Jerry and Scott.

"We'll see you folks tomorrow," Levi said.

"Hey," Gregory said, "aren't you coming to the club?"

Levi glanced at Marissa. "I can't make the club. I'll see you first thing tomorrow."

"What's wrong, man? The woman got her claws in you that fast? What number are—?"

"Gregory!" Charmaine said, shoving him. He moved away. "Marissa, he didn't mean that."

Marissa turned her back to Gregory.

Levi knew differently. "Man, I suggest that you watch what you say."

Grimacing, Gregory snorted. "I gotta talk to you. You gotta come to the club."

He already knew what Gregory had to say. He wasn't interested. "Another time, man."

"Levi," Marissa said, trying to give Gregory the benefit of the doubt. Maybe he did have the jitters. "You should go to the club. He's nervous. You know how you men are about losing your freedom. We can get together later."

"Yeah, you fellas go on," Charmaine agreed. "Marissa, maybe we can talk on the way to my apartment."

"She's not going to your apartment," Levi said, "you'll have to talk here."

"What the . . .?" Gregory started to ask but didn't get the question out. Stumped, he glowered.

"Twenty minutes is all we can spare," Levi added. "How long you gonna be with the minister?"

"Ten, maybe twenty minutes," Charmaine said, looking at Marissa. "Will you wait?"

Gregory started off toward the office.

"I'll wait," Marissa said. "I have to use the ladies' room anyway. Where is it?"

"Use the stairs through that door," Charmaine said, pointing to the door on the far side of the church. "One flight down to the basement. Make a right turn, it's the second door."

"I'll come with you," Levi said, ignoring Charmaine's puzzled expression.

Gregory turned abruptly. "You hardheaded, man."

"My car won't start!" Gail said from the back of the church. "Those guys out there don't know what they're doing."

"I'll look at it," Levi said. "Give me a minute."

"Can you come now? We have to leave."

"I'll be out in—"

"Go on," Marissa said. "I'll be fine."

"The car can wait, you're more important," Levi said.

Charmaine and Gregory looked at each other quizzically.

"Are you coming?" Gail asked.

"Levi, I'm just going down to the bathroom. I'll be fine."

"Okay, but I'll be right back."

"This is real strange," Charmaine said, taking Gregory's hand. "The minister is waiting for us."

They all went off, leaving Marissa standing alone at the front of the church. She felt small in its vastness. She looked up at the depiction of the baptism of John the Baptist. That's what she probably needed—to be washed anew. Maybe she needed to start going to church; she hadn't been since she was a teenager. A faint urge reminded her that she had to go to the ladies' room. She went over to the door Charmaine pointed to and pushed it open. The white-walled and brown-trimmed stairwell was dimly lit. As she descended the stairs to the basement, the sound of her heels clicking on the stone steps bounced off the walls all around her.

Chapter 33

THE BASEMENT WAS morbidly desolate. This was going to be a quick pit stop. Marissa pushed open the door to the ladies' room; it was dark, and the sound of dripping water pierced the quiet. She hurriedly felt along the wall inside to the right of the door for the light switch. Finding it and then flicking it on flooded the room with instant brightness. Everything was stark white—the tiny square ceramic tiles on the floor; the old, wooden partitions between the three toilets; even the cinderblock walls had been painted brilliant white. It could have easily been the men's room as there wasn't a warm thing in the whole room—not a picture, not a flower, not a hint of color. Upon entering the stall, she saw that the toilet seat was far from new. No surprise there. She was careful to not sit down.

After washing her hands, without soap in cold water, Marissa dried them on stiff, white paper towels. She then tried to shut off the leaky faucet, tightening it as much as she could. It dripped faster. She gave up. In the single scratched mirror on the wall above and between the two sinks, she glimpsed her hair. Not a strand was out of place. It was as Louis had said earlier when he tried to talk

her into a lunchtime rendezvous; snatching her hair back into a French twist would not tell on her. It was a mite severe on her round forehead, but she liked it this way; it was sophisticated. She wondered if Levi liked it this way.

That was something new—worrying about what Levi thought. Yesterday she would not have cared, today it meant everything. She had actually enjoyed spending the whole day with him; she had not felt the least bit smothered or uncomfortable. As she walked to the door, she smiled to herself, thinking about how much she was looking forward to being with him tonight. She pulled open the door to leave the bathroom and was about to switch off the light when a wall of opaque blackness slammed her in the face, stopping her dead in her tracks.

Inhaling sharply, she quickly jumped back, pushed the door shut, and stared hard at it as if she could see right through it. She could hear her heart beating loudly in her ears. Someone had turned off the lights. She had been in the bathroom about five minutes. Charmaine could not have forgotten that she was down there. Surely Levi would not have forgotten her.

Maybe the church custodian turned off the lights, not realizing that she was down there. She could kick herself for not paying attention to where the light switch was located. More than likely it was at the top of the stairs, where she would love to be. She could make a run for it, but as chickenhearted as she was, she was not about to go stumbling around out there in the dark. On the other hand, she had no desire to stay in the bathroom, either. She went at the door, slapping it hard several times with the palm of her hand.

"Hello! Hello! I'm down here! Turn the lights back on!"

She stopped hitting the door and put her ear to the door. She heard nothing.

"Hello! Hello!"

She started slapping the door again. *Bang! Bang! Bang!*

Her hand was stinging. She had to stop hitting the door to rub her hand. It hurt. She listened. The *drip, drip, drip* sound of the leaky

faucet was magnified in the eerie silence. She felt like she was in a scene right out of *The Twilight Zone*. She opened the door a crack to see if she could hear anything. She listened with her ear pressed against the edge of the door. She listened hard. At first she didn't hear anything. Then came the sound of someone walking.

"Hello?"

There was no answer, but the sound was coming closer.

"Who's there? Please turn on the light."

The sound of footfalls stopped.

Silence.

She opened the door a few inches wider. She peered around to see if the light was on. Blackness filled her eyes. She quickly closed the door again. Someone was out there. She didn't even want to think who that someone might be. Then the doorknob turned in her hand.

Marissa's heart thumped hard. Fear gripped her. It turned again. "No!" she shouted, holding on tightly to the doorknob. She started screaming, "Levi! Levi! Levi!"

The door started to open. She quickly put her shoulder up against it and tried to close it back. Then, suddenly, *Bang!* The door was bashed up against her, slamming her back into the wall with such force that the back of her head, then her back, hit the wall. The door hit her in the chest. *Whoosh!* The breath was knocked out of her. She was pinned between the wall and the door. For a fleeting second, she thought she would black out. Her chest felt crushed. She tried to push the door away but it would not budge. She could hear someone grunting.

Then it was dark. She wasn't sure if she blacked out or if the lights were turned off. Her eyes felt like they were open, yet she could see nothing. She could hear the entity on the other side of the door breathing just as rapidly as she was.

"Who are you?" she screamed.

Then just as suddenly as the door had slammed her into the wall, it was yanked away from her. Hands grabbed at her. Screaming at the top of her lungs, she started flailing her arms wildly, clawing, dragging her nails through whatever she touched. The hands were

quick, though, and they caught her wrists and held them like a vise. When she started kicking, the entity rammed into her chest, thrusting her hard against the concrete wall. All the fight was knocked out of her. She felt herself letting go. Her knees buckled. The light went out in her head.

Levi cleaned off the tip of the last spark plug and screwed it back into the cylinder head with the socket wrench he took from the trunk of his car. "Gail, I'm surprised this car got any fire at all. Those plugs looked like they were dipped in soot. When was the last time you got a tune-up?"

"I don't know."

"I bet you don't remember when you got your last oil change, either."

"She barely puts gas in it," Lisa said. "Most times it's near empty."

Gail shrugged. "That's not something a woman should have to worry about."

"I tell you what," Levi said, "unless you're ready to put out big bucks for a new car, I suggest you get this car to your mechanic." He slammed the hood down. "Try it now."

Gail got into the car. Turning the key, the engine turned over with a roar.

"Levi!" Brandon shouted, running up to him. "Where's Marissa?"

"Hey, when did you get in?"

"Thanks, Levi," Gail said.

"No problem," he said, snapping his tool box shut. He started to go toward his car to put the box away.

Brandon grabbed Levi by the arm and pulled him back. "Where's Marissa?"

Looking into Brandon's frantic eyes, he froze. "She's inside. What's wrong?"

"Who's with her?"

He could feel the hair stand up on the nape of his neck. "She went to the bathroom. Gregory and Charmaine are inside with the minister. Brandon, she's all right."

"No, she's not!" He took off running toward the church.

Dropping his tool box, Levi sprinted hard behind him.

"What do you think that was about?" Lisa asked Gail.

"Damn if I know. Marissa seems to always have some sort of drama going on around her."

Chapter 34

MARISSA LAY IN A heap like a mound of discarded garbage. The side of her face was pressed into the dusty, rough concrete floor. She could feel her mouth hanging open and her saliva dribbling onto the floor. Slurping, she closed her mouth. Drifting in and out of semiconsciousness, she was afraid to open her eyes. She'd rather see the darkness inside her own eyelids than the darkness of the room. She took a deep breath, then groaned softly. Her whole body ached, especially her chest and back. The back of her head throbbed. She started to reach up to touch it but her arms felt weighted down. They felt like they were twisted behind her.

She was prodded roughly on the hip.

She groaned again.

"I know you're awake, slut. Open your damn eyes!"

Her heart quivered. The voice was the same, the ugliness was the same. What she feared had happened—she was caught. She didn't want to open her eyes, but she had to know. She forced her eyes open. There was light.

"I was hoping you'd never wake up, but then you wouldn't know who killed your whoring ass."

What she saw was the blood-red hem of a choir robe. She tried to roll over so that she could sit up. She couldn't. Suddenly, she was brutally grabbed and shoved onto her back, onto her arms tied behind her.

Groaning pitifully, she looked up the length of the robe into the sneering face of Gregory. She inhaled deep and long enough to practically suck all the air out of the room.

"Yeah, it's me, bitch," he sneered. "You better close your damn mouth before I give you something warm to drink. You'd probably like that, wouldn't you? No telling the freaky things you like to do with all those guys you screw."

She snapped her mouth shut. Her mind was whirling. "This can't be," she said aloud.

"It is, slut. I hate your whoring ass. I never understood why Charmaine had to have anything to do with you. You're nothing but trash."

"I've never done anything to you," she whined, stinging tears washed over the side of her face to the floor.

"Naw, you wouldn't think so, would you?"

What stood before her was slowly beginning to register. "Gregory, why does your voice sound like that? Why are you wearing that robe?"

"I sound just like myself, you just don't know the other me," he said, lifting the hem of the robe out to the side. He curtsied.

She gawked at him.

He stretched his eyes and gawked back at her.

What was he telling her? She tried to sit up.

"Stay still!" he ordered, planting his foot on her chest. He pushed her back to the floor.

It felt like a ton of bricks rested on her chest, cutting off her air. Her chest and back screamed with pain. She groaned.

"You know, I could stand on you and crush your rib cage into your heart and lungs. You'd die slow enough for me to enjoy every minute," he said, pushing harder. "You're lucky I didn't bring my gun. I knew you'd be here, but I thought I could stomach your ass

until I got the chance to kill you after the wedding. But what do you do? You show up with Levi. How did you get him? You have got to tell me your secret. I always liked him myself."

While her breath came in thrusts of painful, shallow gulps, her whole body convulsed. Her tongue protruded from her gaping mouth. Her eyes started rolling back in her head.

"Not yet, slut," he said, lifting his foot off her chest. He stepped back. "I want you to suffer like you made me suffer."

Her lungs felt as if they would burst; her chest hurt. She struggled to breathe normally again. Between gulps of air she cried out, "What . . . did . . . I . . . ever . . . do . . . to you?"

"Shut up! Crying ain't gonna save your goddamn life."

Hoping that someone might hear her, she cried even louder.

"I said, shut the hell up!"

She took a big gulp and clammed up.

"What the hell, ain't nobody gonna hear you all the way down here anyhow, we're in the subbasement. Ain't nobody gonna come down here for a long time. By then, big, old, ugly mangy rats would've ate your whoring ass up."

Brandon and Levi rushed right at Charmaine, startling her as she came out of Reverend Simmons's office.

"Where's Gregory?" Brandon demanded.

"It's Gregory?" Levi asked, his heart racing.

"It's Gregory what?" Charmaine asked.

Brandon grabbed her shoulders. "Where is he?"

"He left! What's wrong?"

"I didn't see him come out," Levi said.

Brandon let go of Charmaine. "He's after Marissa, we have to find her."

"Brandon! What . . . what are you talking about?"

Levi felt like he did once when he fell off a roof he was tarring—like he was suspended in midair waiting for the impact.

"What do you mean Gregory's after Marissa?" Charmaine asked, confused. "What are you talking about?"

"Where is she?" Brandon asked, looking around the church.

Levi made a mad dash for the door to the basement.

"Ple . . . please. . . ."

Lifting the robe he wore, Gregory unbuckled his belt. "That's right bitch, beg," he said, pulling the belt from around his waist. "I told your whoring ass to stay away from my man."

"Oh my God. You're crazy."

"Don't call me crazy!" He kicked her on the thigh.

Marissa grunted. She squeezed her eyes shut until the pain ebbed.

"You are a nothing. You are a slut."

The venom dripping from his lips chilled her soul. She didn't know he hated her so. But it was Charmaine she was worried about. "Gregory, listen to me. You're marrying Charmaine tomorrow—you don't have a man."

"I did until you put your big ass in his face."

God, it had been Gregory all along. That's why they couldn't figure out whose wife it was. That meant . . . "You're gay?" she asked, incredulously.

Baring his teeth, Gregory snatched the belt above his head. "You bitch!"

Marissa's eyes popped. She shrieked. She tried to ball herself up tight, but she couldn't get completely off her back. Straining, she pulled her legs up and forced her hips over so that she turned onto her right side. She winced, squeezing her eyes shut in anticipation of the pain.

Lash! Her hip. Her skin screamed. The tears gushed from her.

"Aaaaaah!"

Lash! Her thigh. Her flesh seared with pain.

"Aaaaaah!" She cried harder.

Lash! Her shoulder. Her body jerked.

"Aaaaaah!"

Lash! Her back. Her skin twinged.

"Aaaaaah!"

Lash! Her back again.

Her skin felt like she had been branded. Her throat was parched—she couldn't scream anymore. Feeling as if she was about to faint, she began whimpering like a wounded animal, and even so, she could hear Gregory. He was panting as if he were out of breath.

Lash! Her body convulsed. It felt as if fire were licking at her skin, burning her alive. The muscles in her legs, her thighs, her stomach were so tight that they ached.

He suddenly stopped.

His breathing was all she heard. She waited for him to hit her again. He didn't. He just stood where he was. But his inaction was just as frightening as his beating. What else was he going to do to her? Fearfully, she peeked up at him. His chest was heaving. His face was a contemptuous mask of hate.

"I ain't no goddamn faggot! Don't call me no faggot, you bitching whore!" he shouted, spit spraying from his mouth. "U'ma goddamn man!"

She cried pitifully.

Gregory fumbled with the belt, trying to snake the end through the buckle. "You ain't gonna call me a goddamn faggot and live to talk about it. What me and Wayne do together ain't nobody's business. Nobody's!"

Did she hear right? She stopped crying. "Wayne?"

"That's right, bitch, Wayne. I knew he was seeing somebody, I just didn't know it was your whoring ass."

"But Wayne's married. He's impotent. How can he—?"

"He ain't impotent!"

Stunned, she gaped at him. Did he know what he was saying? "Wayne is gay?"

"Say that again, bitch, I'll stomp you through the goddamn floor straight to hell."

"But he has a wife. What about his wife?"

"He don't do a damn thing with his lame-ass wife. They go their separate ways. But you, I know he's doing something with you."

"No . . . no! Wayne and I are just friends. Platonic. We have never done anything together. He couldn't, he's impotent."

He lifted his belt. "You're a liar!"

Her body convulsed in anticipation.

He didn't strike her. "You can't leave no man alone, can you, slut?" he asked, quickly buckling the belt so that it resembled a noose. He started for her again. "Why did you have to mess with Wayne? Don't you have enough men?"

His eyes were wild, the sneer on his face was pure evil. The belt in his hand looked menacing. He was going to kill her. Marissa knew it—she felt it. She began to hyperventilate. As best she could, although crying hard again, she tried frantically to push away from him with her legs. But her arms, her back, her shoulders were hurting too badly from scraping against the concrete floor. Unable to do anything else, she started crying hysterically.

"Shut up!" Reaching down, Gregory snatched her up by her arms and pulled her up into a sitting position. Then he dropped down onto his knees and pulled her back up against his own body, holding her with one arm across her breast bone. She tried to pull away. He yanked her hard back up against his chest and held her while he tried to pull the belt down over her head. It caught on her French twist. He tugged on the belt—pulling her hair, hurting her—until it fell around her neck. Holding on to the end of the belt with his left hand, he pushed her off of his chest and yanked the belt tight with a snap, jerking her back up against his chest again. Wrapping the belt around his hand, he began choking the life from her.

Her tongue shot out of her mouth. Her body started twitching.

The door burst open, hitting the wall like a clap of thunder. Levi never stopped running. "Aaaaaaaah!" he screamed. His blood-curdling wail was the hurling force that jetted him across the room into Gregory. Marissa was thrown sideways. She fell like a wet rag doll.

Brandon lunged into the room. He ran straight for Marissa's crumpled body and quickly unbuckled the belt from around her neck.

Gregory fought wildly to regain his balance.

Levi fought harder. He got to his feet and pulled Gregory up with him. Growling, he grabbed him by the upper arm and hurled him face first into the concrete wall, knocking the wind out of him, but

that didn't stop him. Gregory rebounded. He wailed like a wild animal. He started for Levi, but Levi didn't wait for him to get to him.
He charged at Gregory, kicking him square in the chest, knocking
him hard to the floor. Still, Gregory struggled to get up. His face was
streaked red. His breath came in loud, raspy throaty gasps. Levi
stepped up to him while he was still on his knees and grabbed a fist-
ful of his robe while pounding his fist unrelentingly, time and again,
into his already bloody face.

"Stop!" Charmaine screamed, rushing into the room.

Levi's fist stopped in midair. He looked into Gregory's mangled,
droopy face before thrusting him to the floor.

Throwing herself onto the floor alongside her man, Charmaine
screamed at Levi, "Why? Why?"

Turning away in disgust, Levi went to Marissa. Brandon had her
head resting in his lap. He was gently massaging her throat. Her
eyes were closed.

He dropped to his knees. "Is she . . . ?"

"She'll be okay. Another minute. . . ."

Picking up her limp hand, Levi held it. His own throat tightened
as he fought back the tears.

Marissa opened her eyes. "Levi," she said hoarsely.

"I'm here, baby."

Chapter 35

MARISSA HEARD THEM say that Gregory had a broken nose, a broken jaw, broken ribs, and a lot of missing teeth. He was handcuffed and still wearing the blood-red choir robe when they rolled him out on a stretcher.

Levi's swollen, bloody right fist was bandaged, but that didn't stop him from holding her in his arms while she sipped on the last of the peppermint tea Mrs. Simmons gave her. Her chest and throat were both sore, while her whole body ached. Levi had promised the police that he'd get her checked out as soon as possible.

She looked down to the front of the church where Charmaine was being consoled by Reverend Simmons. Her sobbing was pitifully heartwrenching. Marissa hadn't gone to the hospital because she couldn't leave her like that. Not when Charmaine was dealt the devastating blow of Gregory's double life; not when she had been only hours away from marrying him.

The police finally finished with Brandon, and then he went back to sit with Levi and Marissa. Although she was in Levi's arms, he leaned over and kissed her on the cheek. Then he checked the ugly bruise around her throat. "Do you feel nauseated? Are you in any pain?"

She shook her head no because she wasn't ready to leave.

"Yes, she is," Levi said. "I'm taking her to the hospital when we leave here."

"We'll go to my hospital," Brandon said. "She'll be looked at right away."

"How did you know?" Levi asked.

"One of my colleagues told me."

Sitting her cup down on the seat on the other side of Levi, Marissa turned to look at Brandon. "How did he know about Gregory?"

"He works for Corrections, counseling officers who manifest psychosis in their work environment. He didn't mention Gregory by name at first, he was telling me about this officer who had a hard time dealing with his homosexuality and acted out by abusing homosexual prisoners. He targeted them for abuse whenever he was alone with them."

"I can't believe that Gregory is gay," Levi said.

"He hid it well. My colleague told me that on several occasions, Gregory was reported for abusing the prisoners, and because it was thought that his targeting the homosexual population meant that he might be dangerously homophobic, he was sent to be counseled."

She forgot about her pain as she listened to the horror of what was Gregory's secret life.

"After several sessions, my colleague concluded that Gregory was abusing in an attempt to camouflage his own homosexuality."

"Geez." Marissa couldn't believe it.

"See," Brandon continued, "Gregory didn't see himself as gay or even bisexual. In fact, he was angry that he could not resist the desire to be with a man. Eventually, he got himself a secret lover and pretended that they were just friends."

"He told this to the shrink?" Levi asked.

"Well, he never said that they were lovers, he just referred to him as his friend, but he stressed that he could not be gay if he had a heterosexual relationship with Charmaine. That's why it was vitally important, all of a sudden, that he get married. It was the ultimate cover and no one would question his masculinity."

"But that wasn't fair to Charmaine," Marissa said, disgusted. "Look at her, she's crushed."

They all looked down at Charmaine. She was still crying.

"I suspect that Gregory would have lived with his secret indefinitely if he had not found out that his lover was also your lover."

"Oh, no . . . no," Marissa said, shaking her head. "Wayne was never my lover. If you remember what I told you about him, you'll remember that he was impotent with me. We were never lovers. Just friends."

"I know that, but Gregory didn't. He might not have known that Wayne had that problem with women. In fact, Wayne might have boasted about having a female lover in addition to his wife because of Gregory's relationship with Charmaine. He's still a man, and men don't like to admit that they're deficient in any way, shape, or form."

"They both sound terribly conflicted," she said.

"No, they're both crazy," Levi countered. "They ruined other people's lives with their secrets. They should have just come out of the damn closet."

"That isn't as easy as you might think," Brandon said. "When a person comes out, he's not telling the world that he has acne that will clear up after puberty; he's telling the world that he has a sexual preference that's contrary to the teachings of the church, and to what society considers the norm. It's a permanent condition that doesn't fade with blemish cream."

"I understand that," Levi said, grateful that Wayne had never been able to consummate his relationship with Marissa. "But Gregory, what he did, I could beat the hell out of him all over again."

An overwhelming sense of guilt washed over Marissa. "It's not all Gregory's fault. I brought this on myself."

"No, you can't blame yourself for what Gregory did, Marissa. He tried to kill you."

"And I wanna say that I hate him, but I can't."

"Which is good," Brandon said. "Recrimination isn't healthy."

"Oh, don't get me wrong; there was a time when I would have despised him for what he did to me. But I have to ask myself, would

Gregory have wanted to kill me if I had not been seeing his lover, if I had not been such a sl—?"

"Marissa," Levi said quickly, not wanting her to go on, "don't be so hard on yourself."

"The fact is, I haven't been hard enough on myself. I am a—"

"Marissa," Brandon said, "please, don't be a victim. Gregory was not only wrong, he's extremely ill. His attempt to kill you was not a rational panacea for eliminating you as his competition. No matter what you did, killing you should have never entered his mind."

"He's only human, Brandon. Instinctively, we are territorial and we fight fiercely for whom and what we think belongs to us. You know for yourself that there are a lot of people who wish that they could eliminate their romantic rivals."

"Yes, but for most of us, our sense of right and wrong prevails."

"Still, if it had not been Gregory, it could have easily been one of the wives. Each of them were wronged by me."

"Their husbands bear just as much of the blame."

"Yes, the husbands were wrong, but I was more so because I wasn't respectful of any of these women's marriages. In truth, I wouldn't want anyone going behind my back seeing my husband"— she glanced at Levi—"or my man."

Brandon shrugged. "Well, marriage is about fidelity, about trust."

She began tearing. "Why didn't I understand that and respect it? There really is no excuse for what I did. Gregory said I was a slut. He was right."

Levi stared straight ahead. He barely felt himself breathing. She had said it and he did not like the sound of it. He did not see her as a slut, but the truth was, that is what his mother and the wives of the men she messed with would have labeled her as being. Perhaps he did not see her that way because he had never seen her with another man. He hoped that he never would. He squeezed her arm.

"Marissa, tell me," Brandon said, "*are* you one now?"

Marissa closed her eyes. Tears slipped through her lashes. Until all of this happened, she had never felt that she was; but now she understood that she had whitewashed the reflection in her mirror. It

took Gregory's hate to force her to see her true self, but it took Levi's love to show her that she could be a better person. She felt his arm tighten around her. She was safe. It was a good feeling. He didn't hate her; that's all that mattered. Opening her eyes, she wiped them. "No, and I never will be one again."

Taking that as a promise, Levi kissed her on the side of her face.

"My work is done here," Brandon said. "You'll get my bill."

Smiling, she nudged him, but her smile quickly vanished when she looked down at Charmaine. "What about Charmaine? Gregory should not have involved her."

"Honey, he may not have realized what was happening himself way back when he met Charmaine."

"Maybe," she conceded. "But what I don't understand is, if Wayne was impotent with women, then wasn't he the same with Gregory?"

"Marissa, I won't venture to guess if or how they did anything— we are sitting in a church—but it's not unusual for a man who is gay to be completely unresponsive with a woman. When Wayne was younger, he might not have had any problems. That's how he ended up getting married and fathering children in the first place. A lot of men come out later in life, after they've married and had children."

"Wayne is still with his wife—do you think she knows?"

"Maybe, maybe not. Like you, she might just think he's impotent. That happens to a lot of men, straight or gay."

"So if he already had a cover, his wife, why did he want to be around me?"

"Honey, he might've just liked you."

Levi gently stroked Marissa's arm. "Did Gregory tell this psychiatrist about Marissa?"

"Again, not by name. He said that his lover had a lover and that he was jealous. He didn't care that he had a wife, it was the lover that upset him. He thought that Wayne was cheating on him."

"If no names were mentioned," Levi began, "how did you figure out that it was Gregory?"

Brandon glanced down at Charmaine. "After I heard the story and

thought about what was happening to Marissa, I added it all up. I knew that Gregory was a correction officer; I knew that he was getting married; and I knew that the person who was doing the stalking somehow knew Marissa's every move. This person knew where she lived, where she worked, who she was seeing by name, and apparently had all the phone numbers."

"How did Gregory know all that about me? I never talked to him."

"Charmaine. You, my dear, used to tell her all of your business. Remember we talked about that?"

"Oh, God."

"In other words," Levi said, "Charmaine told Gregory everything Marissa told her."

"That's right."

Marissa buried her face against Levi's chest. It all seemed so surreal. If it wasn't for her pain, she would have a hard time believing that any of it had ever happened.

Levi held her close. "The same day I met you, Gregory told me that he hated you."

"He did?" she asked, realizing that he may have never liked her from the start. Why that should bother her she didn't know.

"Yeah, he warned me to stay away from you."

"Marissa," Brandon said, "I know you're not surprised, you never liked him, either. And as for Charmaine, before talking with my colleague, at first I thought it might be her. But then I had to eliminate her because you had seen the 'woman' stalking you. You would have known Charmaine no matter how she was dressed."

"Then I should have known Gregory, too."

"Not really. With makeup on, a dress, Gregory looked nothing like himself. He was truly someone else."

"I know that's right," she said. "You should have seen him in that red dress he wore the night I ran after him."

"I can imagine," Brandon said. "Remember, he was conflicted, as Levi said. On one hand, he was a macho man; on the other, he was a femme fatale. With his lover, who knows."

Marissa shuddered. "That boy needs help."

"Lots of it," Levi agreed.

"Yeah, he was pretty scary there," Brandon said. "That's why as soon as I figured it all out, I tried to call you. When I got no answer at my place or yours, I knew that something real bad had happened."

"Gregory showed up at your apartment waving a gun," Levi said. "I took Marissa to my house."

"From the looks of it, that apparently did more than save her life," he said, observing how comfortable Marissa looked with Levi's arms wrapped around her. "Did we make a love connection?"

Levi and Marissa looked deep into each other's eyes. They liked what they saw. Smiling, they kissed each other tenderly on the lips.

"I'd be honored to give the bride away," Brandon said.

"Brandon," she said, embarrassed. "Don't you think it's a little too soon to—?"

"I don't think so," Levi said, intrigued with the thought of Marissa being his bride.

Taken aback, she blushed.

"It's something we can think about."

"You'd be a lovely bride, Marissa," Brandon said.

Marissa looked from one to the other. The thought of being married to Levi strangely didn't repulse or scare her. But, "We've only really known each other one day."

"How long should it take for one to know that a person is right for her?" Brandon asked her.

"Usually more than a day," she replied, though the idea of marrying Levi was beginning to feel right. What he did for a living was no longer an issue; the fact that he loved her was.

"Baby, I won't rush you," Levi said, kissing her on top of the head. "I'm not going anywhere."

"I hope not."

Placing his hands over his heart, Brandon teased, "How sweet. Marissa, wasn't that sweet?"

"Boy, you better leave me alone," she said, hitting him lightly on the thigh. "Anyway, shouldn't we be thinking about Charmaine?"

Again, they looked down to the front of the church. Reverend Simmons was still with Charmaine.

Brandon started to get up. "I'll go check on her."

"No," she said, gingerly pulling herself away from Levi. "I should do this. I'm the one who is the cause of her pain."

Levi and Brandon both helped her to get up. As she was about to slip past Brandon, he took her hand. "Gregory is the cause of her pain, you just happened to be the catalyst to force him out of hiding. However, don't be hurt if she rejects you."

The thought of rejection had not entered her mind, but if Charmaine did reject her, she'd keep trying—it was her turn to be a friend.

Levi watched Marissa hobble painfully down the aisle. If what he felt for her was love, he was open to it.

Brandon watched him watch her. "You're a lucky man. Marissa's special."

"I know."

They each sat, each with his own thoughts. Levi, unable to take his eyes off Marissa, wondered how he grew to love her so quickly. Brandon, nipping on his thumbnail, wondered if this was the right time to come out to Levi.

"Levi, can we talk a minute?"

"Sure."

He scratched his head. He shifted his weight on the soft cushion. "I . . . well . . . look, I'm gay."

"It's not a problem."

He exhaled softly. "I was hoping it wouldn't be."

"I learned a long time ago, Brandon, that being gay doesn't change who you are as a human being—except for maybe someone like Gregory who obviously has problems. You, I like your style. I like the way you take care of Marissa."

"You didn't do so badly yourself. I want you to know that I love Marissa like she was my sister. That's why I'm glad you were here for her."

"I'm glad she let me."

Brandon smiled. "She can be a handful."

"Yes," he agreed, smiling also, but it was the memory of last night that he was thinking about.

Brandon extended his hand to Levi. "I always wanted a brother."

He took his hand and shook it. "Me, too."

Together they settled back and waited for the woman they both loved.

Marissa eased her sore body down onto the red-cushioned pew next to Charmaine. Her face was buried against Reverend Simmons's chest. She lay her hand gently on Charmaine's back. Her hand shook from her sobs.

Reverend Simmons looked at Marissa. "Are you all right?"

"Yes," she answered softly. "I'm so sorry."

"Don't be. The Lord moves in mysterious ways; he used you to save Charmaine from a life with a man who isn't a man at all. She would have never known happiness because of his deception. It hurts her real bad right now, but she'll understand it by and by. It was better to find out before she took her wedding vows than to find out in a shameful way later on down the road. She's in God's blessed hands, she'll be just fine. Thank the Lord we found out in time."

"Yes, thank the Lord."

"Why don't I leave you two alone," he said, gently pushing Charmaine into Marissa's arms. "I'll be sitting with my wife if you need me."

Charmaine let her body slump into Marissa. She buried her face in her hands and continued to sob.

"I am so sorry," Marissa said, beginning to weep with her friend. She embraced her tightly as their pain echoed throughout the church.

WHY I WROTE *SHADES OF JADE*

A SPECIAL NOTE FROM
THE AUTHOR, GLORIA MALLETTE

As with most writers, it is what I see and hear that inspires me to write.

I heard a woman offhandedly say that her affair with the married man she was seeing had nothing to do with his family. I was intrigued. I thought, His affair had everything to do with his family. Whatever he was giving to his mistress—be it material or emotional—he was taking away from his wife and children. Although he, the husband, took the vow of fidelity, the woman, the mistress, should have had not only a moral sense but a loyalty to sisterhood. Knowing that people never listen to preachy advice, I decided to write a relationship novel showing what could happen if a mistress was stalked by the wife of the man she was seeing. Hence, *Shades of Jade*—a story of jealousy, infidelity, hate, and love with a suspenseful twist.

A CONVERSATION WITH
GLORIA MALLETTE,
AUTHOR OF *SHADES OF JADE*

Do you know any women like Marissa?
I think we all know women like Marissa. At book signings, I have
met women who have told me that they had made choices similar to
Marissa's in the past or that they know someone—a family member
or friend—who is currently choosing to go out only with married
men. Men and women both have bought *Shades of Jade* to give to
the women in their lives who have chosen the misguided path that
Marissa walks.

At one book signing, a woman in her early sixties told me, when
buying *Shades of Jade,* that she had been seeing a married man
for thirty years. She said that she wanted to see what I had to say
that she had not already heard or lived. Before she walked away,
she said that she had no regrets. That did not surprise me. Women
like Marissa have no respect for the institution of marriage. After all,
it's not their marriage that is in jeopardy, it's someone else's. As
long as they get whatever it is they want from that relationship, life
goes on and they don't sweat the small stuff outside of their little
world.

How do you feel about infidelity? Who should bear more responsibility for it?

I feel, in all relationships, that we should be faithful. I think that the individual who makes the commitment to another should bear the responsibility for remaining true and for ensuring that the links of the family chain are not broken because of infidelity, which is usually initiated by lust. The outside lover has no obligation to anyone but him/herself. Thus, no one will be hurt but the lover. But in a marriage or a committed relationship, unfortunately, it is the innocents—the partner, the children—whose hearts will be broken when an infidelity is exposed.

Being in a marriage is a full-time job on all fronts. We take a vow of fidelity and, try as we might, temptation looms all around us. We must be ever vigilant. Wasn't Eve tempted? Didn't she take a bite? And, goodness knows, she had only one test to pass. There are those of us who are strong enough to face down temptation, while some of us give in only after some emotional struggle, and many more of us readily and eagerly give in. We are but mere mortals; we do the best we can and pray for strength.

Who are your favorite authors?

We have been blessed with an abundance of grand wordsmiths. Like so many writers, from early on I have read an array of authors I thoroughly enjoy, from Richard Wright, James Baldwin, John A. Williams, Ralph Ellison, Ernest Gaines, Toni Morrison, Ernest Hemingway, Stephen King, Robert Ludlum, Robin Cook, Graham Greene, Lawrence Sanders, Walter Mosley, John Grisham, and Mary Higgins Clark to romance writers of old like Rosemary Rogers and Barbara Cartland. The list goes on. From each of these authors I've taken something. I have a great appreciation for their varied writing styles, their prolific imaginations, and the excellent way they weave their tales. They have all held me captive between the pages of their books and they have all inspired me to write.

What is your writing process?

For me, the germ of an idea for a story is something interesting I hear or see. It could be a simple statement, an incredible incident, or a news event. My imagination kicks in and once I create my main characters, and perhaps the plot, I get to writing. The first line of the first chapter sets the tone for all the chapters that follow. The characters come to life and seem to mold and create their own personalities. They take over and I let them tell their story. Oftentimes, what I outlined in the beginning is tossed aside by the characters themselves. What they say, I have nothing to do with; what they do, I do not sit in judgment over. I am but a conduit through which the story is told, and my job is to commit to paper the story that unfolds. Sounds a bit surrealistic, but when one creates, one must give oneself over to the process.

What's next for you?

Promises to Keep, my third novel, will be published in 2002. It is quite different from *Shades of Jade,* as I take a look at a family in the aftermath of the murder of a son. The survival of a family is dependent on how they cope with one another when one of their own is brutally and abruptly snatched from their midst. *Promises to Keep* delves into the marriage of Nola and Ronald Kirkwood and their relationship with their surviving son, Vann, while they all try to find out who killed Troy. As in *Shades of Jade,* there is some mystery.

READING-GROUP GUIDE

The questions and discussion topics that follow are intended to enhance your group's reading of Gloria Mallette's *Shades of Jade*. We hope they will provide new insights and ways of looking at this intriguing new novel.

Questions for Discussion

1. In some ways, Mallette has created an unsympathetic character in Marissa. Although we come to understand her motivations, her behavior is still disturbing. Do you sympathize with her? If she were your friend, what would you do?

2. Charmaine values her friendship with Marissa despite her prickly personality, but Marissa does not always reciprocate. Marissa dislikes female friendship because she says it often results in jealousy and betrayal. Is this true? What does Charmaine realize about their friendship that Marissa does not? Is Marissa's friendship with Brandon different?

3. Although Marissa claims to prefer relationships with married men, she eventually realizes how unhealthy they are. Her low

self-esteem and fear of rejection led her into relationships that were increasingly shallow and superficial. How did she become this way? How did her relationship with Wyatt, her first love, shape her attitude toward men? How influential or important are first loves in our lives?

4. From the first time they meet, Levi and Marissa are intrigued by each other, but neither seems to be the other's type. What brings them together? What about Marissa attracts Levi? What does Levi give Marissa that other men do not?

5. Charmaine accuses Marissa of dating wealthy men only for what they can give her. She does accept gifts and money from her male friends. Does this make her a prostitute? Does giving money to Marissa make Louis or Wayne feel better about cheating on his wife? How are their perceptions of the relationship different from Marissa's?

6. When a woman has an affair with a married man, who is more at fault, the man or the woman? What would Levi's grandmother say?

7. When Marissa finds out Eric is not married—he's just been busy building his new dental practice—she is not pleasantly surprised. His attempt to take the relationship to a deeper level is quickly rebuffed and Marissa breaks off the whole thing. Why? What is she afraid of?

8. After Charmaine and her bridesmaids get together to try on their dresses, they tell the real truth about marriage. They blame men for not taking an active role in the house but admit they sometimes don't demand that their husbands do so. What is the right recipe for marital happiness? Whose responsibility is it to set the rules?

9. Marissa's mother told her she should make her own money, make her own rules, and never let a man make her his servant. Is that what Marissa is doing? Who is using whom in her relationships?

10. Charmaine and Gregory seem to be in love and Charmaine is sure he is the one she wants to spend her life with. Yet Gregory has been keeping things from her, and his secret life ultimately destroys their relationship. Is it possible to keep such a secret? Was there any way for Charmaine to know? Why couldn't Gregory admit his true feelings to himself?

11. Marissa's threatening phone calls set into motion a series of events that force her to completely reevaluate her lifestyle and explore her own motivations and history. Had she not been stalked, do you think Marissa would have changed? If she hadn't changed, what kind of person would she have become?

ABOUT THE AUTHOR

GLORIA MALLETTE lives with her husband in
Brooklyn, New York. This is her second novel.
She would love to hear what you think of
Shades of Jade and can be reached via e-mail at
gempress@aol.com.